The Prince's Man

The Gareth and Gwen Medieval Mysteries:
The Bard's Daughter (prequel)
The Good Knight
The Uninvited Guest
The Fourth Horseman
The Fallen Princess
The Unlikely Spy
The Lost Brother
The Renegade Merchant
The Unexpected Ally
The Worthy Soldier
The Favored Son
The Viking Prince
The Irish Bride
The Prince's Man

The After Cilmeri Series:
Daughter of Time
Footsteps in Time
Winds of Time
Prince of Time
Crossroads in Time
Children of Time
Exiles in Time
Castaways in Time
Ashes of Time
Warden of Time
Guardians of Time
Masters of Time
Outpost in Time
Shades of Time
Champions of Time
Refuge in Time
Unbroken in Time
Outcasts in Time
This Small Corner of Time

A Gareth and Gwen Medieval Mystery

THE
PRINCE'S
MAN

by

SARAH WOODBURY

The Prince's Man
Copyright © 2020 by Sarah Woodbury

This is a work of fiction.

www.sarahwoodbury.com

To Gareth, Heidi, and little Gwen

Cast of Characters

Gwen –Hywel's investigator, Gareth's wife
Gareth –Hywel's steward, Gwen's husband
Llelo – Gareth and Gwen's son
Dai – Gareth and Gwen's son
Tangwen – Gareth and Gwen's daughter
Taran – Gareth and Gwen's son
Meilyr –Gwynedd's court bard, Gwen's father
Saran – Healer, Meilyr's wife
Gwalchmai – Gwen's brother

Hywel – Prince of Gwynedd
Owain – King of Gwynedd
Cynan – Owain's son
Madoc – Owain's son
Cristina – Owain's wife
Susanna – Owain's sister
Madog – King of Powys, Susanna's husband
Iorwerth – Owain's son
Marared – Madog's daughter
Mari – Hywel's wife

Gruffydd – Rhun's former captain, Dragon member
Cadoc – Assassin, Dragon member
Steffan – Dragon member
Iago – Dragon member
Aron – Dragon member
Abbot Rhys—friend
Marged – Tangwen and Taran's nanny
Cian – Marged's son

Cadwaladr ap Gruffydd – King Owain's brother
Alice – Cadwaladr's wife
Deri – King Madog's court bard
Nest – King Madog's court bard
Andreas – Deri and Nest's steward
Manon – Andreas's wife

The son of Cynan has fallen.
The conflicts of princes
appeases the black-winged raven.
The power of our lord
with his men about him
subdues his peers.
Faced with his resolution
and his furious hand
they retreat cautiously.
A fearsome lion.
Hope of the nations.
Dragon of the men of Gwynedd.
In his place stands Owain
the despoiler of the English

--Meilyr Brydydd, *Elegy for Gruffydd ap Cynan*

1

Denbigh

December 1148

Gareth

"Gareth!" Gwalchmai's tenor penetrated the room, along with a soft but persistent tapping. "Are you there, Gareth? We need you!"

Gareth had been awake for a while, trying to pretend he didn't have a headache from staying up too late to hear the music in the hall—and drinking too much while he was at it, though he hadn't realized he was doing so at the time. Having married into a family of bards and in the service of another, Gareth heard beautiful music on a daily basis, but the singing leading up to the wedding of King Owain Gwynedd's son Iorwerth and King Madoc of Powys's daughter Marared was not to be missed. Unfortunately, the mead had been particularly excellent as well, a fact which Gareth was currently regretting hugely.

To make matters worse, and in typical small-child fashion, Taran had been awake more than usual in the night. At the moment, both he and Gwen were finally sleeping solidly. As it was still dark, Gareth hoped they could sleep some more.

For Gareth's part, rather than pull the covers up over his head as he wanted to do, he admitted that the only way he was going to reduce his hangover was with food, copious amounts of water, and by thinking about something else. That Gwalchmai could ask for him, and that Gareth would oblige without question, was what made them a family.

To that end and trying not to awaken the rest of his children and servants, who were strewn across the floor on pallets between him and the door, he swung his legs out of bed and stood up. His family had been given a small room in the guesthouse, one hardly more than ten feet by twelve, and he carefully skirted the sleepers as he made his way to his wife's brother.

Gwalchmai, having received no response yet from Gareth, cracked open the door to the room and peered inside.

The nanny, Marged, slept closest to the door, and she opened her eyes at Gareth's approach. When he made a calming motion with his hand, she nodded and closed her eyes again, though not before reaching out a hand to Tangwen, who lay nearby, and adjusting the little girl's blanket up over her shoulder.

Marged had been with them since the summer, and Gareth and Gwen were relieved to have finally found someone who might stay with them longer than a few months. Some years past forty, Marged had three grown children plus a youngest son, Cian, who'd just turned seventeen. With a long-dead father and as the last child of four, Cian had been leaning towards a vocation in the church until Gareth had offered him a position as Prince Hywel's clerk. To Gareth's mind, that Cian was so young made him more suitable for the position rather than less. He was eager and trainable. He'd also become good friends with Gareth's son Llelo.

Gareth shooed Gwalchmai out of the doorway and then angled his body to block the light coming from the lantern Gwalchmai held, so it wouldn't shine into the room.

"What is it?"

"Murder."

Though Gwalchmai was visibly hopping with impatience, Gareth put up one finger to tell him to wait and turned back to the room to gather up his discarded clothing, boots, and weapons. Then he returned to the door, eased through it, and closed it with a click of the latch.

"What time is it?" Gareth pulled on his breeches right there in the space outside the door.

"Still over an hour until dawn."

Over an hour until dawn this close to the Christmas feast didn't mean what it meant in summer. Today, Wales would see fewer than eight hours of daylight. Thus, for many, the day was already well under way, despite the darkness.

Blergh. He put a hand to his head, moaning a little and knowing Gwalchmai wouldn't have woken him for a less urgent reason. Gareth needed more than a few moments to force his mead-soaked brain into its usual pathways, but murder meant he didn't have even that amount of time. Few people had ever seen Gareth drunk—let alone hung over—and he was embarrassed enough at how he felt (and likely looked) to hope they might think him ill instead. Gareth would have cursed at how far behind he was before he even started, if there hadn't been a chance doing so would wake his family.

With the rest of his clothing bunched under his arm and holding his sword belt in one hand, Gareth went with Gwalchmai down the stairs to the common room. When he'd come into the guesthouse, Gwalchmai had left the exterior door partly open, and a quick glance outside revealed an unrelievedly dark sky, without moon or stars. Clouds covered the sky from horizon to horizon, as they had the night before when Gareth had gone to bed. It wasn't raining currently, but Gareth had been awake in the night and had heard the thundering of rain on the roof and the whipping of the wind through cracks in the shutters. Another glance showed him puddles in the courtyard and, if the bruised roil of the clouds was any indication, more rain was coming soon.

The royal *llys* at Denbigh was one of King Owain's grandest palaces east of the Conwy River, and many of its wooden structures had been rebuilt in the last decade after a fire had destroyed much of what was inside the wall. The guesthouse reminded Gareth of a Danish hall, in that it was two-stories high with a central room on the ground floor. A stairway led to rooms above, accessed by a walkway with a railing, which circled the hall and overlooked it. The ten rooms along the walkway each had walls and doors that provided some privacy, but, like Gareth's room, every one was overfull for the wedding.

Gareth had been glad to have been given a room at all, rather than sleeping in a tent outside the palace or on the floor of the great hall. But accommodation had been made for them because they had small children. The same was true for Hywel's wife, Mari, and their two boys, and Prince Cadwaladr's wife, Alice, and their children. Despite her husband's disgrace, she was still the daughter of a powerful English lord, and to treat her with anything less than utmost courtesy risked an unnecessary dispute with her brother. Besides, she herself had not chosen Cadwaladr for a husband, and his treason was not her fault.

Turning back to the room, Gareth was glad to see the fire in the hearth had been stoked already, in preparation for more people than just him waking and wanting a buffer against the damp. Dumping his clothes on a nearby bench, he began to dress completely, starting with his boots.

Gareth firmly believed that every crisis should be met fully dressed. As much as Gwalchmai's hopping about implied they should already be on their way, Gareth had learned long ago that a man was taken far more seriously when he was wearing boots than when he wasn't. It was the reason the tapestry he'd seen on the wall of Robert of Gloucester's castle in Bristol, depicting the first meeting of Robert's ancestors with the lords of Gwent, had shown the Welsh rulers without shoes. The presentation had irked Gareth at the time, and the more he thought about it, the more angry it made him. But it also was a good life-lesson as to what the Normans really thought of the Welsh—and the importance of putting on one's boots whenever called to action, even if there were no Normans in Denbigh this week.

"I sense from your uncharacteristic silence, that you don't want to tell me about the murder, but before I leave the guesthouse, I'd better know who's dead." Gareth wrapped his sword belt around his waist. As with the boots, the authority conveyed by wearing a sword was almost more important than knowledge of its use.

Gwalchmai was still shifting from one foot to another, much as he had outside Gareth's chamber. Now, however, his stance implied uncertainty rather than urgency. Under Gareth's gaze, he finally stopped moving, took in a breath, and said, "It's a dog. Her name was Annwyn."

Gareth had been adjusting his belt, but now he froze, staring at Gwalchmai and thinking he'd misheard. Then Gwalchmai's expression turned sheepish, and Gareth realized his brother-in-law was serious. "You woke me about a dead dog?"

"Fetching you wasn't my idea! Queen Cristina demanded it."

Gareth's annoyance with Gwalchmai vanished. "Then we would be wise not to keep her waiting a moment longer."

Cristina had been a force to be reckoned with from the moment she'd become betrothed to King Owain. They had all learned long ago that giving Cristina what she wanted, if it was at all possible, was always the best course of action. If King Owain objected to her activities, it was up to him to rein her in, not Gareth or his family.

As he and Gwalchmai crossed the courtyard, Gareth was glad he'd left his cloak hanging over the back of a chair in the common room. Last night he hadn't noticed how warm the air had become but, after a night of rain, the icy patches in the courtyard were gone, and he had no fear of slipping on the flagstone path. The warmth wouldn't last more than a day or two—it never did in winter—but he welcomed it after the knee-deep snow they'd experienced for much of November and the early part of December.

If the warm air and rain continued throughout the day, on top of what had fallen in the night, the melting snow would make the rivers rise and the roads impassable for a time. It was a good thing, then, that the last of the royal guests had arrived the day before. The wedding wasn't for two more days, but nobody wanted to miss the event of the year—not to mention the free food and lodging provided by King Owain. It had been many years since anyone in Gwynedd had been allowed to go truly hungry, but they were coming up on the time of year when belts would be tightened, as the community looked ahead to several more months of winter.

Marared and Iorwerth had been kept waiting for their wedding. At first, this was because it was seen as unseemly to marry before a year had passed since the death of King Owain's heir, Prince Rhun. Then, the negotiations over the dowry had dragged on miles past the point of reasonableness. King Madog of Powys, King Owain Gwynedd's longtime rival, brother-in-law, and occasional friend resented Owain's reach and power, along with the fact that the Kingdom of Powys acted as a buffer between Gwynedd and England. Madog didn't see why he should take all the risks in their alliance for too little reward.

The kings had finally resolved the details of the marriage contract enough to placate, if not satisfy, both parties, though not before the second anniversary of Rhun's death had cast a pall over the whole of Gwynedd again. Gareth's lord, Prince Hywel, had been perpetually angry for nearly a month. Sometimes Gareth thought he was more angry now than when Rhun had died.

Gareth couldn't blame him for feeling the way he did. Rhun had been Hywel's brother and his best friend. Even when the rest of the world was ready to move on, Hywel was not. Matters hadn't been helped by the fact that King Madog had attempted to murder Hywel himself two years ago.

Even though Hywel was dealing with all that, his mood had lightened a little over the course of the last week, indicating the wound from Rhun's death had scabbed over again. It would always itch and would never heal completely. Such was the way of grief, which was really love in disguise.

As Gareth and Gwalchmai approached the entrance to the hall, the shouting going on inside was audible even through the closed doors. The commotion was so loud, in fact, that it was a wonder Gareth hadn't been able to hear it all the way up in his bedchamber.

Gareth crossed the final distance to the great door in two strides, and then, as he pulled it open, a scream in a register that hurt his ears split the air.

It was followed by the words, "Murderer!"

Near the dais at the far end of the hall, Cristina had set herself between two combatants, Deri and Nest, brother and sister musicians from Madog's court in Powys. The queen's arms were outstretched as far as they would go, keeping the siblings apart, and each was a mere inch away from the flat of her hands. The two singers gave the impression they were only moments from evading the queen and attacking one another outright.

Even so, Gareth was glad he'd delayed long enough to put on his boots and sword.

"It's just like Dinefwr all over again!" Nest went on. "My cousin died, and now I almost died! When will it end?"

Gareth's stomach clenched at the mention of Dinefwr. He'd been present when a celebration in the great hall had been laid waste by poison. Many guests had died including, apparently, Nest's cousin. At the moment, nothing about the current state of Denbigh's hall reminded him of the carnage there, so he wasn't sure how seriously to take her words. She had a habit of speaking in hyperbole.

"I had *nothing* to do with this!" Deri, the elder of the two, was forty if he was a day, balding and overweight, his belly stretching his tunic in a manner that indicated he might need a larger size soon. "I think you were trying to murder *me*!"

His sister was a good ten years younger, in a fine wool dress a spectacular shade of blue, with her blonde hair piled on top of her head in an elaborate style, even at this early hour of the morning. Her skin was clear, her nose long and straight, and her eyes the perfect distance apart. In short, she was at the height of a beauty some women achieved as they matured. For Nest, thirty was better than twenty had been and forty might see her more beautiful still. Gwen was another so blessed. Cristina was somewhat less so, at least to Gareth's eyes.

It was only Deri who was the official court bard to King Madog. His sister, who had a beautiful voice in her own right, sang on the dais most evenings and would have been named *bard* if a woman was allowed such a station. As with Gwen's family, music was in their blood, and brother and sister served King Madog in much the same way Gwen's family served King Owain, though Gwen rarely sang on the dais these days, by her own choice rather than her father's or brother's.

At the moment, Nest was glaring at her brother, not giving a single inch, in the manner of all siblings everywhere, no matter, apparently, their age. Gareth could have told them that attacking each other wasn't going to make anyone feel better, even if it felt good in the moment.

The dog was nowhere in evidence.

For the first time in her life, Cristina looked pleadingly towards Gareth.

At first, Gareth had assumed the queen had summoned him about a dead dog because she liked to poke at Gareth at every opportunity and make him do her bidding. She saw him as firmly on the side of Hywel, whom she hated, since he was the *edling*, the heir to the throne, and was thus favored by her husband over her young sons.

She didn't like Iorwerth either, of course. He was her husband's eldest legitimate son—and Gwalchmai's best friend. While legitimacy wasn't worth a great deal in Welsh law, since a son could inherit no matter the circumstances of his birth as long as his father acknowledged him, and Hywel's mother hadn't been married to Owain either, the Norman Church was reaching its fingers more and more into affairs in Wales, and *it* cared.

The Church saw Owain's marriage to Cristina as incestuous, since she and Owain were first cousins. Fortunately, the Archbishop of Canterbury couldn't say the same about Iorwerth's marriage to Marared. Although she was Madog's daughter, she too was born out of wedlock, and thus not a natural daughter of Madog's wife, Susanna, who was also Owain's sister. To the Welsh, even the use of the English word, *illegitimate*, was misguided: by the very act of acknowledging a son or daughter, the father made him or her *bonheddig canhwynol,* innately family.

However, what Cristina hated more than Hywel and her own ambiguous status (which she endeavored to ignore) was disorder, and she saw herself as the perfect hostess. At the very least, a dead dog in the hall might threaten that. Gareth, for all that he was her hated stepson's steward, knew what to do with unexplained death.

Though Gareth owed his livelihood to Hywel, not Cristina, Hywel's life went more smoothly when the Queen of Gwynedd was happy. Having braced himself to maintain a conciliatory attitude, Gareth strode down the hall to come to a halt a pace in front of Cristina.

"My lady, I am here to be of service. What exactly has happened?"

Really, he should have known better than to ask that question so baldly. It was obvious the situation was out of control.

Sure enough, rather than allowing Cristina to answer, both Nest and Deri instantly turned on Gareth, shouting at the top of their lungs, such that he could neither make out what they were saying nor get a word in edgewise. Some diners might have left the hall as the argument between Deri and Nest had escalated, disconcerted by the discord, but far more had gathered to watch. In winter, any form of entertainment was better than no entertainment, and, even in this regard, the pair gave good value.

Gareth had met both bards several times during the years he'd served Prince Hywel, but had never had a conversation with them beyond an exchange of a few polite words. They were musicians; he was a knight. They had their duties; he had his.

Because he was all but a stranger to them, it was perhaps no surprise they didn't take him seriously as an authority figure (despite his reputation), or maybe their disregard stemmed from the fact that Gareth was married to the daughter of one of Deri's chief rivals—that being Gwen's father, Meilyr, who had become so famous in the service of the kings of Gwynedd that more often than not these days he was known as *Meilyr Brydydd*: Meilyr the Bard.

So Gareth accepted the barrage for a count of ten, hoping it would lessen.

It didn't.

Cristina's eyes found Gareth's. "Please."

"Of course, my lady."

She hadn't needed to ask him again. Her doing so revealed her desperation.

He allowed the siblings to scream at him for another three heartbeats. Then he drew himself up to his full height, taking in everything they said and everything they were, and said, "Quiet!"

2

Gareth

Gareth's voice resounded throughout the hall and resulted in a gratifying silence.

As was made clear every time he joined in song with Gwen's family, Gareth was no bard and not much of a singer either (at least, no more of one than any other Welshman) but he had learned a thing or two since his marriage to Gwen about making his voice carry. In his reply to Nest and Deri, he had supported his breath with the muscles in his belly and thrown everything he had behind the word.

In response to his command, Deri and Nest stopped talking. Their mouths remained open, however, as they gaped at him a bit with their eyes wide. Well aware that the silence wouldn't last long, he put up one finger to tell them to wait, and then he gestured for Cristina to step a few paces away with him so their words couldn't be heard easily by anyone else. He was hopeful that he'd shocked Nest and Deri enough that they no longer felt the need to shout, and he was further heartened by the arrival of Manon, the wife of Andreas,

Deri and Nest's steward (for want of a better word). Such was the pair's glory that they had to be *managed*, and Gareth took a moment to wonder where Andreas was. If any moment called for management, it was this one.

"In as few words as possible, my queen, perhaps you could tell me what this is about?" He accompanied his request to Cristina with a bow, just to smooth over whatever unpleasantness was inherent in any conversation the two of them might have.

As before, Queen Cristina kept her disregard for him out of her face, and she answered straight-forwardly. "Nest's dog was poisoned by eating Deri's porridge and died immediately thereafter."

"You are certain the dog ate of it?"

She nodded.

"Did Deri?"

"He says no."

"Is anyone else ill?" At Dinefwr, one man had been poisoned before the rest, and that could be the case here too.

"No."

"I am very glad to hear it. But even so, why is everyone still eating?"

"The poison was in a bowl of porridge prepared exclusively for Nest and Deri, with ingredients they themselves supplied. I myself was eating porridge at the time and—" she spread her hands wide, "—as you can see, I am well. Everyone but the dog is well."

"Where is the dog now? Gwalchmai tells me her name was Annwyn." The victim might be only a dog, but Gareth had found that people responded more respectfully to death when the one who died had a name.

"I told one of the servants to wrap her in a cloth and take her to the laying out room."

Gareth found his lips pressing together for a moment as he struggled to reply in an even tone. He ended up asking very carefully, "Do you mean the laying out room next to the chapel? The one for people?"

He was pretty sure he hadn't done a very good job disguising his incredulity, but rather than punishing him for it, Cristina waved a hand, dismissing his concern. "It isn't as if it's occupied at present."

"I suppose not."

He knew the dog in question, a little white terrier, because Nest so rarely could be found without it. Glancing around the room at the other diners, he acknowledged that she was hardly alone in keeping a pet. Of the sixty people present, fully a quarter were accompanied by a dog. They came in all shapes and sizes. Some were small like Annwyn had been, more akin to the size of a cat, and belonged, like Annwyn, to ladies. Others were working dogs, sheepdogs being most common, as this was Wales. King Owain himself owned nearly a dozen dogs, whom he loved unreasonably. All of his dogs aided in hunting: terriers for small game, spaniels for birds, and hounds for deer and boar.

Many of the residents of the hall had fixed their eyes on Gareth and Cristina, their expressions a mix of curiosity and concern, and most had full platters in front of them. Gareth's stomach roiled at the thought of food, and even more at the smells that permeated the hall. Even so, he knew he needed something to eat, and quickly, if he was to maintain control of himself and the situation. Water, too, would help.

As if summoned by the very thought, Gwalchmai appeared at his elbow with a full cup. "Drink."

Gareth obeyed the boy—who wasn't really a boy anymore but a very grown up seventeen-year-old. Gwalchmai had also spent his life singing in great halls from Gwynedd to Aberystwyth, entertaining drinking men. He hadn't needed to be told what was wrong with Gareth.

After Gareth had drained the cup, he gave it back to Gwalchmai, who refilled it immediately. "Where is their bowl of porridge now?" Gareth was starting to feel a little better, especially after Gwalchmai next thrust a hunk of fresh bread into his hand. Fortunately, bread was nearly impossible to poison.

He took a bite as Cristina pointed to the end of one table, near where Nest and Deri were standing. "There."

Coming more and more to himself with every passing moment, Gareth reached the bowl in a few quick strides, picked up a cloth that had been used to cover a basket of buns, and laid it over the porridge bowl. Wrapping it carefully in the cloth, he handed it to Gwalchmai.

"Take this to your stepmother. At this hour, she's usually in the herbalist's hut outside the palace walls."

"I know it." Gwalchmai set off for the door.

Secure in the knowledge that Gwalchmai was capable and knew the importance of his task, having helped with investigations before, Gareth turned back to Cristina. "Where are the Dragons?"

Although Cristina's nose turned up at the mention of them, she answered easily enough. "I heard they rode out early this morning."

It had to have been early if they'd risen before these events. Gareth was surprised Hywel hadn't mentioned the desire to do so last night, but Gareth was no longer the captain of his guard, so the prince's safety was the Dragons' domain and that of the current captain of his *teulu*, Hywel's foster father, Cadifor. Selfishly, Gareth would have liked to have had their assistance, and it was only now that Gareth realized he hadn't seen Dai sleeping on the floor of their chamber when he left it, which made sense if the boy had risen early to ride with the Dragons.

Then his stomach roiled again out of concern that Hywel *had* told him where he was going, and Gareth had been so drunk he couldn't remember it.

Gareth shook off the fear. He'd been able to walk without assistance to the guesthouse and find his bed. Hopefully, in another hour or so, he would be feeling so much better that how he felt now would be a fading memory. If Gareth's closest friend and favorite Dragon, Evan, had been at Denbigh, he would have looked out for him and stopped him drinking sooner. But Evan's wife had given birth to a daughter, who was still too young to travel, so Hywel had ordered him to stay behind. Hywel had decided, perhaps mistakenly, that the potential danger at this particular wedding didn't merit leaving a wife and new baby.

Gareth wanted the Dragons' help, but he would have to make do without it.

As Gareth swallowed the last bite of bread, which landed in his stomach like a rock, he glanced to where Nest and Deri stood, alone now, morose expressions on their faces. They'd been watching him too, and, at his moment of attention, they opened their mouths again to speak. He put up a hand to stop them, and while they subsided immediately and appeared subdued, the glares they were shooting in his direction spoke volumes.

Because of their shared profession, Gwen had known Nest and Deri longer than Gareth had. In the course of the last week, she'd told Gareth a little of what she knew of their history, just as a by-the-way. The rest he had figured out for himself.

Their shouts and accusations were a boiling over of the long pent-up resentment each held towards the other. While Gareth had plenty of experience sorting out fighting men during his years as the captain of Prince Hywel's guard, his men were rarely as opinionated, strong-willed, and attention-loving as Deri and Nest. Every conversation in which either took part centered around themselves and, more often than not, involved one of them breaking into song or showing off their talents in an attempt to put their own skills on display and outshine the other. Naturally, in so doing, they became the center of attention once again, something they invariably enjoyed. It was as if they were always auditioning for the position of court bard, even though Deri had held his post in King Madog's retinue for at least ten years.

Gareth himself had never sung before a crowd, but he'd seen the outright joy singing in front of others gave Meilyr and Gwalchmai—and Gwen herself to a lesser extent. He could appreciate how it might be something to which a person grew accustomed, to the point that he or she was compelled to pursue it until it became unseemly.

Then Llelo, his hair sticking up on end, entered the hall at a run. He saw Gareth and made a bee-line towards him. "I heard screaming. What's happened?"

"Enough so I need your help."

Llelo looked pleased, as he would, though really it was Gareth who was happy to see him, since it saved him from having to ask a random person in the hall, or (God forbid) Queen Cristina herself, for help. In a few sentences, Gareth explained what he knew so far, little as it was, and then sent Llelo off to the kitchen to appropriate the remainder of the porridge, if there was any, and to warn the staff of what had happened.

Finally, with that situation as settled as he could make it, Gareth returned his attention to the bards and jerked his head in the direction of the back door to the hall. "Please come with me, so we can discuss this matter in private."

In the last few moments, Gareth had come to the conclusion that the only way to prevent Deri and Nest from getting the upper hand in an interview was to separate them from their audience. As long as they remained in a hall filled with people, whatever they said would be said for effect. While their lies and half-truths might be instructive, even informative, he'd rather hear something resembling the facts first.

Typically, instead of following Gareth, both protested that they'd done nothing wrong and didn't see why they should not stay right where they were. Such was their petulance that their voices overrode one another's as before.

Then Nest said, in a too-loud voice, "I didn't touch the porridge! I wasn't even in the hall when it was delivered! I wouldn't kill my own dog anyway!"

Rather than leaving the matter to Gareth as he'd intended, even hoped, Cristina waded into the altercation again and cut off their protests with a command of her own. "Follow Gareth now and do exactly as he says. Or do I have to wake Queen Susanna and have her tell you to do it?"

Identical looks of consternation crossed Deri's and Nest's faces. Cristina shot Gareth a satisfied smile before motioning with her head that he should lead the way.

"Thank you, my lady." Gareth couldn't remember a time when Cristina had so readily gone along with anything Gareth did or said.

He walked just ahead of Cristina to the rear door to the hall, and he reached it before glancing back to make sure Nest and Deri really were coming. Typically, they had taken a few steps, but their progress had been slowed further by various hangers-on who had moved closer to offer their condolences.

Cristina made a sound under her breath that sounded like a snort.

Gareth had never seen her so human, and he ventured a comment. "When Gwalchmai told me my investigation would be of a dead dog, at first I thought he was in jest, but now I see you did the right thing to wake me."

"I was afraid that if their argument went on any longer, they would strangle each other with their harp strings. Then we really *would* have a murder." Cristina had made a jest of her own, but she'd also spoken something of the truth, tinged with that same desperation he'd noted earlier.

"Do *you* know what this is really about?"

"It's about a dead dog." She seemed genuinely confused as to why he was asking the question again.

They'd stopped in the middle of the floor of the adjacent receiving room, built for private audiences, since some guests shouldn't be received—or at least conferred with—in the great hall itself with everyone watching and listening. A fire burned in the grate, making the room a bit too warm. Gareth was again glad he hadn't worn his cloak.

"Well, yes, my lady, but each is accusing the other of attempted murder."

Cristina's expression turned rueful. "Do you really have to ask? You've seen them together this week. You know what they're like."

"I suppose." Gareth believed he knew what she was implying, since he'd just had similar thoughts, but he wasn't sure how much was safe to admit. He never spoke to Cristina if he could help it. He certainly never let her into his mind, so to have a real conversation with her like this felt like sailing into dangerous waters. On the other hand, the queen was right that the pair had been at each other's throats from the moment they'd set foot in Denbigh. It was one of the first things he'd noticed about them.

Cristina was watching his face, and likely some of what he was thinking crossed it, resulting in a more audible snort from her. "Deri and Nest compete against each other, as siblings often do, but their rivalry is made worse by their differing and unequal stations. While Deri holds the position of official court bard for King Madog, Nest's talent far exceeds his."

"Do you really think so? His voice is one of the best I've heard. That's why I stayed so late in the hall last night, much to my regret. I thought the same when I heard him for the first time years ago. As far as I can tell, nothing has changed."

"I grant that he has a spectacular voice. I might even admit, if pressed, that Deri's voice is better than Meilyr's, if even to think such a thing wasn't forbidden by my husband and a betrayal of my country." Now Cristina genuinely grinned. It was shocking how personable she was appearing to be. "But I also know, from Nest, that he hasn't written a song in more than two years. Everything they're singing these days is hers."

"So she says."

Cristina laughed. "True."

His hands on his hips, Gareth watched the doorway, which Nest and Deri hadn't yet come through. Beyond the opening, he could see them talking to each other, suddenly in lower voices, and from this distance he couldn't hear what they were saying. He contemplated going back into the hall and forcibly removing them, but to do so would cause a scene—or more of one, rather, than had already been caused.

"I wondered why each seemed to behave as if the other was on stage only out of charity."

Cristina flicked out her fingers. Twice in one morning that dismissiveness hadn't been directed at Gareth. "Nest resents needing Deri—but need him she does. Without her brother, she would have no position anywhere."

"Her husband—"

"Died. Conveniently enough, I thought at the time."

Gareth turned his head to look fully at Cristina. "You suspected foul play?"

"He got drunk and fell off a wall. This was years ago."

That sounded like possible foul play to Gareth too, but what a dead husband years ago had to do with a dead dog today, he couldn't begin to say. "Female bards are rare and always accompanied by a male relative, but a lesser lord might consider sponsoring her anyway, especially if she's as good as you say. Winters are long and dark in Wales."

"She has seduced far too many husbands and angered far too many wives for any lord, high or low, to want her in his house without her brother *and* Andreas present to rein her in." Though initially Gareth had sensed Cristina was admiring of Nest, her tone had turned derisive.

For his own part, he just managed not to roll his eyes. "I can see why that might be a difficult task."

"Regardless, King Madog likes her on the dais."

Gareth knew better than to ask Cristina if King Owain had strayed in Nest's direction. Cristina kept Owain on a tight leash, but she didn't always come with him as he journeyed around his kingdom, preferring to stay most of the time at Aber. The king, meanwhile, wanted a woman in his bed, even if she wasn't his wife. Gareth hadn't heard rumors that Nest had been one of Owain's women, nor that she'd been Madog's, who also had many children born outside of wedlock. But if the Powysian king favored her this much, it seemed likely she'd shared his bed at one time, even if she wasn't his current mistress.

"And you see it as my job to keep her there?"

"Our job," Cristina said. "No matter what comes of this, she cannot be allowed to forgo her duty. She *must* keep singing."

"I'm not sure I understand why that is so important," Gareth said, speaking slowly as he attempted to be diplomatic. "We have other bards. Deri's voice aside, we have better ones, in fact."

"Of course we do." Cristina sniffed. "Though Meilyr was once the drunkard Deri is, he has reformed, and Gwalchmai's voice rivals an angel's. But one condition of having the wedding here at Denbigh, rather than at Dinas Bran like Madog wanted, was that Meilyr, Gwalchmai, and Hywel were not to sing. He made Owain put it in the marriage contract itself."

Gareth's mouth fell open.

At his reaction, the corners of Cristina's mouth turned down. "I am as disgusted as you, believe me. It's unconscionable. Yet for Madog, it's a matter of pride, or some such thing. Powys must always appear equal to Gwynedd. If Deri and Nest don't perform, Madog might even cancel the wedding. The contract gives him that power. Gwynedd can provide the bards only if Powys agrees, which you know Madog will never do. As I said, he got Owain to put the condition in writing."

"Why would King Owain agree to that?" Gareth knew he was still gaping, but he was having trouble swallowing down his surprise. "Why not simply hold the wedding at Dinas Bran?"

"Owain will never go to Dinas Bran again." Cristina's voice was flat, without any emotion. "It might look to outsiders as if the entire affair has been swept out with the ashes. It might look like that to Madog, and he might have convinced himself it's true. But *we* haven't forgotten that Madog arranged to have Hywel killed at Dinas Bran."

Gareth along with all his friends and companions felt the same way. "King Owain holds that truth in reserve, does he?"

"You do see." Cristina nodded, as if it was no more than she'd expected. "Madog has to be catered to if we want the wedding to go forward, and Owain does want it." She released a reluctant laugh. "*I* want it. Marared is a sweet thing, and the two are in love. Iorwerth has to marry someone, and a daughter of the King of Powys makes an excellent match. At the time, who was to sing at their wedding seemed like a small price to pay, in comparison to Madog's concession of having the wedding here at Denbigh."

Cristina was right that the pair truly wanted to be together. Gareth knew from Gwalchmai that Iorwerth had talked about eloping with Marared. If the deliberations had gone on much longer, they really might have, and it looked now as if perhaps they should have.

"All it takes for them to be married is for their fathers to agree they are. That we do all this—" he waved a hand to indicate the hall, the event, the guests, and everything else involved with the celebration, "—is immaterial in the end."

"Of course it is. That's not the point." Her laugh this time was entirely without amusement. "Madog wants always to get the better of Owain. My sense, and I told the king this, is that Madog is here at all because *Susanna* wants Marared and Iorwerth married. Any excuse to leave Denbigh with the wedding vows unsaid, forcing Owain to come to the table again and concede more for Marared, would please Madog very well. We cannot allow that to happen—and certainly not over who sings on the dais or a dead dog!"

Cristina jabbed a finger at Gareth's chest. "I'm counting on you to put a stop to any further nonsense from Nest and Deri."

Gareth just managed not to take a step back at the force of her words—and her poking finger. Singing was a serious business in Wales. He couldn't have been in love with Gwen for a decade and not know it. And that made him wonder why Meilyr had come to Denbigh at all, if he was just going to be outshone every night by Deri.

"I will do my best."

"I know you will. You always do. *That's* why I summoned you."

3

Llelo

Llelo was still waking up, and it was taking more than a few breaths to get his head around the fact that his father was handing him a piece of a murder investigation—albeit of a dog—so early in the day.

But this was what he was training for, so he stopped at the basin of warm water (intended to allow diners at the high table to wash their hands before eating), splashed some water on his face, smoothed down his hair as best he could, and proceeded out the side door to the kitchen. He told himself the fact that his heart was beating a little faster than usual was not to be taken as a sign that he was nervous. He was merely excited.

They'd had a few minor investigations since the murder at Prince Godfrid's wedding, and this could well turn out to be the same. But assisting his father with counting cattle and sheep on Prince Hywel's estates, while something Cian was very good at, was something Llelo tried hard not to despise. Investigating death was what he'd put his name down for.

Denbigh's kitchen was separated from the main hall by a covered walkway, necessary to protect the food from the weather as the servants took it to the great hall, while still preventing the spread of flames should a fire in the kitchen get out of control. The scene as Llelo stepped through the door was a familiar one of controlled chaos. The current hour was the height of the breakfast rush, and the eight workers in the room were moving purposefully from one task to another.

Llelo didn't have the authority of his father, but the head cook knew who he was from when Llelo had served at Denbigh under the command of Cynan, another of King Owain's sons. Thus, Llelo had no trouble walking right up to him and telling him the truth. In a way, it was surprising nobody had told him already.

"Alun, I have some bad news. Nest's dog died after eating the porridge made for Nest and Deri. We fear poison."

There really wasn't any good way to break this kind of news, so Llelo had thought it best to say it straight out. He was also careful to couch the words in such a way that no blame was laid. He didn't say, *You sent poisoned porridge to the great hall,* or *You killed Nest's dog with poisoned porridge.* It was something he'd been working on of late, at the behest of his mother, who sometimes had a lighter touch than his father when it came to putting witnesses at ease. People were more likely to cooperate when they didn't feel threatened.

But bad news was bad news, no matter how it was said. At first it didn't appear that Alun had even heard him, because he kept chopping onions on the table in front of him. But then he stopped in mid-chop and turned his head to look at Llelo. "What did you say?"

Llelo repeated his message, in an even more urgent tone.

His attempt at circumspection did no good in the end, however, because one of the servers burst through the door at that very moment and announced, "Nest's dog is dead from eating poisoned porridge!"

The uproar was instantaneous, much like it had been in the hall, and Llelo just managed to stop himself from glaring at the server, who was looking very satisfied at the effect of his announcement. Instead, Llelo decided the time had come for more commanding action.

He put his arms up over his head and said, "My father, Gareth, who as you know is Prince Hywel's steward and investigator, asked me to secure the pot in which the porridge was made. We understand the porridge was cooked especially for Nest and Deri."

His words could barely be heard over the hubbub. Llelo wouldn't have thought ten people could make that much noise. He himself often liked to linger at the table in the kitchens of the castles they visited, watching the activity, and he'd seen many crises over the years, from spilled vegetables to burned bread to entire dishes ruined because someone put too much salt in the pie. He'd even been at Dinefwr when the residents of the castle had been poisoned during a victory celebration.

In this instance, Alun showed why it was he who had been promoted to head cook. He put down his knife and came around the table to stand beside Llelo.

Pointing a finger at the servant in the doorway, he said, "Shut the door, Brychan."

He hadn't even shouted, but the room quieted instantly, and the young man obeyed.

"I want everyone to stop what they are doing and look at me, except you, Bronwen. Keep turning the crank."

Bronwen was roasting several chickens on a spit over the fire. She nodded, though her eyes were on Alun too.

"If there's something that needs my attention, raise your hand. Otherwise, be still."

Such was his command of his kitchen that everyone obeyed, and nobody appeared even slightly resentful.

Alun looked now at Llelo. "Is anybody else in the hall showing signs of illness?"

"No."

"Thank the Lord for that." Alun heaved a sigh.

Turning back to the servant Brychan, he asked, "Where are Tomos and Pawl?"

"Still in the hall. They were collecting dishes." Brychan paused. "Really, they were doing little but gaping at the queen and Lord Gareth." The young man gestured to Llelo. "I was the only one who thought to come tell you what had happened."

Alun turned back to Llelo. "Are we to shutter the kitchen?"

Llelo was momentarily flummoxed. An abundance of caution might require it, but he didn't want to overstep his authority. "Nobody said."

Alun rescued him. "For now, we will bring no more food into the hall until I speak to Queen Cristina. It doesn't sound like anyone is interested in eating at the moment anyway." With a gesture at

Llelo, he added, still making it easy on him, "Ask the questions you came to ask, and we will answer the best we can."

Llelo felt on more solid ground. This he knew how to do. "First, where is the cooking pot that held the porridge meant for Deri and Nest and were there any leftovers?"

"No leftovers, and the pot has been washed already," Alun said immediately. "It was a small pot, and we needed it for other things." He turned to one of his underlings. "What's in it now?"

"Water, sir," the man said. He was red-headed, in his late twenties, tall and thin. "I was about to boil more onions."

"Take it off the fire and set it aside. We will use a different pot until that one is thoroughly scrubbed again." Alun turned back to Llelo. "What next?"

Alun's acceptance of Llelo and respect for his authority was giving him confidence, and Llelo endeavored to return the compliment by being as straightforward as he could, without emotion or accusation. "Who among your people made that porridge?"

"I did. I've done it every day they've been at Denbigh." Bronwen, the woman at the spit, put up a hand.

She was middle-aged and comfortably stout, with gray hair pulled back into a bun. Today, her brow was furrowed, which was not usual for her, as she was a person who was always laughing. Bronwen had been the one who'd fed Llelo and Dai extra food in the months they'd lived at Denbigh before Prince Rhun's death. All they'd had to do was plop themselves down at the kitchen table, and fresh bread and mead would appear before them. More importantly, she'd listened to their woes, patched up their cuts and bruises and, in short, been a substitute mother to them when they'd needed one.

"Everything was as usual. I put grain and milk in the pot, boiled them, added a pinch of salt, and set the bowl on the table to be taken into the hall."

"Where is the bag of grain?"

Rather than make Bronwen leave her post, Alun answered for her, striding across the kitchen to a shelf from which he took down a jar. Lifting the lid, he showed the wheat grains to Llelo, who frowned at how few were left. "This is all you have? It doesn't come in a large sack?"

"It does, but this is all that steward, Andreas, provided for us. It seems Nest and Deri require special grains for their breakfast. They won't eat from our stores." For the first time, Alun allowed a tinge of opinion—in this case, unfavorable—to color his tone. "Tomorrow I would have been asking for more."

Llelo was still frowning slightly. "Are you saying that not only the porridge destined for Nest and Deri wasn't taken from the communal pot, but the grains from which you made it weren't either?"

"Exactly. It's all special to them. We were serving oat porridge this morning to everyone else."

Llelo felt a rush of relief, and it must have shown on his face, because Alun nodded. "We did everything they asked."

"Could anyone have tampered with the contents of the jar?"

"Of course. It sits on a shelf here. We are busy—and sometimes we sleep." Alun shot Llelo a quick grin.

Llelo made a feeble attempt to return it and then got back to his questions: "How long did the porridge sit on the table in the kitchen after it was cooked?"

For the first time, Alun had no easy answer, and his workers looked at each other with some consternation too.

Finally, it was Bronwen who replied. "I remember seeing it there for a little while, but it wasn't long, well less than the time it took the bread to bake."

"Who took it into the hall?"

Brychan, who was still standing with his back to the door, raised a hand. "I suppose I did, with two spoons and two bowls, one for each of them, on a tray. That was a requirement as well, and they wanted it to be exactly the same every day."

Llelo wasn't surprised to hear it. His grandfather was very particular too about how things needed to be done. Llelo had supposed it was a product of moving about so much, or maybe superstitions were universal to bards.

"Did you see the dog eat the porridge?" He was still speaking to Brychan.

The server shook his head. "I set it where Deri told me to. He was the only one about. At the time, he didn't seem interested in eating it. I almost said *don't let it get cold*, but decided it wasn't my place to tell him what to do. As I said, he wanted things the same every day, so he would have known it was hot."

"Where did you go after that?"

"Back to the kitchen for another tray."

Alun intervened. "Brychan is a good boy. He didn't do any-thing."

Llelo put up a hand. "I wasn't suggesting anything by these questions. I'm trying to establish a timeline of events, so we can fig-ure out when the poison was added to the meal."

"None of us here would do such a thing," Alun said stoutly.

Again Llelo was soothing. "I never said so or that you had done anything wrong. There's no reason for the food not to sit on the table for a short while before being served, nor for Brychan to leave the tray where Deri indicated. He did his duty." Llelo looked again at Brychan. "Did anyone stop you along the passage from here to the hall?"

"No." He was sure about that.

Llelo gestured broadly to the rest of the workers. "Do any of you remember anyone coming into the kitchen who isn't one of you here now? Guests at the palace, for example? Or others who aren't normally ones to come to the kitchen? I'm particularly interested in the moments between when Bronwen started cooking and when Bry-chan took the porridge to the hall."

Alun's expression turned dubious. "Queen Susanna was here earlier, to discuss the day's menu. So was Queen Cristina."

"A young woman came in whom I hadn't seen before," the red-headed worker said, "looking for tender meat for a child."

In turn, each of the workers put forth a memory of someone they'd seen at some point that morning, such that Llelo finally had to put up a hand again. "Is it usual to have so many people passing through the kitchen in such a short time?"

That hadn't been the case that he remembered when he'd lived at Denbigh, but then, a wedding hadn't been scheduled those months either.

"When we have guests, yes. Everybody wants something special, which is why we didn't blink at the rules for the porridge for Nest and Deri, especially after Queen Cristina told us to accommodate all requests if we could." Alun paused. "Come to think on it, this was the first morning that Andreas, Deri's steward, didn't oversee the cooking."

"Did either Nest or Deri come in?" Llelo's father had explained they'd each accused the other of murder, so he supposed it was a question he might have asked sooner.

"No." Alun was certain, and the nods from the others indicated they agreed.

Llelo believed them, for no other reason than neither bard could go anywhere at any time without calling attention to themselves.

"The same could not be said of Andreas's wife. What's her name?" Alun snapped his fingers.

"Manon," Llelo supplied.

"She was feeling unwell and wanted honey in warm water to settle her stomach."

Llelo glanced over at him. "Unwell, how?"

Alun bit his lip before answering. "Nauseous." He put out a hasty hand. "Nothing to do with our food! She said she was sick before she rose from her bed."

Llelo really hoped that was the case, and he made a mental note to check.

Then Alun asked, "Where is the dog now?"

Before Llelo could reply, Brychan said, "Queen Cristina told me to find a cloth to wrap the dog in and take it to the laying out room by the chapel, which I did. That's why I wasn't back sooner." He sniffed. "I assumed Tomos or Pawl would have told you what was happening."

He appeared to want some kind of commendation for being so helpful, so Llelo gave him another opportunity to answer a question. "Did you see the dog die?"

Brychan's expression turned regretful. "No, my lord. It happened in the time it took for me to go to the kitchen, load up another tray, and return to the hall."

"How long might that have been? A quarter of an hour?"

"Oh no! Nothing like that long. I'm quick!" Brychan spoke with pride, as a man who was good at his job and knew it. "I'm sorry I can't be of more help."

"It really is only a dog that died?" Alun said.

"So far." Llelo said. "We'd like to keep it that way."

"Me too," Alun replied fervently. "Me too."

4

Gareth

Nest and Deri finally appeared in the receiving room, where Gareth and Cristina had been waiting, followed by their manager, Andreas. He was large, blond, with hair a shade darker than Nest's, and handsome (according to Gwen, though, always the diplomat, she'd added, *if you like that type)*. He was also closer in age to Gareth than Deri and suited for his job in that he was entirely unflappable. After some study, Gareth still hadn't decided if that was a matter of tactics or the result of a deficiency in intellect and/or emotion.

At the moment, Andreas was somehow managing to be apologetic yet unaffected, as if everyone was getting upset over nothing. "Sorry this happened. Annwyn was a sweet dog."

"Sorry! You're sorry?" Nest turned on him. "I wish I'd died instead of her!"

The door to the great hall was still open, meaning untold numbers of people had heard her lament. Gareth took several long strides and closed the door between the rooms.

"I don't know what else to say, Nest." Andreas put up both hands, seemingly on the verge of laughter at her vehemence.

"Nothing will bring her back." Nest turned away, harrumphing and folding her arms across her chest.

Andreas swallowed down his levity and bowed, though Nest couldn't see that part. "Apologies, I didn't mean to offend you."

"You should be sorry."

"Where were you this morning anyway?" Deri eyed Andreas with something like distaste. "Normally you make sure they've cooked our porridge correctly."

"Again, so sorry." Andreas's words were contrite, but amusement more than sorrow still showed in his face. "I should have checked in with the kitchen this morning. It won't happen again."

"Why didn't you?" Gareth was taking a risk in intervening, since it might stop them from talking to each other, but the question was an important one to have answered, and Andreas had avoided it once already.

"I was at the church, speaking to the priest about the order of the service. The wedding will take place at the church door, before mass, and there was some question as to whether the priest wanted only Deri to sing or both Deri and Nest."

That sounded reasonable enough on the surface. It would be a strange situation if Andreas wanted either singer dead. While he was employed not by them but by King Madog himself, without Deri, he would have no job. When Gareth had first heard of the arrangement, he'd been skeptical, but it took only a few moments in Deri's or Nest's company to realize why the presence of Andreas was necessary.

As to the two bards, now that they were away from their audience, their behavior was more normal. They weren't screaming at each other or even speaking in loud voices and had listened to Andreas's explanation without interruption (or complaint).

"It's just you've never absented yourself before, in all the years I've known you." Deri eyed Andreas, suspicion in his face.

"Really?" Andreas shrugged. "I wouldn't have said that was true."

Deri tsked under his breath, but then appeared to dispense with the issue because he said to Nest, taking a leaf from Andreas's book, "I don't see what all the fuss is about, Nest. She was an old dog. Dogs die all the time."

"You are a cold, heartless man!" The words were dramatic, but for all that, they were heartfelt. "All of you!"

"What are you going to do, Nest? The dog *is* dead. No point in going on about it." Deri really was sounding exactly as his sister described.

Andreas, for his part, stood looking on impassively, as if her complaints about her dead dog were something he'd heard a thousand times before. As they'd been talking, Gareth had been switching his attention from the bards' faces, to Andreas's. With the most recent exchange, he had begun to watch them all more closely, in addition to listening to what they were saying. Suddenly, it was obvious that, while Andreas may not have poisoned the porridge, provided he was telling the truth about not going into the kitchen this morning, he wasn't sorry the dog was dead.

All in all, Gareth could understand why Nest might be irritated with both of them.

Now she shook her head. "How can you not see that it isn't just about the dog, though I loved the sweet thing? *I almost died.*"

"I don't understand why you keep insisting that is the case," Deri said. "*I* was the one who was lifting a spoonful of porridge to my mouth in the moments before Annwyn died. While you didn't touch the porridge in the hall, as you yourself said, you could have entered the kitchen earlier and poisoned it. You said only last night that you wished someone would murder *me.*"

Gareth blinked. "Is that true?"

Nest shrugged. "It was a turn of phrase, nothing more."

"Why would you say such a thing?" Cristina had been uncharacteristically silent up until now, but her question was on point.

"He accused me of murdering the last verse of a song." Nest tossed her head. "I told him he was mistaken. That's all."

Deri appeared unconvinced, and while Gareth could see him working up an ire before he voiced it, Gareth himself couldn't think of a reply quickly enough to cut him off.

"Clearly, the poison was meant for *me.* A moment ago, you called me a murderer, but it's sounding more and more to me as if *you* are the one responsible and are trying to cover it up. Why else would you choose this morning of all mornings to declare yourself too fat to eat?"

"I don't know what you're talking about. I never said I was too fat. I merely said that I wanted my blue dress to fit properly for the wedding reception, and that meant I wasn't going to eat today."

The pair was almost at their former crescendo. In that moment, Gareth wished he'd taken them farther from the hall. While the door was closed, preventing any of the other guests from witnessing their conversation, it would be impossible for them not to hear it.

Still, that the argument was starting again, even without an audience, did give some indication how seriously Nest was taking the death of her dog.

Andreas made one more attempt to smooth things over. "I'm sure this is all a big misunderstanding that will be sorted shortly."

"Sorted!" Nest's voice rose another octave. "What does that even *mean*? My dog is *dead*!"

She had a point. It was also a very English phrase, and not one Gareth would have applied to this situation. Nest was right that the death of a beloved dog wasn't something that could be *sorted*.

Though he hadn't given it any thought up until now, so far Gareth wasn't particularly impressed with Andreas's ability to rein in his bards' worst impulses. While his organizational skills appeared to be adequate, and he was always at their beck and call, whether bringing them a different instrument, a glass of mead, or reminding them of the order of the songs they were to sing, appeasement wasn't control. Neither viewed him as having any genuine authority over them.

In short, they were both spoiled. Given their ages, it was likely to be a permanent condition.

Then again, Andreas might have been hired for precisely the qualities he was currently displaying, and King Madog might not want someone to control them.

It wasn't Gareth's place to discipline them either. They weren't his children. Though he was exhausted already, and his headache had not improved in their company, he was tempted to let them go on as they were until they ran down just to see how long it would take. He had to think it would happen eventually.

Cristina, however, had been looking from Gareth to the three Powysians like someone watching a game of catch. Her brow was furrowed, for once not in anger or irritation, but worry. "I have guests who must be soothed." She spoke in an undertone, as if afraid Nest or Deri would overhear.

She needn't have bothered. Neither was in the least bit concerned about anything but their own umbrage. Gareth wouldn't have said either that Cristina had ever spoken to him so politely. In that instant, he decided that, if this was some new accord, he would be wise not to fight it. Cristina was King Owain's wife, whether or not any of them liked it. Gareth would do virtually anything to make Prince Hywel's life easier.

"I'm sorry this is taking so long," he said, though it wasn't really his fault. "Please, feel free to do what you need to do elsewhere. I will deal with them."

"Perhaps the guardhouse would be a better venue? More private."

With the palace complex full to the rafters, there was definitely a limited number of spaces that could afford anyone a quiet place to talk. If Gwen and the children hadn't been asleep in the guesthouse, Gareth might have suggested they retire to the common room there, but he was loath to inflict Nest's and Deri's screeching on anyone else, much less his own family.

"I will see to it, my lady." He put out a hand. "And if I may ask, if you have a moment, would it be possible for you to look in on the kitchen? Llelo will have spoken to the cook and the rest of his staff, but Alun will need to know if his people can keep cooking or if we must be concerned about the safety of the food."

Initially, Gareth had intended to do this himself, and would have preferred not to set the queen on his son, but he was going to be occupied with Nest and Deri for some time.

"Are we? Concerned about the safety of the food, I mean."

"I leave that to you, Madam. Nobody else has fallen ill, as you said, and the porridge was made specifically for Nest and Deri. Regardless of what Nest said, this doesn't appear to be another Dinefwr."

"I will see to it." Cristina made a move towards the door, but then turned back before she'd gone more than a pace. "I will have them scrub every pan, utensil, and dish in the place."

"That's probably wise. And it's what we have done in the past, after which we were spared any further incidents."

"The meat and bread should be fine, though, don't you think?" Her brow was furrowed.

"I would like to think so, my lady. I myself ate bread just now. If nobody in the hall is ill, then we would not be out of bounds to believe the poison was truly meant exclusively for Nest and Deri's porridge."

Further astounding Gareth with her even temper, she gave him another approving nod. "Please sort this out. The king will be grateful for whatever you can accomplish—as will I."

5

Gareth

Gareth waited until the door had closed behind the queen before shaking his head. Cristina had said *please* to him. Twice. It was unprecedented. He wanted to trust that this was an indication of a new accord. He didn't know if he could. In fact, he was pretty sure he couldn't. Right now, Gareth had what she wanted, which hopefully was a quick way out of an uncomfortable situation. Past experience told him that if he was slow in his task or in any way failed to live up to her expectations, she would be the first to leave him hanging.

Still, she was correct that he had a job to do, and he would have done it regardless of whether or not she'd been polite when she asked him.

He turned back to Nest and Deri, who were as close to screaming at each other as to make no difference, their faces a foot apart, while Andreas tried ineffectually to get between them. As with most things, he didn't believe the need was urgent enough to truly assert himself.

As Gareth watched, deciding how best to intervene, Nest put a hand on Andreas's shoulder and shoved him towards Deri. "You should be doing something about *him*, Andreas, not *me*."

Deciding there was no help for it, Gareth put himself between the two siblings, took each by an elbow, and turned them forcibly towards the back door. He'd dithered long enough with them that as he stepped outside, he was just in time to see Cristina entering the kitchen. She didn't close the door behind her, so he hurried Nest and Deri past, not wanting either of them to wonder what was going on inside, decide that Annwyn's death was the kitchen's fault, and get caught up in a new argument there.

In addition, *he* didn't want to get caught up there—not because he wasn't interested in what was going on and how the poisoned porridge had come about—but because he wanted Llelo to believe he trusted him fully. Being left to his own devices with the queen should be evidence enough of that.

"Let go of me." Nest pulled her elbow out of Gareth's grip, and he thought himself lucky not to have received a sharp jab to the ribs. "I am perfectly capable of walking without help."

"Pardon me, madam, I was concerned about the number of ears listening to what really should be a private matter."

As they came around the corner of the kitchen, Nest was tossing her head again to show Gareth how little she thought of him and his privacy concerns, when they almost ran over the ewerer crossing the courtyard from the well, buckets of water hanging from both hands. It was his job to keep the washbasins throughout the palace supplied with warm water.

At the sight of Nest, he stopped abruptly, sorrow in his face. "Madam, I heard what happened. I am so sorry!"

"Thank you, my dear." Nest's anger at Gareth immediately gave way to an appropriately mournful expression.

"Anything I can do for you ... anything. Please let me know."

Nest put a gentle hand on the man's arm. "You are very kind."

The man bobbed his head, and they separated, the ewerer heading for the massive cauldron that hung over a fire night and day and supplied the palace with warm water and the rest continuing to the gatehouse.

As they walked on, neither Nest nor Deri said anything about the exchange that had just taken place, and as Gareth looked from one to the other, he realized that it was so commonplace as to be unremarkable. Nest drew male attention wherever she went—and she encouraged it.

Once at the gatehouse, Gareth slowed, feeling some relief to have achieved the journey without encountering anyone else. At least now, if more screeching were to occur, the thick stone of the barbican would prevent the sound from being heard throughout the palace. Andreas had come with them and stopped a few paces away. His head was high, and he looked around with a pleasant smile on his face, enjoying the warm air and the morning, to all appearances completely unconcerned about why they were here. He made no move to open the door to the guardroom, instead waiting for Gareth to do it.

As Gareth gestured the three Powysians inside, he watched their faces in turn, wondering at their motivations. He was beginning to understand Nest and Deri, but Andreas remained a closed book, and that included his marriage to Manon. Though Manon herself had once been a musician of some renown, she had ceased to perform. Gwen had known her well because, as with Nest, their fathers were bards. Similarly to Deri, Manon's father had felt himself in competition with Meilyr and had discouraged their friendship, much to Gwen's disappointment.

Though she could have been lovely in her own way, since they'd arrived at Denbigh, Manon had slunk around the palace with a worried, cowed look to her, like a dog who'd been kicked too many times. That certainly had been her look this morning in the hall. Gareth was worried it was a result of Andreas's treatment of her. Greed, jealousy, and hatred were motives for murder—but so was desperation. While Gareth saw no motive for murder in Andreas, he hadn't settled on how significant were Manon's resentments. If Nest or Deri were the ones who'd done her wrong, he might need to take a closer look.

Denbigh was one of the few royal palaces under Owain's control that he'd surrounded with a high stone curtain wall. With twenty-two palaces in Gwynedd alone, all could not be fortified so strongly and few needed to be. While each had some kind of restrictive fortification, more common was either a wooden palisade or a lower stone wall. The wall at Rhosyr, for example, was no more than eight feet in height and was more a matter of discouraging unauthorized entry to the compound than a structure designed to resist a concerted attack.

Location was the reason Denbigh needed an intimidating stone wall. These lands along the River Clwyd had gone back and forth between Norman and Welsh control for centuries. At times, even Gwynedd and Powys had fought for control of it, and Owain, now that he was securely ensconced, wanted to keep it. That was also the reason Denbigh was located to the west of the river on the highest point of the whole region, overlooking the valley below. The plateau on which the palace had been built had long been known as one of the more easily defensible strategic positions in eastern Gwynedd, since cliffs protected it on three sides. It was accessible only from the north, where a village had grown up, with its own parish church, in which Iorwerth and Marared were to be married.

Of course, by having the wedding here, King Owain was giving his main rival, King Madoc, an intimate view of the inner workings of the palace and what Madoc would have to do if he wanted to take it.

Alternatively, Owain was showing Madoc all the reasons taking it would be impossible, and why he shouldn't try.

Gareth followed the others into the guardroom and was pleased to find Conall, Leinster's ambassador to the court of Gwynedd, already there. As they filed inside, Conall was tipped back against the wall and was nearing the end of a tale set in Ireland. He finished his sentence before bringing the front leg of his stool down to the floor. Gareth could tell the story had been a particularly outlandish one because the taller the tale, the thicker Conall's accent became.

Gareth had never known Conall to shout, scream, or cry (in contrast to Nest and Deri), but he liked an audience too, in this case composed of Madoc and Cynan, two of Hywel's younger brothers, to whom Denbigh was home for most of the year. It was into their hands that King Owain had placed the eastern defense of Gwynedd.

All three men rose to their feet, and everyone's eyes were on Nest. If Gareth hadn't spent the last quarter of an hour trying to quell her emotions, he might have been looking at her admiringly too.

"Miss." Conall bent over Nest's hand, which he'd taken in his. "Your singing last night was glorious."

Nest simpered, and Gareth had a moment's fear Conall would fall for her ploys. Looking at him now, to some degree in his element, Gareth acknowledged how much he still didn't know about his friend.

But then Conall straightened and shot a wink in Gareth's direction, albeit behind Nest's back because she had already turned to Madoc and Cynan to receive their accolades.

Deri, meanwhile, looked on with a stoic, if not resigned, expression.

"If you'll excuse us, boys." Nest's smile widened, and she actually batted her eyelashes at Owain's sons.

Neither brother was a boy any longer, but they were younger than Hywel, and thus close enough to boys to react more to her tone than her accompanying smile. If they had been Gareth's sons, he might have taken them aside later to warn them not to look in that direction for affection. Still, it was too early to judge whether Cristina's assessment of Nest was entirely accurate. She couldn't really help what she looked like, and, as a widow, she had every right to preen under male admiration. In addition, Nest's husband could have died of natural causes, particularly if he was a drunkard, and Nest could simply be happy to be free of him. She was a lovely young woman, and there was no real reason she shouldn't make the most of it.

In truth, however, neither Cynan nor Madoc looked displeased to be leaving. Conall moved to follow, but Gareth put out a hand to stop him and said in rudimentary Gaelic. "It may be I could use your help."

Though his eyebrows went up, Conall immediately turned back and didn't feel the need to ask why Gareth wanted him to stay. Even more than when he had been the ambassador from Leinster to Dublin, Conall had an enviable autonomy in Gwynedd's court. Dublin was Leinster's vassal state, and Dublin's king was subservient to Leinster's. Between Gwynedd and Leinster, however, there was no such power relationship. Conall was here because he wanted to be, and because it pleased both Owain and Diarmait to have him here. Gwynedd's ties to Ireland were wide and deep, and more communication was always better than less.

The reason Conall stayed when Gareth asked, then, was not because he had specific political obligations to Gwynedd, but because he and Gareth were friends. Conall had taken part in several investigations over the years. At the moment, Conall's eyes held a look that asked if this was another, told Gareth he wasn't displeased about getting to tag along, and thought it might be an amusing diversion. Gareth decided not to dissuade him of that notion, since he would discover how wrong he was as soon as Nest and Deri started talking.

Gareth pointed to chairs on one side of the table that took up a portion of the room, indicating Deri and Nest should sit beside each other, while he walked around to the other side and took the seat intended for the garrison captain. The guardroom was similar in size to Gareth's bedchamber in the guesthouse and looked as if it had been used similarly too, given the stacked sleeping pallets in the corner. Otherwise the room was plain, with whitewashed stone walls and a wooden floor and ceiling. Thick beams supported the next floor above. Coals glowed in the grate, which gave off just enough heat to cut the coolness that remained in the air.

Andreas hovered at first between the door and a bench set against one wall but then chose the bench, his hands resting on his thighs, relaxed and expansive as always. He appeared to have no concern that somehow he was to blame for Annwyn's death. So far, Gareth wasn't seeing anyone to blame—or behaving as if they were to blame—though he instantly reminded himself that everyone lied and it was too early to tell.

Conall took it upon himself to close the door and lean back against it. Nest then crossed her legs, straightened her skirt, and put her clasped hands on the table, like she was about to recite a lesson for her tutor. She seemed to realize there was no point in trying to put on airs with him, and the change in her demeanor was refreshing.

"To begin—" Knowing better than to ask a general question like he had earlier, Gareth looked at Deri. While Nest would feel put out at not being allowed to go first, and he preferred not to alienate her any more than he already had, he needed a few details clarified before he spoke to her. "Describe to me how the dog died."

Deri's brows came together. "I told you it was poison."

"And I heard you, but I want you to tell me the sequence of events from the arrival of the porridge to the death of the dog."

Deri drew himself up straighter and genuinely appeared to have a desire to comply. "The servant brought the porridge and set it on the end of the table where I indicated. Annwyn had been somewhere around my feet, snuffing about. Then she jumped on the bench and onto the table to put her nose in the porridge. She took a few bites. Then she died."

"Immediately?"

The frown was back, but this time because he was thinking. "She ate of it, a few bites only, and then got off the table, which surprised me because she usually eats more than that. Now that I think about it, she seemed to be shaking slightly. At the time, I didn't think anything of it, and seeing as how I had the porridge to myself, I scooped out a spoonful. I was about to lift the food to my own mouth when I heard Annwyn under the table, choking and gagging. I bent down in time to see her body convulse. There was blood spewing from her mouth and saliva too."

"Oh, Deri!" Nest put the back of her hand to her forehead and looked like she was about to faint.

Andreas moved to where she was sitting, shooting daggers at Gareth with his eyes. "Must we discuss this?"

Gareth wanted to say, *Yes, really, we must!* Instead he made a little motion with his hand at Deri. "How long was she like this before she died?"

"It took the length of a ballad, no more." A ballad was the shortest of a bard's songs, a matter of a few verses in most cases.

"What did you do?"

Deri spread his hands wide. "What could I do? I pulled her out from under the table, but she was already going limp. And then she stopped breathing entirely."

"It's so awful." Nest had her face in both hands.

Gareth could only agree, but he couldn't allow the awfulness of the death to deter him from his job. First, he motioned to Andreas that he should move back to his place. Then Gareth leaned forward, his hands clasped before him as Nest's had been earlier. "I'm so sorry to have to do this, madam, but now I must hear what happened this morning in the hall from *your* point of view."

At first Nest kept her head down as if she didn't hear him, but she was simply gathering herself. Throwing her head back, she looked across the table at him, her cheeks still wet with tears but not openly weeping. "Every morning my brother and I share a meal of porridge with honey. We have eaten it for years."

"It's good for the throat," Deri put in.

Nest nodded her agreement, calmer now that they'd moved on from the specifics of the dog's death.

"Go on," Gareth said, feeling a little less like a fiend for torturing her. He already knew that a drink of warm water and honey was good for the throat. His family of bards, along with Prince Hywel, drank it in quantity in the midst of a performance, or if one of them came down with an illness, but he was unsure why the addition of porridge might be helpful. Still, he wasn't going to argue now that she was talking. "That you eat this dish was common knowledge in the kitchen?"

"We made it clear to the cook when we arrived a week ago that it was a requirement for our services. King Madog knows it well and has never begrudged our peculiarities."

And since their services were a condition of the wedding going forward, nobody, least of all Denbigh's kitchen staff, was going to object. Gareth didn't add that comment to the pot, however, knowing it would only make the dish before them more bitter. To be conciliatory seemed the better option. "Surely eating porridge for breakfast isn't such a great request. I have eaten it many mornings myself."

Deri lifted a hand. "We do not eat of the castle stores. We buy our own grain from a supplier in Shrewsbury, who brings it from Kent. We are very specific about the flavor and the density. Anglesey wheat simply will not do."

As Anglesey was part of Gwynedd, Gareth had cause to wonder if the decision to use a non-Welsh supplier was made by them or by King Madog.

"It is the same with the honey," Nest said. "We have a favorite producer."

Gareth couldn't wait to hear who that might be, but since Nest wasn't immediately forthcoming, he prompted, "Who is—" He left the sentence hanging.

"The monks of Llansilin. They supply mead to Dinas Bran as well. Their honey has a delightful apple blossom flavor."

Gareth endeavored to maintain his benign expression. "So you're saying the porridge prepared for your meal—and the accompanying honey—would not have been served to any other diner, a fact the whole kitchen would have known and anyone could have learned with a few simple inquiries."

"Yes," Nest said.

"Does the kitchen add the honey to the dish, or do you do so yourselves?" The honey was definitely a complicating factor, one Gareth hadn't yet considered.

"We keep it in our wagon and bring it to the meal ourselves," Deri said. "I wouldn't trust the kitchen with it."

Nest nodded her agreement.

"Where is the honey now?"

Andreas coughed into his fist. "I saw Manon pick it up before she left the hall."

Conall straightened in the doorway. "I'll get it." He left.

Gareth wasn't particularly pleased to be left alone with his victims/suspects, but he didn't argue with Conall about the need to secure the honey. "Tell me about your dog."

Now Nest's expression crumpled. Since her only audience was Gareth, admittedly with Andreas and Deri looking on, he believed it reflected her genuine emotion. "Annwyn was the runt of the litter, hardly bigger than a loaf of bread. I'd had her since she was weaned, a week after my husband died—eight years ago now."

"She ate with us every morning." Instead of reflecting Nest's grief, Deri's tone implied that he looked upon that fact with something of an unfavorable eye, though given that it had gone on for years, his disdain sounded a bit well-practiced and perfunctory.

"This is also something everyone would have known?" Gareth asked.

"I suppose." Nest looked dubious. "Though I still don't see why anyone would want to harm her. She was such a sweet thing."

"She defecated under the high table the other day," Andreas said in a tone that was very much by-the-way. "Queen Cristina was quite put out."

Nest turned to her brother, threw her arms around his neck, and wept, but her words could be heard through her tears. "If Queen Cristina murdered Annwyn, nothing will ever come of it. King Owain won't hear a word against her."

Gareth didn't reply. Nest wasn't wrong, though he'd had just about enough of the drama. Tangwen's ability to carry a tune at the age of three implied she might be able to join the family business sooner rather than later, but if she showed signs of anything resembling Nest's proclivities, he'd put a stop to it right quick.

At this point, Conall returned—empty-handed.

"You didn't find her?" Gareth asked.

"I found Manon all right. She was waiting outside. It seems everyone knows where we are and what we're discussing." If Conall hadn't been the ambassador to the court of Gwynedd from Leinster, Gareth would have said he rolled his eyes. Then, at their expectant looks, he spread his hands wide. "Manon says she doesn't have the honey and doesn't know what became of it."

This news brought a fresh burst of tears from Nest.

Deri patted her back. "I'm sure Gareth will do his best to discover who killed your dog." He glanced at Gareth. "You will, won't you?"

Gareth drew in a long breath through his nose. "Of course I will. I am truly sorry for your loss, Nest."

Nest nodded and dabbed at her cheeks with a handkerchief. By this point, her eyes were genuinely red—unattractively so—and Gareth further revised his estimate as to the extent of her grief. Some people loved their pets more than they loved their own children, which neither Deri nor Nest had anyway. Gareth hadn't had a dog of his own since he was a boy, but he knew that King Owain was very attached to his dogs, even when he cursed them for lying under his feet and tripping him. None, as far as he knew, had ever defecated under the high table.

"When we are done here, I'll get her favorite blanket and have the carpenter craft her a coffin so she can be buried properly." Nest turned anxiously to her brother again. "Will the priest let me bury her in holy ground? She must be buried next to the church or her soul won't be able to properly rest."

"I'm sure he will," Deri said magnanimously.

Gareth chose not to comment on that either. It felt as if the only practical thing he'd done so far was bite his tongue over everything unsaid and the continual absurdities.

"Father Adam has a sheepdog of whom he is inordinately fond," Conall said, in a calmer tone than Gareth would have managed. "It might well be that he will understand."

"Regardless, I cannot possibly sing tonight at dinner." Nest put the back of her hand to forehead again. "It would be too painful."

Then, once more, she burst into tears.

6

Llelo

Llelo had learned within the first day of his arrival at Aber as a newly orphaned twelve-year-old that Queen Cristina was a force to be reckoned with and definitely not one to be crossed. While from the start his parents had warned him to be respectful of her, his knowledge hadn't been a result of his parents' attitude, but was a product of what he himself had witnessed.

That first day, he'd been playing with Dai, wrestling in a grassy space near where the horses were picketed, when he'd heard yelling behind the kitchen. Cristina had been giving one of her maids a lashing with the rough side of her tongue, calling her names like *lazy, worthless,* and *stupid.* When it was over and once Cristina had stormed back inside, the maid had remained cowering near the corner of the woodshed.

Llelo and Dai had crept carefully to where the girl was weeping.

"What did you do?" Dai had asked, in his forthright ten-year-old way.

"I was laying out a dress for the queen to wear, and I caught the hem on a nail and ripped it."

It was a major offense. Even Llelo knew that.

"What are you going to do now?" he'd asked.

"I'll wait out here until the bell tolls for Nones, and then I'll go back inside. She holds a grudge, does our queen, but not for things like this. When she is really angry, she berates me with the back of a hairbrush, not just her tongue. Honestly, she was pretty calm, considering what I'd done. She didn't have to bring me out here when she could have humiliated me in the middle of the hall for all to see."

Then the girl had wiped her tears and walked off. Llelo had seen her hardly an hour later, laughing with one of the boys whose job it was to chop wood.

Llelo had never been able to do that. When someone was angry with him—especially when they'd said cruel things—he couldn't brush it off and pretend it didn't matter or hadn't happened. Even if the one who was angry forgot about it a few hours later, the accusations burned in Llelo's belly for days afterwards—years sometimes, depending on the offense. And yet, by her behavior, the girl really thought everything was going to be fine, as it turned out to be. Even before the evening meal, he saw her following after the queen, evidently returned to Cristina's good graces.

Thus, in the moments immediately after Queen Cristina appeared in the doorway of the kitchen today, Llelo had forced himself not to cower. He told himself he'd been assigned a task by his father, who'd been assigned *his* task by Cristina herself. Any anger she might be feeling right now—or might direct at him—had nothing to do *with* him.

So he straightened his shoulders, stepped forward, and bowed slightly. "My lady."

"What do we know?"

Taking her question for the command it was, Llelo gave her a rundown of what he'd learned.

She gave him a nod in reply—it was a quick one, but still a nod—and said, "Well done for taking care of things so ably. You can leave the kitchen to me now. Undoubtedly your father will have need of you more than I."

"Yes, my lady." Llelo gave her another quick bow and escaped, thinking himself lucky to have gotten off so easily *and* with a compliment.

Though it was hard to tell with the cloud cover so absolute, the day had dawned. At times in winter, Llelo felt his bones aching for the sun. His only consolation was that it wasn't cold today. And really, though he enjoyed reading and writing at times, any day not spent sitting at a desk was a good day. Oddly, Cian, his father's new clerk and Llelo's friend, didn't agree.

Llelo found himself in the courtyard a moment later, watching his father's retreating back as he walked with Andreas, Nest, and Deri under the gatehouse and into the guardroom. In that moment, he wasn't sure if he was supposed to join them, or if he should wait for further instructions. He dawdled so long before following, in fact, that he was still deliberating when Cynan and Madoc came out, Madoc with his hand on his brother's shoulder.

They were laughing.

Llelo pushed off from the post against which he'd been leaning at the corner of the blacksmith's works and went towards them. The blacksmith's apprentice was working the bellows while the blacksmith himself was pounding loudly on iron, making it impossible for Llelo to be heard above it when he stood nearby.

"There's our miscreant!" Cynan bounded forward and wrapped Llelo up in a hug that involved rubbing the top of Llelo's head with his knuckles. As these days Llelo was four inches taller than Cynan, it was something of a feat. Of course, Cynan weighed half again as much as Llelo did, so Llelo had little choice but to accept the treatment, barring a few flailing attempts to shove him away. Besides, he knew whatever abuse Cynan meted out came from a well of affection.

"Your father just booted us out of our room," Madoc said.

Madoc was far harder to read than Cynan, and he spoke as if he resented what Gareth had done, but there was a twinkle in his eye that told Llelo his true feelings were the exact opposite.

"Nest's dog died, and Queen Cristina wants us to investigate what happened."

"*That's* why we had to leave the room?" Cynan laughed. "Ambassador Conall was in the midst of one of his better stories."

Llelo knew all about Conall's stories and was almost sorry he had become caught up in the investigation instead of loitering in the guardroom with Cynan and Madoc. Then, since they were here, he decided it was as good a time as any to ask some questions, especially since the brothers were among the few people in the palace Llelo was certain would answer truthfully. "Were you watching the gate this morning?"

"We are always watching the gate, though I confess not this last half-hour." Cynan draped an arm around Madoc's shoulders. "Conall's stories put us to shame, brother. We need to do better if we're going to keep up."

Madoc took the affection of his brother stoically, as if it wasn't even happening. "Why do you ask, Llelo? Surely it can't be because of this dead dog."

"Surely it can." Llelo explained what he'd learned in the kitchen, exactly as he had just related it to Queen Cristina. He saw no reason not to tell it all. Maybe that was naïve of him, but if either Madoc or Cynan had tried to murder Nest or Deri by poisoning their porridge, Llelo would never trust anyone again.

"Fifty people passed through the courtyard and gatehouse while it was still dark," Madoc said after Llelo's recitation wound down. "Many were servants, but the great hall is full of nobles and peasants alike."

"We couldn't tell you the names of most of them, much less where they're from," Cynan said. "We are leaving the postern and gatehouse gates open at all times. You can ask the guards on duty, but I don't know what you'd be looking for. Even if someone was out and about at that early hour, the issue would be whether or not they entered the kitchen, and surely those who work there would know that best."

"We're headed to the hall now." Cynan transferred his hand to Llelo's shoulder in a manner reminiscent of Prince Godfrid, almost buckling Llelo's knees with its weight. "Why don't we listen to what people say about what has happened and report back?"

"Would you?" Llelo brightened. "When you talk to people, it comes off differently than if the questions are coming from me. When I first apprenticed to my father, I found people told me things because I was young, and they didn't realize I was part of the investigation too. These days, everyone here knows who I am and who I'm working for and they aren't as open."

Madoc spoke one word for every five of his brother's, but the ones he put forth tended to be thoughtful. "I dare say you're right, but you have to remember what your father says: you can learn something from a witness, even when all they're saying is *no*."

7

Gwen

"Oh no." Gwen shook her head rapidly. "Gareth, for me to be the one to speak to Nest would be a very bad idea."

Gwen had woken to find Gareth gone, which wasn't particularly unusual. They tried to go to sleep at the same time, but because of the children, they rarely rose together. Last night Gareth had come to bed very late, mumbling apologies. At least he hadn't snored. It was so rare for him to drink to excess, she was a little concerned that his heart was hurting over something she didn't know about.

She looked at him now with that in her mind, trying to see beneath his request.

Gareth had arrived in the guesthouse common room to find his family occupying one end of the long table, which, for the moment, they had to themselves. Everyone else had drifted off to the great hall, for the simple reason that the gossip about the drama of earlier that morning was too delicious to miss. And that was on top of the details of the wedding, what the guests were wearing, who was sleeping with whom, and, in a pinch, the mild weather, all of which was already more than enough to keep their minds and tongues occupied.

From across the table, Gareth appeared to be trying to speak obliquely so their very curious daughter wouldn't understand what he was talking about. They'd taken to spelling out words for things that were particularly frightening or unsavory, though to do so now would be far too unwieldy. Now, he switched to English, which Tangwen didn't understand. Yet. Or so they thought. "The woman's dog was killed. Both she and Deri have to be interviewed separately, but not so forcefully that it puts them off their singing. Cristina was quite adamant about that."

"My father and brother, not to mention Prince Hywel, are perfectly capable of taking their place," Gwen said, not bothering to hide the genuine pride in the truth of her words. "More than capable."

She glanced at her father, who was eating quietly at the end of the table next to Tangwen. He looked up, his expression turning rueful. "I'm compromised, I know, so I can't possibly talk to either of them. Deri has resented me ever since I won a contest for best up-and-coming bard. That was the contest that brought me to King Gruffydd's attention all those years ago, before the war in Ceredigion and all the rest. Deri is ten years younger than I am, so his resentment then was absurd. I believe I told him so at the time. On top of which, under different circumstances, if Deri were to refuse the stage, it would be Gwalchmai and I who would take his place."

As King Owain's court bard, Meilyr received a stipend for his daily living. But if he were to sing for the wedding, he would receive a further gift—from both King Owain and King Madog. If past events were any indication, the amount given would be considerable. Only Hywel never received compensation for his work. Although an accomplished singer and poet, with a voice equal to any in Wales, he was royalty, and thus not a participant in the order of bards, the *urdd bardd*. It was the reason, back before Rhun's death, he had performed at his *eisteddfod* but not competed.

"I know that, and you know that," Gareth said. "*Everybody* knows that except, apparently, the King of Powys. In truth, he does know it, but he simply refuses to acknowledge it. Worse, Queen Cristina told me when we were still in the hall that the wedding contract King Owain and King Madog signed states that Powys will provide the entertainment. It is part of the deal. If Nest and Deri do not perform, there is no wedding."

"You can't be serious!" Gwen's mouth opened in surprise. "I've never heard of such a thing. Are you sure it isn't the other way around? It would be more sensible for the contract to stipulate that if Madog doesn't provide the music, Owain can call off the wedding."

"Not according to Cristina," Gareth said. "Madog resents the inferior position in which he often finds himself in relation to Gwynedd. For some reason, it has to be played out in the entertainment for his daughter's wedding."

"I suppose that's preferable to on the battlefield," Gwen said ruefully.

Her husband grunted, apparently not so sure. "Besides, if anyone wants the wedding to go forward, it's King Owain."

Once again, Gwen looked down the table to her father. Except for his brief comment, he had spent the last quarter of an hour eating quietly, listening to their conversation without participating in it. He was still doing it, to the point that he was refusing to look into her face.

Her eyes narrowed. "You knew about this already, didn't you?"

He didn't answer, instead picking out another piece of bread for his granddaughter and very carefully scraping an appropriate amount of butter across it.

"Father," Gwen said, trying, and failing, to stop her impatience from affecting her tone.

Meilyr kissed Tangwen's cheek before finally looking up. And sighing. "Of course, I knew. King Owain had to tell me, so I wouldn't rail at him about why Gwalchmai and I were being set aside. I didn't tell you because he swore me to secrecy." This time, he spoke in French. While he understood English well enough to follow along with what Gwen had been saying, he didn't speak it well enough to answer. French would confuse Tangwen equally well. Or, worst case, Tangwen would understand everything they said and be fluent in three languages before she turned five.

"So King Owain does know the provision is mad," Gwen said.

"Of course, he does. He explained that he could do nothing about it." A wry smile touched Meilyr's lips. "You may be happy to know I'm getting paid anyway."

Gareth laughed. "I hope the king isn't angry at Cristina for telling me."

"The queen can take care of herself, as you well know." Meilyr said.

"What have you been telling people when they ask why you aren't singing?" Gwen asked.

It was Meilyr's turn to laugh. "The same thing *you've* been telling them: the truth, as far as it goes. King Madog agreed to provide the entertainment, and for once Gwalchmai and I are content to join the audience. Nobody believes me, of course, but they can't argue either."

"I'm pretty sure nobody has believed me either." Gwen turned back to Gareth. "You're saying all Madog has to do to stop the marriage is to prevent his own bards from singing?"

"It seems so," Gareth said.

"Well, it isn't quite that simple." Meilyr finally set down his knife and met the incredulous gazes of his family. They had given up on their complicated dance of languages and were back to speaking Welsh, Tangwen or no Tangwen. At least the topic wasn't murder anymore. "It's quite a long provision—you know how jurists can be—and the marriage can't be called off simply because they refuse to sing. It has to be a result of something external, something done *to* them. In addition, no other bards from Powys can be available to step in."

"Are there any here at present?" Gareth asked.

"None in the Order," Meilyr said, "which are the only ones who matter."

"The implication is that Owain is the one the contract is written to counter," Gwen said, "as if he, rather than Madog, might want to stop the wedding."

"Yes." Meilyr snorted. "As if our king would be involved in this attack on Madog's bards."

"King Madog, on the other hand ..." Gwen's voice trailed off as she thought about what she was saying. "Madog likely made sure no other bards from Powys came."

Gareth had been looking from Gwen to her father and back again, and now he let out a puff of air. "I hadn't yet made the leap to that particular conclusion."

Gwen shot her husband a grin. It was nice that an idea could still surprise him, especially when it was an evil one. "Madog knows Nest and Deri better than any of us—better than anyone at Denbigh except for Manon and Andreas. He knows they eat porridge every morning. But would he go so far as to poison his own bards to get out of the marriage contract?"

While she'd asked her family the question sincerely, from the looks on everyone's faces, they all thought the answer was obvious.

Gareth, who'd settled his back against the wall, was the one to say it. "Yes. Of course, he would."

Conall had also been uncharacteristically quiet throughout their conversation. Now he reached across the table to the platter of mutton, stabbed a chunk of meat with his belt knife, and brought it to his trencher. "You say that so calmly, even as all of us merrily continue to eat food brought from the kitchen. *That* is what is truly mad." Just for a change of pace, he chose to speak in Danish. He also didn't stop eating, taking a big bite of his meat with an accompanying grin.

"And yet, the method would be unlike him." Saran, Meilyr's wife and Gwen's stepmother had been settled in a corner during their conversation, drinking a hot herbal concoction of her own design. It was more normal for her to be silent as her family bantered at the table, but when she did speak, everyone listened. Gwen didn't actually know if she'd understood Conall's words, but her point was well taken anyway.

"While Madog is most certainly capable of murder, poison is a very round-about way of getting what he wants. When Madog wanted to murder Hywel, he sent his own men to do it in his own guesthouse at Dinas Bran. It would have been far smarter—and more subtle—to have followed Prince Hywel's party from the castle when he left the next morning, or better yet, gone ahead in order to ambush them on the road. His men could have buried the bodies, and all King Owain would have known was that his son had disappeared."

"If Madog is involved, likely we can't do anything about it." Gareth ran a finger around the rim of his cup. He was drinking only water this morning, Gwen noticed. "I should tell you as well that Cristina thinks Madog is looking for any excuse not to go through with the wedding. It's her opinion that only Susanna wants it."

"I still think it is nonsensical for Owain to have agreed to what you describe." Gwen slumped forward, her chin in her hand. "But I realize there's nothing at this point we can do about it."

"Thus, my request to have you speak to Nest. We are charged with the investigation, and we have an obligation to pursue it fully. A bard's daughter is the perfect person to speak to a bard's sister."

Gwen laughed, now speaking English. "You would think, wouldn't you? But I am my father's daughter." She motioned down the table to Meilyr. "He can't speak to Deri; I can't speak to Nest."

Gareth frowned. "Has she given you reason to think she doesn't like you?"

"So far, she has refused to speak to me other than a few semi-gracious words at our introduction, implying she didn't remember me," Gwen said flatly. "Yesterday at breakfast she turned her back on me rather than answer my polite inquiries about her health and well-being."

"That might also be my doing, above and beyond my relationship with Deri." Meilyr had returned to French.

"I'm happy to blame some things on you," Gwen said. "But I'm not so sure about this."

"At one point she made an overture in my direction." He sucked on his lower lip. "I refused her, of course."

Into the silence that followed that outrageous comment, Tangwen piped, "Qui Tadcu a-t-il répudié?" She pronounced the French perfectly.

Meilyr, her *tadcu*, because that was the Welsh word for grandfather, gave a full belly laugh and swept his granddaughter into his arms. "You are a smart one, aren't you. Take after your mother, you do."

Tangwen giggled up at him. She would be four in another month, though much of the time it seemed she was really four going on fourteen. At least Taran, at one year old, remained oblivious. He did everything his sister told him to do, naturally, but understood far less of what his parents said. Or so Gwen hoped.

"Nothing to worry about, *cariad*," Meilyr said. "Grownups talking."

"They do that a lot," Tangwen said prosaically, taking another bite of her bacon. If she'd been older, she might have been speaking facetiously, but she was actually very serious.

"Just try, Gwen," Gareth said, resorting to pleading. It wasn't like him either and further indication of his rough night with the mead.

"All right, but I can't promise she'll talk to me. What are you going to do?"

"I must try to get something approximating the truth out of Deri. And after that, I need to speak to King Madog, God help me." He put his hand to his head and moaned.

"As I said before, I'm no good with Deri," Meilyr said, "but if you like, I can take on King Madog."

"Are you sure, Father?" Except for the occasional times when he couldn't help but be present, Gwen's father rarely participated in their investigations. Taking it upon himself to question the King of Powys was unprecedented.

Meilyr patted Tangwen on the head as he released her. "It's the least I can do."

8

Llelo

Llelo hesitated with his hand on the latch of the common room door. His grandfather had just offered to speak to King Madog, which Llelo thought all to the good. It certainly wasn't a task he felt comfortable taking on.

Through the open window, he could see his family gathered around the breakfast table, and a flood of warmth filled his heart. Before that first day, back in Newcastle-under-Lyme, when he and Dai were newly orphaned, he hadn't known he was lucky. He'd never had any luck before. But then a genuine Welsh knight had come to the friary and transformed his world.

"Have you talked to the cook yet?" Gwen asked Gareth.

"Not yet. I sent Llelo to—"

At the mention of his name, Llelo lifted the latch and took a step into the room.

"And there he is!" The smile on Gareth's face at the sight of Llelo coming through the door would have brought tears to Llelo's eyes if he wasn't a sixteen-year-old man, charged with investigating the poisoning of a dog and the attempted murder of two bards.

Gwen looked up too. "Hello, son." She held out her arms, and he bent to to give her a hug and a kiss on the cheek.

"Hullo, Mam."

"Are you all right?" She patted his arm.

"I'm fine, Mam." He squeezed her once before letting her go and looking at his father. "I did what you said." Then, standing at the end of the table, he related what he knew. This was the third retelling, after Queen Cristina and Prince Hywel's brothers, but the first time in French, which his mother insisted he speak so the children didn't get an earful. He also explained that Cynan and Madoc had gone to the hall to eat and gossip.

"I love those boys," Gwen said with a smile. "Two peas in a pod."

"They are if it's possible to have one pea green and one purple in the same pod," Gareth said with a laugh and gave Llelo a quick rundown of what he had learned from Nest and Deri, so they would all have the same knowledge going forward.

Then Gareth rose to his feet, having finished his meal. "More to do." He tipped his head to Conall, indicating they should leave. "Shall we?"

"We shall." Conall rose.

"What about me?" Llelo knew he had an expectant look on his face, but he couldn't help it.

Gareth studied him. "How would you like to take a look at the dog?"

Llelo's jaw dropped. "By myself?" This was unprecedented, since he was still seen as an apprentice to his father, not a full-fledged investigator.

"Why not? I have to speak to Deri, and we'll talk about it afterwards."

Llelo swallowed. "I will do my best, Father. Thank you."

His father pointed to the bench he and Conall had just vacated. "Breakfast first, though. It sounds like you haven't eaten today."

"Yes, Father. Thank you, Father."

Gareth and Conall departed.

Gwen looked up at her son. "Are you sure you wouldn't rather eat afterwards?"

Llelo pressed his lips together as he thought. She was right that examining a corpse was best done before a meal rather than after, but he was hungry now—almost to the point of nausea. He was *always* hungry, which his mother knew and why it had been a genuine question.

"I'd better. Father put me to work the moment I entered the hall." Having sat at the table where his father had indicated, he pulled a trencher towards him and began loading it with food. "The kitchen is still cooking, and nobody is sick. He eyed his grandmother, who was sipping her usual hot drink in her usual corner. "What do you say, *Mamgu*?"

"This morning before we knew any of this had happened, I ate my own porridge with no ill-effects," Saran said. "If nobody else is ill, I say go ahead. I think we're going to find there is more going on here than meets the eye."

"There always is," Gwen said.

Llelo was inclined to agree, but he was already wolfing down the piece of buttered bread with honey his mother had handed him, so his mouth was too full to talk.

Meilyr slapped his thighs and stood. "That's settled then." He gestured to Saran, who gave him a long look before rising to her feet and taking his hand. They left without a backwards glance.

Llelo frowned at the speed of their departure. "Was it something I said?"

Though from the moment they'd met, his parents had showered love and affection on him and had made him feel securely part of the family, his grandfather had been much more difficult to get to know. They got along well enough, but Meilyr wasn't a demonstrative person, nor one who was forthcoming about what he was feeling. Llelo couldn't recall a time he'd seen Meilyr hug anyone other than Tangwen.

Gwen smiled. "I'm pretty sure it was something your grandfather said." Somewhat hesitantly, she explained that Meilyr had spent some time with Nest before his marriage to Saran, enough for her to be interested in him.

It was something Llelo was having a very hard time picturing, and that must have shown on his face too because his mother smiled. "It's hard to believe everyone was once your age, isn't it?" She got to her feet. "I can't believe I agreed to visit Nest!"

"You will be fine." Llelo lifted the jar of honey he was holding and attempted to jest. "Do you need to take some with you? Nest has a sour tongue."

Gwen stuck out her own tongue at her son. "Very funny. Watch out, or I'll make you come."

He swallowed quickly, half rising from the table. "Whatever you need—"

"No." Gwen put out a hand. "Your father gave you an important job, and I won't interfere with that. I'll find you when I'm done."

Llelo subsided, relieved that she trusted him and glad he had time to eat a little more. Sometimes during these investigations, there was far too little of both eating and sleeping. He'd learned to take advantage of the opportunities given him.

His mother's departure meant he was left at the table with only his sister and brother and their nanny, and he took a moment to make Taran laugh with a poke in the belly.

Then, almost immediately, Cian, Marged's son, plopped himself down in the spot where Gwen had been sitting. He was shorter than Llelo by several inches and rail thin, despite the fact that he ate his weight in food every day. "What is everyone so serious about?"

Llelo told him. By his count, this was the fourth time.

Cian was new to investigations, and that made him appropriately open-mouthed at Llelo's recitation. Really, it was very gratifying. There was plenty that Cian did better than Llelo when it came to book work, and Llelo couldn't handwrite to save his life, but he did generally have the better of Cian in terms of exciting news to report.

"I want a dog, but I don't want it to die." Tangwen kicked her heels against the bench, for all appearances completely unconcerned by the subject of conversation.

Llelo had forgotten he probably shouldn't have said all that in Welsh in front of her. He looked at Marged. "Sorry."

Marged shook her head. "I'd heard stories, so when I first came to your family I was wary of what living with you might be like and worried that I wouldn't like it."

Llelo was confused. "We have a wonderful family."

Marged waved her hand back and forth. "I see that now. But back then, I wasn't sure how you could. Now, I know that what you do is very important, and I simply *worry*." She gestured to Taran and Tangwen. "I worry for you and about what your job means for them."

"I want to help," Cian said, showing he had no such concerns. "What can I do?"

"Cian—" his mother started to say.

He turned on her. "What? You just said that what he does is important. I'm here, aren't I? With the wedding so close, I have no letters to write or sums to calculate." He looked at Llelo. "Put me to work."

Llelo studied his new friend. "You're sure?"

"Of course!"

"Then come with me to the laying out room. You can take the notes."

9

Gwen

Although court bards weren't dependent on the kindness of strangers in the way Gwen's family had been before Meilyr and King Owain had made their peace, the kings they served had many palaces and castles. Thus, a king himself was itinerant, journeying every few weeks from one location to another—and when a king traveled, his court bards went with him.

Thus, like itinerant workers everywhere, bards included, Nest and Deri owned a covered wagon in which they slept when not at their home (wherever that was) or at Dinas Bran. Approximately fifteen feet long and six feet wide, with a thick tarp stretched around a wooden frame for protection from the elements, the wagon not only provided sleeping quarters for Nest and Deri but space as well for their possessions and gear, which in their case consisted primarily of costumes and musical instruments.

Meilyr, Saran, and Gwalchmai had traveled to Denbigh in a similar wagon, though Gwalchmai was sleeping in Iorwerth's room to keep him company until the wedding. Gwalchmai was Iorwerth's closest friend and would stand up with him as he married Marared. Because of that, Gwalchmai's family had seen little of him this week as the young men spent Iorwerth's last days as a bachelor together.

Of all of them, Gwalchmai seemed to mind his banishment from the dais the least. For him, singing wasn't an occupation so much as a way of life. The wedding contract hadn't said anything about forbidding him to sing in the latrine, the stables, or a nearby field. He didn't need an audience—though if he kept it up long enough, a crowd usually gathered anyway.

Nest and Deri's wagon was parked within the palace walls by the stables, close to several others, including Meilyr's wagon, which was new and much nicer than the one Gwen had traveled in with her father and brother before their return to Gwynedd. Nest and Deri's also appeared to be only a few years old.

Usually Nest was a permanent fixture in the hall, always desiring some sort of social interaction. Thus, the hall had been where Gwen checked first, and after a quick look in various other possible locales, including the latrine, she rapped on the wooden frame of the wagon and heard Nest's resulting, "Come in."

A wooden step stool had been set at the base of the wagon, and Gwen climbed it to find Nest sitting on a closed trunk at the end of her bed, holding a length of rope and weeping.

Gwen took in a deep breath, bracing herself for Nest's emotions, and sat on Deri's trunk two feet away. "I'm so sorry for your loss."

Nest's weeping became great heaving sobs of bottomless grief. "Annwyn was a true friend. My only one."

Gwen didn't reply, just gripped Nest's hand tightly and allowed her to sob as long as she needed to. This was quite a long time, which allowed Gwen the opportunity to inspect the interior of the wagon, which was highly organized in a way Gwen found pleasing. The two pallets had been raised up on wooden frames so items could be stored underneath them. Both beds were made, the blankets straightened and pulled tight.

"I should have protected her. I should have known something was wrong. It's my fault she's dead."

Those same words had been said a thousand times by survivors, though usually in regards to people. But grief was grief, and Nest's mourning had brought empathetic tears to Gwen's own eyes. "Annwyn's death is nobody's fault but the one who poisoned her. And if you think about it, if she hadn't eaten the porridge, it could have been you or your brother in the laying out room, instead of her."

Nest straightened from where her forehead had been pressed against her knees. Tears still rolled down her cheeks, but the heart of the storm had passed, giving way to outrage, which hadn't at all been Gwen's intent. "She was an innocent!"

Gwen paused. "Does that mean you are not?"

The words were out before Gwen thought about them, and certainly came out more bluntly than Gwen had intended. They weren't even what she'd meant to say. Now that she'd spoken, however, she watched Nest's face intently.

At first, it was as if Nest hadn't heard her, and then another moment before Gwen's words penetrated her grief, which gave way, as before, to anger: "What's that supposed to mean?"

"Is there some reason someone would want to murder you?"

"Don't be ridiculous."

"Annwyn sacrificed her life so you might live. If she loved you anything to the degree you loved her, that would be a trade she would willingly make. Gareth tells me that, earlier in the hall, you accused your brother of murder. You're saying now you don't think he tried to kill you?"

Gwen had been prepared for her words to feed Nest's anger, but instead they sobered her, and her blue eyes gazed at Gwen out of a very white face. "I—I don't know. I was angry and sad. Sometimes I say things I don't mean."

"So you don't think your brother was trying to murder you?"

"I don't know!" The words burst out of her with force. "I just told you that. I don't know what happened."

"In which case, I do need to ask again if you think the murderer meant to kill Annwyn ... or you."

"Annwyn often shares our porridge, but not always. *The poison was meant for me.*"

"I hear what you're saying, but I have to wonder: if you're so sure about that, why do you say nobody would have a reason to murder you?"

Nest didn't respond, and now her chin stuck out a bit.

Gwen tried again. "Why do you assume it was you who was meant to die, knowing that your brother would have eaten of the porridge too. In fact, from what I understand, he would have eaten of it first."

Nest's eyes went to the floor, which for some people meant a lie would soon be forthcoming. "If he'd died …" She shook her head, silent a moment. "Nobody has any reason to kill him."

"Again, is that in contrast to you? That's what you're saying, isn't it? Annwyn was innocent, Deri is innocent, but you are not." It was the third time Gwen had asked essentially the same question and caused Nest to swallow hard. Whatever animosity she may or may not have had for Gwen was put aside, and they were speaking woman to woman, as intent a conversation as Gwen had ever had with anyone.

But then Nest's spine straightened, she rose to her feet, and put her nose into the air, as if realizing only now to whom she was speaking. "I don't know what you're talking about or why you're asking me these questions. I don't feel like talking about this anymore. It's your job to find out who did this, not mine!"

Gwen remained seated on Deri's trunk and looked up at Nest. The transformation was startling, though in keeping with what she had seen of Nest so far. Gwen wasn't done with the questions, and she hoped Nest's ingrained manners would prevent her from leaving the wagon with a guest still inside. "Poison has been known to be a woman's weapon—more than a blade, anyway. Would a woman have wanted to poison you?"

Nest snorted, well in control of herself now. She didn't give the question serious thought. "Of course not."

It was time to change direction. "Why did you tell your brother you weren't eating this morning?"

Both Cristina and Meilyr believed Nest to be free with her virtue, but it didn't mean she was. That line of questioning could always be pursued later, and right now, Gwen needed more basic information, without alienating Nest completely. As it was, Gwen thought it unlikely she would be getting anything out of Nest that had even a passing resemblance to the truth if Nest didn't want her to know it.

"It is as I told your husband." She smoothed her hands down her belly, which was enviably flat. Having produced two children, Gwen's belly was not and never would be again. "I have a dress that I want to fit into for the wedding, and I have only two days in which to do it. I suppose it doesn't matter now, since I won't be singing anyway."

Gwen pressed her lips together before she spoke, wanting to ask her next question in exactly the right way to get the response she needed. "You would let your brother carry on alone, you mean?"

Nest frowned. "What do you mean by *carry on alone*? Neither of us will be singing."

"That isn't what I heard. He has said he will sing without you if he has to. The wedding must go forward." This was entirely untrue, as Deri had said no such thing, but Gwen wanted to see what kind of reaction she engendered by telling Nest that he would.

So she took it a little further. "As you well know I'm sure, it is a bard's duty to take the stage, regardless of his personal circumstances."

This edict was, in fact, genuinely part of the covenant a bard swore when he joined the order of bards. As a bard's daughter and sister, it was something Nest would know, just as Gwen did. Really, with their common upbringing, Gwen and Nest should have been the best of friends. It was really too bad their personalities had diverged so profoundly as to make that impossible.

The resulting aghast look on Nest's face was gratifying.

Gwen believed Nest loved her dog—and she appeared to quite enjoy her fit of pique—but not so much she would allow her brother to claim the dais without her.

10

Meilyr

While Susanna had her own quarters within the palace, King Madog slept separately from his wife, residing in a palatial tent in the field outside the walls. Meilyr wasn't entirely sure why he'd volunteered himself and Saran to talk to the king. Gwen's look had told him how surprised she was to hear it. Not that he hadn't been peripheral to her investigations all these years. He himself had been the subject of one at Carreg Cennen, before their return to Gwynedd. That investigation had set her on the path she now trod. She'd looked so comfortable sorting through the various aspects of the investigation, it made him almost forget that, underneath her calm exterior, was pain at all those deaths and an intimate knowledge of grief and loss.

He knew as well, however, that her work made her stronger than he could ever have imagined his daughter being. Really, he should have known better, since at ten years old Gwen had weathered the death of her mother and taken on the raising of her infant brother. Saran had been there too at Carreg Cennen, and it had been

Saran, in fact, who'd pushed Gwen to find the truth in order to save *him*. From a certain point of view, everything that had happened since that day was the product of that single moment.

Meilyr thanked God every day he'd not been so much of an imbecile that he couldn't recognize Saran's worth and marry her.

He himself had behaved foolishly towards Saran for many years. To state it bluntly, he'd behaved foolishly full stop for many years, drinking himself out of his position as Gwynedd's court bard. For a long time, he'd blamed everyone but himself for that failure. At least he hadn't fallen so far as to blame Gwalchmai for his mother's death in childbirth, as some men did. He shuddered to think how close he'd come to destroying not only himself but his children.

It was another testament to his daughter's strength that she'd forgiven him before he'd asked.

Saran hooked her arm through his as they left the guesthouse. "You are very thoughtful this morning."

"I was thinking of Carreg Cennen."

Saran put her head on his shoulder as they walked along. "I often think of those days."

"I was thinking how close I came to losing you forever."

"Is that what prompted you to volunteer us to speak to King Madog? It isn't like you."

"I thought the children could use the help."

Saran laughed. "I love you, Meilyr, but the reason you volunteered us is because you're bored."

Meilyr wrinkled his chin, trying not to be offended. "You don't think I want to be of service?"

Saran patted his arm where she still held it. "You are frustrated, and to your credit, you are doing this rather than let those frustrations boil over."

Meilyr allowed himself to grump along another few paces—but at Saran's continued serene expression, he had to laugh and throw up his free hand, disgusted and at the same time entertained by her insight. "How do you know that? I didn't know it until just now when you told me!" He kicked a pebble off the flagstone path, the stones for which had been brought by wagon to Denbigh from mines in Snowdonia on the other side of the Conwy River. "Deri is a drunk. Gwalchmai and I—or at the very least Prince Hywel—should be singing in the hall."

Saran eyed him. "And what about Nest?"

He came to a dead halt. This was what they'd been navigating to since he'd mentioned he could have had a relationship with Nest. He turned fully to his wife, took her by the upper arms, and looked deep into her eyes so she would know he was telling her the truth. He didn't care who was watching. "I spoke of Nest now to Gwen because to not tell her would be a kind of lie. I promised never to do that—never again—to her or to you. I'm sorry you had to learn of it that way—" the words stuck in his throat, but he managed to add, "—I assure you nothing happened between us."

Saran reached up and patted his cheek. "I know that, husband. You are an open book to me."

"I am?" He eyed her, suspicious of her calm demeanor.

She smiled. "Was this before you and I married?"

"Yes!"

"Do I have anything to worry about?"

"No!"

"Well then." She tipped her head towards the main gate to the palace. "Should we see about this poisoning?"

"We should. We definitely should." Thanking the saints for getting off that easily, and relieved that Saran was being so understanding, Meilyr started walking with her again, directing their steps towards the gatehouse.

Nobody stopped them as they left the palace proper—or even looked twice at them. It was to allow the free comings and goings of Madog's people that virtually all watch on the gate had been forgone.

All things considered, Meilyr decided he'd gotten off more lightly than he deserved. Though really, the interlude with Nest had been short, a matter of sharing a few meals when the King of Powys had brought his bards with him in a visit to Deheubarth during a time Meilyr was singing for Prince Cadwaladr.

Now, as they walked along, Saran had a pleased smile on her face. He kept glancing at her, until finally he could be silent no longer. "Why are you so happy?"

"Like you, I enjoy being of use. And it occurs to me that this forced absence from the dais could be good for you—and for Gwalchmai as well."

"Gwalchmai is a good boy. A good man." Meilyr might have protested, but she'd made him think. "I would ask why you say so, but I suspect I can guess: you don't want him to become like Deri."

"He would have to fall a long way to become like Deri. Truly I cannot see it from where he sits now. It's Nest I was thinking of."

"She does screech very loudly."

Saran swallowed down a laugh. "A bard has to be confident to do what he does, but sometimes he can be too confident."

"I don't know what you mean." He put his nose into the air in a gesture of mock superiority. "Besides, a bard has a great many responsibilities."

"I don't mean the tutoring or the song writing, though that's important too. I mean to stand on the dais each night and perform requires a certain ... *something*. Confidence is a valuable quality, one you have rightfully cultivated in Gwalchmai. The concern, however, is that he could become so focused on what others think that he loses part of himself, namely the reason he started singing in the first place. Like Nest."

"That won't happen to Gwalchmai."

Saran pursed her lips, clearly not agreeing. "Gwalchmai wants to be perfect."

Meilyr didn't say *as he should* because he knew what Saran meant. "That's my fault."

"It is," Saran said simply. "You were and still are a hard taskmaster. Too hard at times. More than ever, Gwalchmai feels it. In the last year, he has also become more ambitious for himself, which on the whole is a good thing, because it gives him direction. But do you remember the last time he did something mischievous?"

Meilyr grunted. "It's been a long while."

"Too long. But like you, boredom might push him to remember what else he liked to do. Music will be his life. When you are gone, he will become King Owain's bard, and then Hywel's in his time. But he is too young to think there's nothing more to life than work."

As usual, his wife spoke wisely. Meilyr himself hadn't always remembered to look around at the beauty of the world, even as he sang about it. It was possible to write about it *without* seeing it.

Which was another reason he'd volunteered the two of them to speak to King Madog. A person who saw the world the way it was, rather than the way he wanted it to be, was rare in Meilyr's experience. Even more rare was a person who saw the world with all its flaws and loved it anyway.

Like Saran did. He hadn't volunteered *himself* to speak to King Madog. He'd volunteered *Saran.*

As sometimes happened, a stray thought gave him an inspiration for a new song, and he started humming it to himself, trying to work out the lines before he forgot them: *I have drunk from a bright cup, with fierce and warlike lords …*

He startled as Saran poked him. "We're here."

Blinking, having no memory whatsoever of arriving at the King Madog's pavilion, he smiled at the guard, who was standing at the entrance and looking distrustfully at them. "We have come to see the king. Is he within?"

"He is busy." The words were perfunctory and unnecessarily rude. If nothing else, it told Meilyr the true state of relations between Powys and Gwynedd.

"I would hope he would speak to us," Meilyr said. "We have come at the behest of Queen Cristina."

This wasn't expressly true, but he doubted anyone would argue, even if it ever came to light he'd used her name. Gareth was tasked with getting to the bottom of the dog's death, and he'd directed them to follow their current course.

Then words came from inside the tent, big and bluff. "My lord, the dog's death has nothing to do with us." It was Andreas speaking. "Let Gwynedd sort it out."

Saran, showing all of the confidence she'd ascribed to him and Gwalchmai, stepped past the guard and through the tent flap without waiting for permission.

Meilyr had no recourse but to follow, cursing and admiring his wife at the same time. Upon entering the pavilion, he found Andreas standing before King Madog, with his legs spread wide and his hands resting at his sides, relaxed as always. Servants milled around the large space, all of them, Meilyr noted, young and attractive women.

Madog's proclivities in that direction were well known, though Meilyr couldn't help but notice that none of the women looked particularly overjoyed to be where they were.

Madog himself was seated in a cushioned chair next to a glowing brazier, a carafe and cup on a low table beside him. While it was a warm day for winter, sitting outside without some extra warmth wouldn't be comfortable for long.

The king's expression was mild as well. "I wasn't blaming you, Andreas. *Someone* is responsible for that damned dog's death, and I want to know who."

The implication was that it had nothing to do with Madog himself. Of course, the king was unlikely to claim responsibility in broad daylight.

Then Madog noticed Saran and Meilyr entering the tent, and his eyes narrowed. As Meilyr had suspected, the attitude of the guard at the entrance came from on high.

In response, Meilyr bowed deeply. "Pardon, my lord. We couldn't help but overhear Andreas speaking. As we were sent by Queen Cristina to apprise you of what Gwynedd knows of the matter, I hope you'll excuse our intrusion."

Madog shifted in his chair. Like Owain, he was quick to anger—a kingly prerogative. Unlike Owain, however, he was slow to forget. Even so, Meilyr wasn't regretting Saran's initial boldness. Yet. And Saran's curious expression told him she wasn't either. But surely Cristina would look unfavorably on any of them getting on the wrong side of the King of Powys.

At the moment, he seemed peaceable enough and said, "Andreas was just telling me how upset Nest and Deri are about the loss of their dog. Both are refusing to sing." Madog usually had excellent control over his features, but a shimmer of glee overcame his expression before he smoothed it. "They fear their lives are in danger."

"We do have some concern in that regard, my lord," Meilyr said. "Queen Cristina wanted me to assure you that we are doing everything in our power not only to uncover who is responsible for the dog's death, but to ensure the safety of Nest and Deri *and* everyone else at the palace too."

Improvisation had always been Meilyr's strength when it came to music, and he was pleased to see it working for him now.

Madog's face still held a satisfied look, and Meilyr didn't have to guess why: Nest and Deri had a genuine grievance that could stop them from performing, in which case, the wedding could be called off. The longer the danger went on—if anyone really *was* in danger— the stronger Madog's position *vis a vis* King Owain. It was a place Madog didn't often find himself occupying.

"My lord, if I may ask, did you see anything unusual in the hall this morning?" Saran said.

"I have not been in the hall this morning. I breakfasted in my tent."

"I understand you weren't in the hall either." Saran turned to Andreas.

"I was not." Looking at her with undisguised amusement, he put his heels together and gave her a short bow. It was so well done that Meilyr couldn't tell if Andreas was truly being respectful or was, in fact, mocking. "Normally I would have been, but with the wedding two days away, I have many things to see to. As I explained to the king, and to Gareth earlier, I was speaking to the priest about the or- der of service."

"What of Manon?" Meilyr said. "She was there, I understand."

"In this, I cannot speak for her, beyond the brief observation that she knows nothing about the dog's death."

"Has she any insight into the conflict between Deri and Nest?"

"No." Andreas's expression turned rueful. "They do not listen to her like they listen to me."

"Then you are the one whose task it is to persuade them both to sing again, is it not? Singing itself should not be dangerous." Saran was one to look on the world with amusement sometimes too, and this question came from a well of playfulness. While Saran was motivated by a love of people, Meilyr rather thought Andreas's perpetual amusement stemmed from a conviction that people were absurd. On the whole, Meilyr couldn't blame him for thinking it.

Now, however, Andreas's expression turned dubious, as if the thought hadn't occurred to him before. "I suppose."

Madog snorted. "It is near impossible to convince either of those two to do anything they don't want to."

"You are their liege lord, sire." Saran's expression was one of surprise. "Surely if *you* ordered them to perform, they would have to."

"I suppose that's true," Madog said slowly.

Meilyr gave a little internal cheer. His wife might be middle-aged, growing stout, and with a kindly face, but her mind was as sharp as ever. She was easy to underestimate. Madog mightn't again.

"The death of a dog is a grievous matter," Saran went on, now sounding pious, "but surely not more important than one's duty to one's lord."

"Surely not." Now Madog himself sounded amused, realizing he'd been out-flanked. "If they are still recalcitrant this afternoon, I will speak to them."

Saran curtseyed. "You are a wise man, my lord."

"How kind of you to say so." Madog's eyes had turned watch-ful—and a little dangerous.

Meilyr nudged Saran's elbow. "Thank you for your time, my lord. With your permission, we will take our leave. Queen Cristina may have more need of us." With another bow, and after a wave of Madog's hand, they were out of the tent and headed at a fast walk for the gatehouse.

"Ooh, I'd forgotten how much I didn't like him." Saran forged ahead, taking long strides. "I see why, in all your rambling about Wales, you never ended up at Dinas Bran."

"I was a drunkard, but I was never stupid." Meilyr said. "Even at my lowest point, I knew better than to knowingly get in bed with a snake."

11

Gareth

“What are you hoping to get out of Deri?” Conall loped along beside Gareth. Today he was wearing his *court* clothes, as he called them, which meant a long robe with a knife belted at his waist rather than armor and sword.

“Whatever I can.” Gareth wasn’t wearing armor either, since he hadn’t returned to his room after he’d followed Gwalchmai out of it. He was still glad of his boots, since any detour off the slate pathways put them three inches deep in melting snow and mud. Because of the balmy weather, many of the children were barefoot, and their play had left them dirty to their knees.

“I suppose it is probably best to tackle him while Gwen is speaking to Nest,” Conall mused. “That way they won’t have time to align their stories.”

“It may well be too late for that,” Gareth said.

They had been delayed in their quest to find Deri by Queen Cristina, who’d insisted on going over everything they’d learned so far. That Gareth had escaped once again with not only his life but his pride and honor intact appeared to him as something of a miracle. For Cristina's part, she reported the kitchen was hard at work scrubbing every utensil and pot. She herself, alongside Alun the cook, had searched the kitchen from top to bottom for anything resembling poison and found nothing. She was confident the noon meal could go forward as planned.

Deri wasn't in the hall, the washroom, or his wagon, which they hadn't had to approach very closely, since Nest's voice carried to them even though they were outside. She didn't sound happy. Nor did Gwen, though Gareth couldn't make out her words because of their softer tone. Truthfully, he didn't want to, and he hustled Conall away before they'd eavesdropped on more than a few sentences.

In the end, they found Deri in the chapel, which was located on the opposite side of the palace from the guesthouse, in its own domain within the complex. The church where Iorwerth's wedding would be taking place was outside the palace walls and further down the slope towards the village. Owain, who'd ordered the chapel built, had done so in order to provide the residents of the palace a private place to pray. The two places of worship shared a priest, who came to the palace when the king requested it. The village had its own laying out room by the church too, one Gareth very much hoped he would never need to see. One corpse, even that of a dog, was one too many.

Judging by the boxes of instruments and folios of written music that surrounded Deri, he and Nest had claimed a section of the chapel for themselves as a place to practice and prepare without all eyes on them, for once. Having himself married into a family of bards, Gareth didn't begrudge them the need. Even performers such as these two couldn't be performing all the time. They certainly didn't want everyone in the palace to have heard their latest song before they'd had a chance to perfect it.

At the moment, however, Deri was sitting on a bench against the wall and staring at the floor, not doing much of anything. As often was the case, he was taking occasional sips from a flask resting on his thigh. His graying hair was particularly lank, and a length of it had fallen across his face. As he swept it back, Gareth noted that he was quite bald and had grown the hair on one side of his head long so he could sweep it over the bald spot on top.

It was something Gwen had probably noticed long ago and not commented on, preferring not to gossip or be unnecessarily catty. Gareth had to admit it looked like a pathetic attempt on Deri's part to pretend to be younger than he was and to keep up with Nest. In that moment, Gareth swore, if he ever started balding, he would cut his hair even shorter and live with it.

Although they were thirty feet away in an otherwise empty church, it didn't seem Deri had heard them come in. The door had even banged against the inner wall of the chapel's entry way, caught by a sudden gust of wind. Soon, they'd have rain again. Even Gareth, who was no weather-sayer, could tell that.

Gareth and Conall approached slowly, not wanting to startle the old bard. When they were only twenty feet away, he finally caught sight of them out of the corner of his eye and looked up.

Gareth put up a hand. "I'm sorry to disturb you, Deri, but I have more questions I was hoping I could ask you."

Deri motioned with the flask. "Ask away."

"Why would someone want to kill you?"

"They wouldn't." He paused. "Well, I take that back. I have the most beautiful voice in Wales, so another bard might do away with me out of professional jealousy. With me gone, my station as court bard to Powys would be vacant."

Gareth's family might have a few objections to what Deri had just said, but Gareth wasn't going to contradict him today. "Do you know of anyone in particular who might want to kill you and is *here*?"

"No." The word was accompanied by a shake of Deri's head. "Meilyr and Gwalchmai are almost as accomplished as I, but they have a position in Gwynedd, and I can't see them exchanging it for one in Powys, even if Madog would have them. Prince Hywel is even more unlikely. So no. I don't know of anyone."

"What about your sister?"

"What about my sister?"

Gareth fought for patience. "Would she want you dead, as you suggested in the hall?"

"No." He drew out the word a bit, speaking slowly, though it wasn't clear if that had to do with his lack of confidence in his answer or because he was loath to admit his sister wouldn't want to kill him. "She would have no position at all without me."

"Why then did you suggest it earlier?" Conall asked.

Deri scoffed, looking affronted. His range of expression was vast and served him well on the dais. Gareth needed to keep in mind that Deri could prevaricate at will. A bard had to sing when he didn't feel like it and call up emotion when he didn't feel anything in order to engender emotion in his listeners. "I was angry, and she did refuse to eat the porridge, for reasons I think are absurd. The blue dress fits fine."

Gareth refrained from raising his eyes to the ceiling and merely said, "Can you think of who might want to see your sister dead?"

"That I don't know." At last, Deri turned serious rather than dismissive. "There was a time my first thought would have been a jealous wife, but it's been years since she had a liaison that I know of."

"That you know of," Conall said flatly. "Wouldn't you know?"

Deri took a long drink from his flask and then set it aside on the bench. When he looked back at Conall and Gareth, a smile hovered around his lips. "I know what you're thinking: I'm a drunk. Well, you'd be right, and if you know drunks, you know that we are sometimes unreliable witnesses. We sleep hard and long, wake late, and stumble through the day, just waiting until we can have our next drink. If Nest was seeing someone, I wouldn't necessarily know if she saw fit to keep it from me. She lies better than I do."

He was being honest and straightforward—and it broke Gareth's heart, which he'd thought was hardened to this sort of thing. In point of fact, he wanted to shake the bard, because he did have a beautiful voice, and he was drowning it in mead.

Gareth wet his lips before saying, somewhat cautiously. "Have you spoken to Nest since last we talked?"

"We went our separate ways. We have nothing to prepare, since we're not singing tonight."

"Really?" Conall stepped in again. "Nest said she was. You'd let her perform without you?"

Gareth put his fist to his lips to cover the smile he couldn't otherwise hide, since Conall's strategy had come as a surprise. Gareth was nearly certain he would have been unable to lie so boldly himself. He didn't say anything to Deri or correct his friend, however. Really, if he'd thought about it, this was why he'd asked Conall to come with him in the first place.

"Nest told me she was too grief-stricken to sing." Deri's brow furrowed, unaware of the deception—and why would he be? Conall was the ambassador from Leinster. While King Owain didn't necessarily *trust* the King of Leinster, without most people speaking the truth most of the time, little could be accomplished in the world. By lying, Conall was breaking that social compact. For his part, Deri was not acquainted with Conall and would have no reason to assume he was lying through his teeth.

Conall had the grace to look slightly embarrassed at what he'd wrought, but that didn't stop him from adding, "Nest says she changed her mind because, without a performer, the wedding won't continue, and she can't bear to break poor sweet Marared's heart."

Again, Nest had said nothing of the kind. It was something she *might* have said if it would have endeared her to her audience, and Gareth could even hear her voice behind Conall's words. He hoped Deri could too.

Gareth felt able to participate at this point, and he spread his hands wide. "She understands if you are too distraught to join her. She's happy to manage this all by herself tonight."

Deri's eyes moved from Conall to Gareth and back again. Gareth hoped they weren't spreading the butter on too thick. Deri appeared confused more than anything else. "I told her I supported her decision."

"But you are not grief-stricken," Conall said, not as a question.

"The dog is dead." Deri had begun fidgeting with the bow to his *crwth* and now he lifted both and played the first verse of a song, absently, as if it wasn't one of the most beautiful things Gareth had ever heard. "Nothing to be done about it now."

"So you're ready to sing?" Gareth said.

"I suppose I am. Though ..." Deri stopped playing and thought for a moment, "if someone is trying to murder us, would it be folly to stand on the dais and make ourselves more of a target?"

"I thought you said nobody would want you dead." Conall had been doing a good job taking turns with Gareth asking the questions. It was a useful technique for keeping a suspect on the back of his heels. For the most part, Deri was not a difficult subject. He had drunk too much mead, and his guard was too far down, to need much in the way of tricking.

Deri didn't answer right away, instead setting down the bow and taking a long swig from his flask, seemingly emptying it because he looked inside the opening before turning it entirely upside down over his mouth.

Gareth waited. Deri was doing a much better job of hiding he was bald than hiding he was a drunkard. Gareth had long experience questioning men deep into their cups. One had to give them the space to answer in their own time.

Finally, Deri looked up, somewhat blearily, and said, "I suppose I did."

"Why *did* you accuse your sister then?" Gareth said.

"Because I was angry she would accuse me of trying to murder *her*!" The words burst out of Deri like water flowing through a broken dam. "As if I would. She's my sister! What kind of man does something like that? All I'd have to do to get rid of her is tell Madog she was more trouble than she was worth, and he would send her away."

"Is that something you've considered doing?" Gareth asked with real curiosity.

Drunkards had a hard time not telling the truth, even when they wanted to hide it, and Gareth saw the struggle for control on Deri's face before he grudgingly admitted in a calmer tone, "Of course I've thought about it. We think about things all the time that we would never do. And I would never abandon my sister, no matter what she did. I thought we were getting along better these last few months too."

"No matter what she did?" Gareth said, all innocent. "Earlier you talked about jealous wives. You have more reason to think someone might want her dead?"

"No, no." He shook his head vigorously and almost fell sideways off the bench.

Conall and Gareth exchanged a glance. There was something behind Deri's words, but neither knew what it was, and Gareth wasn't sure how to get it out. For now, he left it.

"So you don't think she tried to murder you?" Conall was using another interrogation technique, which was to ask the same question in different ways over the course of an interview. It was surprising how often the answer wasn't quite the same the second time.

"No." At first Deri shook his head. But then he paused, flask halfway to his mouth before he remembered it was empty and set it down beside him on the bench. "I don't know what to think."

He was frowning, and Gareth could practically see his mind struggling to work through the problem. Gareth didn't begrudge him the time or the effort. He himself was struggling too. He didn't interrupt, on the chance that some new thought, or better yet, a confession, was forthcoming.

But then Deri surged to his feet, more agitated than at any time previously. "Maybe she really was trying to murder me, and when that failed, she told me she wasn't going to perform to get me to agree not to. I would sit here, drinking myself into a stupor, and by the time I knew she was going to sing without me, it would be too late for me to join her. She *does* want to get me out of her way!"

Gareth was startled by the sudden change in attitude, and though he appreciated that he was hearing Deri's true thoughts, he didn't necessarily like the direction they were taking.

He put out a calming hand. "We don't know that."

"She appears truly to be mourning her dog," Conall said. "Would she have murdered Annwyn to get to you?"

"No." Deri's shoulders sagged. "She loved that dog more than any person. Certainly more than me." He sighed. "I'd better find her so we can get to work. The wedding ballad still isn't quite right, and we've been so focused on that, we've let the songs for tonight slip!"

Deri seemed to want to leave right that instant, but Gareth wasn't done and stepped in front of him to block his way. "One more thing."

"What?" Deri made a motion as if to move past him, but he wasn't stable enough to push Gareth out of the way.

"Have you talked to Meilyr?" Gareth deliberately made his tone gentle and unassertive.

It didn't work. The mention of the rival bard's name, made Deri sneer. "No. Why would I want to?"

"When he lost his wife, he began drinking overmuch," Gareth said simply.

Deri couldn't maintain his sneer at that news, though he did give a little snort. "I'd forgotten that."

"My wife raised her brother much of the time, except for the music, of course, because drink made Meilyr unreliable."

"What does that have to do with me?" Though he had admitted he was a drunkard earlier, Deri was fully belligerent now.

"Eventually he was able to stop drinking too much."

That got Deri's attention, and his eyes focused on Gareth's face for the first time. "How?"

Gareth turned up one hand, glad he'd guessed right that Deri might truly be at a point where he not only could use help, but would take it when offered. "That's what I thought you might want to ask him."

12

Llelo

Llelo led the way to the laying out room, confidence in every stride.

Though, of course, that had more to do with wanting to make Cian believe he was confident than because he was genuinely feeling that way. He'd never examined any kind of dead body by himself before, beyond a frog that had been squished in the road. His father had always been there, looking over his shoulder. And unlike some fathers, his was a comforting presence.

The laying out room was located near the chapel. As they passed by the open window, he could hear the murmur of a conversation, presumably between his father and Deri. Then Deri strummed on one of his instruments, and the beautiful sound wafted through the window too. Llelo found his tension easing to hear it.

Although Llelo himself hadn't been raised with music during the first twelve years of his life and had merely an acceptable voice, both Tangwen, at almost four, and Taran, who was only one, were able to carry a tune. Meilyr, Llelo was sure, had grand hopes already for Taran to follow in his and Gwalchmai's footsteps. To Llelo's mind, that would be a good distribution of the family labor for Gareth's sons: Llelo would become an investigator like his father; Dai would become a full-fledged Dragon and protect the prince as Gareth had done when he'd been captain of Hywel's guard, before his promotion to steward; and Taran would become a bard. Each then could have a piece of their family's history as their own.

The weather had remained warmer than it ought to be in December. Suspecting rain was in the offing sooner rather than later, Cian had fetched his cloak from their quarters before coming out with Llelo and now pulled up his hood against the drops which had started to fall. Llelo didn't do the same, stumping along bareheaded beside his friend. He might not even have been wearing his cloak if Gwen hadn't made him put it on. He knew his parents thought he refused his cloak out of an adolescent disdain, but really, he was hot all the time, and the rain felt good on his head.

They arrived at the laying out room to find the door had been left open, the better for keeping the air fresh. Llelo had every intention of walking right up to the dog and getting to work, but when he poked in his nose and saw the forlorn lump on the table, covered with a sheet, he found himself hesitating. While he was proud that his father trusted him, he had to admit he'd been half-hoping the servant had made a mistake and put the body somewhere else. There was something so much more pathetic about the little dog's corpse than he expected.

Cian rarely looked worried, but a flash of concern crossed his face. "You may need more help than from just the few of us here. Where have Prince Hywel and the Dragons gone off to?"

"Queen Cristina said they rode out this morning before sunrise."

Cian guffawed. "Our prince is as smart as I already thought him to be. Good for them for being as far from here as possible."

"Though you're right we could use their help if the investigation gets any bigger, for now, it's a single dead dog."

"What are you waiting for?"

Llelo thought for only a heartbeat about how to reply before he said, "Courage."

Cian was not a friend to tease him, which was why Llelo had spoken the truth. Probably Dai would have punched him in the shoulder and pushed past him. Instead, Cian eyed the lump. "Not what I expected to be doing today either."

"Sadly no, but it's better than having Nest or Deri here."

"Have you ever examined a dead dog before?"

"Actually, I have. I know well the Church's strictures against intensive examination of people, particularly to the point of looking inside them, but it does not forbid cutting into animal remains. My father and I have made a study recently of a variety of animals. Sheep and pig carcasses are commonly available. The butcher always stands over me as I do my work, thinking us very odd, but it's a good way for my father to teach me."

Cian looked as if he was about to gag, which prompted Llelo to tsk through his teeth. "I'm not saying we make a habit of dissecting every animal we come across, but we've all shot deer. We've speared a boar. If the opportunity presents itself, I see no reason why I shouldn't learn what I can, the better to serve my lord when a person lies dead on that table."

"Do animals decay at the same rate as humans?"

"In many cases, they decay faster, but the dog died this morning. I still have time before full rigor sets in."

"Do you really intend to cut into it?"

"Not if I don't have to."

"Why would it be necessary in the first place? We know how the dog died."

Llelo glanced at him. "Do we?" At first he spoke just to be contrary and make Cian think, but the more Llelo thought about it himself, the more he wondered how much they really did know.

Cian blinked. "Don't we? The dog was poisoned."

"So everyone says. But even I know better than to take Deri and Nest at their word. That's why we need to inspect the dog in order to make sure. Maybe we can even determine the type of poison used."

"What are signs of poisoning?" Cautiously, Cian entered the room and approached the table.

Llelo allowed his friend his curiosity before following him inside. "In people? Frothing at the mouth. Vomit. The condition of the eyes. Things like that."

Cian looked at the sheet with a dubious expression. "Wouldn't it be better to have your grandmother here? She's the one who knows about poisons, isn't she?"

"I will fetch her if I need her, but right now she's speaking to King Madog."

"She probably knew what she was doing going off with your grandfather." Cian gave a mocking laugh. "It sounds like your father wanted to put this off as long as possible too."

"You mean he gave me the dirtiest job?" Llelo considered the idea for a moment. "I suspect you're right."

"You don't resent it?" Cian turned his head to look at Llelo.

"Do you resent it when he gives you jobs he doesn't want to do himself?"

"I like writing and figuring."

"Well, it's the same here. This is what he's training me for. I'm honored that he would consider giving me something he doesn't want to do since I would prefer not to be an afterthought. Normally he takes on everything himself, even the worst jobs." Llelo paused. "Especially the worst jobs, which means we should get to it before he comes and takes the responsibility off my shoulders."

Having grabbed one of the lavender sachets from a dish on a small table set against the wall and put it to his nose, Llelo threw off the sheet, ready to get the task over with—and swallowed down a curse he didn't dare say so close to the chapel.

Where the dog should have lain was simply rolled up sacking.

Cian had his hand to his mouth, not really believing what he was seeing. "Where's the dog?"

Llelo picked up the sacking, noting the few wafts of hay drifting to the floor, and laughed. "Not here, apparently." He felt bad now for hoping the dog had been taken somewhere else, as if by wishing he'd made it so.

"Your father is going to be angry." Cian bent to pick up the piece of hay and twirled it in his fingers.

Gareth rarely lost his temper, but Llelo himself was angry enough that he might have swept the sacking to the floor in a fit of pique.

But that would not have been mature. Llelo had felt the back of his birth father's hand more times than he could count, and he tried very hard never to exhibit anything like that degree of temper. Thus, since the sacking was evidence now, he folded it neatly and set it on the table with exaggerated gentleness.

"But he won't be angry at me."

13

Gareth

Everyone met back in the common room a little before noon. At first Gareth feared they wouldn't be left alone, but he should have known that he and Gwen (and all their friends and companions) had solved too many murders and brought too many killers to justice for everyone in the palace—even those from Powys—not to know what they were doing. And to know better than to disturb them when they were meeting. Even the other residents of the guesthouse seemed to be giving it a wide berth.

Then again, it would soon be afternoon, and the midday meal was a form of entertainment in and of itself, all the more so on the day of a murder.

Gareth and Conall had taken the longest to return, and the moment Gareth walked in the door he could see Llelo hopping with impatience, much as Gwalchmai had been doing when he woke him. It would have been cruel not to allow him to go first, and he spilled out the bad news the moment Gareth looked expectantly at him.

Gwen folded her arms across her chest. "We are certain the dog's body was placed in the laying out room to begin with?"

"That's what the servant told me in the kitchen," Llelo said. "I believed him then, and believe him now."

"I feared we'd delayed too long and the body was going to be stiff." At Llelo's news, Conall plopped himself down in a nearby chair and kicked back against the wall. Gareth sometimes sat like that, but he never managed to make himself look quite as perfectly casual as Conall.

"I should have inspected the body myself." Gareth sighed. "Conall and I popped in on our way to speak to Deri and saw the dog's body as a shape on the table. That was all I thought I needed to know."

"You had given the job to Llelo. You knew he was coming in a moment and would do what needed to be done." Gwen eyed the men around her. "Nest was never going to like it if we had to cut Annwyn open anyway."

That prompted Saran to tap a finger to her lower lip. "Perhaps she knew what might be in store for Annwyn and took her before any of us could touch her?"

"That would be the best-case scenario." Gareth looked at his mother-in-law for a moment, frowning, and then he glanced around the room quickly, knowing all the while that Gwalchmai was nowhere to be seen but looking anyway.

And then, as the first real moment of wondering what had become of the boy passed through Gareth's head, Iorwerth dashed through the door of the guesthouse. "Come quickly! Gwalchmai is hurt!"

Gareth gaped at him, his mind churning, and then he surged to his feet, cursing his stupidity for letting the memory of the porridge, and what he'd asked Gwalchmai to do with it, slip from his mind.

"It was Gwalchmai whom Queen Cristina sent to wake me," Gareth said to Saran as they followed Iorwerth out of the guesthouse and across the courtyard. "Once I ascertained the situation, the very first thing I did was give him the bowl of poisoned porridge and send him to find you at the healer's hut. Are you telling me he never arrived?"

Saran's headshake revealed her confusion. "When was this?"

"Before first light."

Saran was still shaking her head. "I have been in the healer's hut most mornings, but Meilyr and I went for a walk in the warm air, down to the river. Did you know it's in flood?"

Gareth motioned with his hand, brushing away the issue and wishing yet again he hadn't drunk so much mead last night. Food and water had helped his headache, but it was still there, reminding him of his incompetence. He had to think that, if he hadn't been feeling so ill, he would have remembered Gwalchmai sooner. Nobody else had given him a thought because only Gareth himself knew what he'd asked of him.

A moment later, they arrived in the kitchen, where Gwalchmai, not atypically, had taken refuge.

"Son!" At the sight of Gwalchmai slumped on a stool by the fire, a folded cloth to the back of his head, Meilyr pushed past Gareth and fell to his knees in front of him. "What happened?"

"I don't know, other than I was hit on the back of the head." He lifted the cloth to show his hair matted with blood. "It hurts."

Gareth had no doubt it did. His own head ached just from looking at the bloody cloth. He'd suffered a similar injury, potentially for very similar reasons, back before he and Gwen were married. "What happened to the porridge?"

Gwalchmai looked up at Gareth, his mouth dropping open as memory returned. It was some comfort that his memory *was* returning at so little prompting. Gareth had obviously been a complete dolt all morning, and he had merely drunk mead. The blow to Gwalchmai's head could have been much harder and caused much more damage. Truthfully, it could have killed him.

"I don't know! I was on my way to the herbalist's hut like you said." He paused. "I never made it."

"Where did you wake up?" Gwen rubbed her brother's arm.

Saran meanwhile had been bustling about, getting warm water and a clean cloth, at which point she shooed everyone back five feet and got to work on the wound. "You are very lucky to be alive, young man." She dabbed at Gwalchmai's head, her cloth coming away with more blood, though not as much as on the cloth Gwalchmai had been holding. Head wounds bled like no other, but this one had mostly stopped.

Gwalchmai answered his sister's question rather than responding to Saran's admonition. "I woke up against the garden wall, rolled in a thick sacking. I think I was awake on and off much of the morning, but I kept going back to sleep. I wasn't cold, and the layers of sacking and my cloak kept me dry." He pointed to his stained and muddy cloak, which had been hung on a hook near the hearth.

Gareth put a hand on Gwen's shoulder. "All of you stay with him. I will have a look."

Two paces past the kitchen door, Conall fell into step beside Gareth. "Are you all right?"

"I'm shaking with anger." It was the truth, and he could say it to Conall. "Here we were thinking this investigation involved only a dog. Dead, yes, but otherwise no harm done." Gareth barked an unamused laugh. "Whoever poisoned the dog is a true coward. Gwalchmai is a boy. He's not involved in my investigations. I just used him today because he was handy."

It was as if he had a fire burning up his insides, and he wanted to shout and curse and stamp around. Not that he would.

"What was in that porridge?" Conall shook his head wonderingly.

"I don't know. I fear now we will never know, though if whoever did this believes that taking the evidence is going to slow the investigation, he is going to be very surprised. He should have known it would only encourage us to redouble our efforts."

They arrived at the postern gate, which had been left open—and was being left open at all times—to give access to this section of the plateau outside the wall. While King Madog's pavilion and his people's tents were located to the north of the palace, accessible through the front gate, the postern gate led to where more wagons had been parked, along with a few small tents that had been set up for servants and guardsmen for whom there was no room elsewhere. With so many people moving in and out of the palace at all hours, all the gates were patrolled but not guarded.

Beyond was the herb garden, with its own wall and southern exposure, which aided in the growth of the plants during the limited growing season in Gwynedd. A few paces from the garden gate, Gareth crouched to the ground. With all the rain they'd had, the remains of many boot prints were outlined in the mud, but there was only one double track of drag marks. Conall passed Gareth, following the tracks around the edge of the wall. When Gareth went after him a moment later, he found the Irishman standing over the hemp sacking, of which Gwalchmai had spoken, and a flattened place in the grass where he must have lain all morning.

A thick piece of wood, three feet in length, with square edges, indicating it had been milled for building, lay on the ground nearby, and Gareth bent to pick it up. Grimacing, he held out the end to show Conall the splotch of blood and bit of hair lodged six inches down from the end. "The weapon."

"We must be thankful his attacker smote Gwalchmai with the flat side rather than the corner, or he really might be dead." Conall stood with his fists on his hips, still looking down at the spot where Gwalchmai had lain. "How did the person who did this think he was going to get away with it?"

"It was still dark when it happened." Gareth bent to push aside the hemp sacking; Gwalchmai was right that it was thick and bulky, of a type used all over the castle to keep out the rain and damp. A very similar piece was laid over the firewood near the blacksmith's works.

Once Gareth swept his hands through the grass and came up with nothing more than dewdrops, he continued to contemplate the scene, scratching the back of his head.

"What is it?" Conall asked.

"This investigation is different from previous ones in ways that make me uncomfortable."

"You mean because of Gwalchmai? Or is it the dead dog?"

"That Gwalchmai was attacked makes it more in line with previous ones. It's the fact that our victim is a dog that has thrown me off."

"It made all of us take the situation less seriously. I certainly did."

Now Gareth scrubbed at his hair with both hands. "I told you earlier I was angry, but really, I'm more angry at myself than at the attacker, whoever he may be. I have been behind from the start and making poor decisions from the moment Gwalchmai rousted me from my bed." He dropped his hands. "I should have known better than to have that last cup of mead."

"You didn't know we'd have an investigation today," Conall said. "And once you did, you did take it seriously. From where I stand, you did everything you would normally have done if the victim was a person. You will get your man. You always do."

Gareth wasn't entirely ready to be cheered up and made a motion as if to slough off Conall's reassurance. But then he arrested the movement halfway through. "Thank you, my friend. I appreciate your confidence. And you're right that we have to face the truth of the situation: while we can't change what happened during the course of the morning, we *can* start again.

"Until now, we weren't sure murder was intended. We weren't even sure this was murder. I was still holding in abeyance the idea that the dog had been poisoned at all. Now we must be certain of it. Whoever attacked Gwalchmai has made a huge mistake."

14

Llelo

Llelo was disappointed in himself for not discovering sooner that Gwalchmai was missing—and even more for not *remembering* him. Though only half a year apart in age, Gwalchmai was Llelo's uncle, which made them friends—brothers even—instead. It was almost worse that, by the time anyone spoke of him, Iorwerth had been walking into the guesthouse to find them.

"If it hadn't been such a warm morning, Gwalchmai might have frozen to death beside the palisade," he said to his father as they left the kitchen for the laying out room. They were headed there not because Gareth didn't believe the dog was missing, his father had assured him, but because he needed to see it with his own eyes and see if anything had been left behind.

"You are blaming yourself," Gareth said. "That's my job. I was the one who sent Gwalchmai off with the bowl of porridge. I should have remembered what I'd done."

"You were busy."

Gareth scoffed—not at Llelo, he knew, but at the situation. "You are kind, but that is no excuse. What I really am is hung over."

Llelo glanced at his father. "You rarely drink too much mead. Why did you last night?"

"That's a son for you." Saran was walking a few paces behind them. She'd left Gwen with Gwalchmai, since there wasn't anything more she could do for her stepson. He needed rest; he needed food and water; and he needed someone to sit beside him through the rest of the day and perhaps the night to make sure that, when he slept, he didn't descend too deeply into unconsciousness. "Makes you practice what you preach."

Gareth came to a halt some yards from the laying out room, shaking his head. "I have counseled you never to drink to excess, and then I go and do it myself."

"You might consider, Gareth," Saran said, "that you perhaps *didn't* drink all that much more than usual."

He looked at her through narrowed eyes. "I don't understand what you're saying."

"If it was possible for someone to poison the porridge, it is equally possible for someone to have put something in your drink that would make you stagger. Poppy juice would do it, maybe with a touch of hawthorn. If I was planning to murder Deri or Nest in the morning, I would make sure the prince's man charged with investigating death would be several steps behind from the start. If not dead himself."

"I surely wished I was dead this morning when I woke." Gareth looked rueful. "You are both trying to make me feel better, as Conall did earlier, and I appreciate it."

"It's more than that, Gareth," Saran said. "I am genuinely concerned that the scope of this investigation is far broader than we have considered up until now."

"Which also means, as you've told victims many times in my hearing, that the only one to blame for the attack on Gwalchmai is the one who did it," Llelo said staunchly.

Gareth let out a breath. "You are right, of course."

Llelo had seen Gareth rubbing the back of his own head, feeling for the indent of that old injury. Llelo had a sudden thought that if he continued in his service to the prince, he might experience something similar. And when he did, it could kill him.

It was as if a bucket of cold water had been dumped over his head, and he genuinely shivered.

Gareth noticed. "Son?"

"Gwalchmai could have died."

"Yes." Gareth was looking at Llelo, but Llelo didn't meet his eyes, instead dropping his gaze to his feet. "Are you thinking that it could have been you?"

"Yes." His admission wasn't grudging so much as subdued. "I honestly never thought about it before, not even when Dai was in trouble last summer. I've been stupid."

"You have not been stupid." His grandmother's arm came around his waist. She wasn't tall enough to put an arm across his shoulders. "You are a trustworthy, serious, loyal companion and an able investigator in your own right."

Llelo believed she meant it, but still he frowned. "It's different for Dai as a Dragon. He could have died in Dublin, and he knows it. As a soldier, he knows death is always around the corner. But this person we're chasing—" he paused as he fought for the right words, "—he's sneaking around like a coward. It's wrong!"

"Yes, it is," Gareth said, "and that's why we have to catch him."

Llelo grunted. "I suppose I knew that." He looked at Saran. "Is Gwalchmai going to be all right? I mean, really all right?"

"When we left, he was humming a tune I hadn't heard before. I think we have a song coming on, so if I had to guess, I'd say yes."

Relief flowed through Llelo, and he let out a sigh.

Gareth eyed him again. "You still with me?"

Llelo did a sweep around his emotions and thoughts and was relieved to discover his sense of surety remained. He nodded, and then said more firmly, "Yes. Yes, I am."

They reached the laying out room, and Saran shook her head as she stepped inside. "Both the porridge and the dog. What on earth is going on here?"

Llelo put out a hand to his father. "Before you say it again, this isn't your fault either."

"He's making me look like a fool," Gareth said, charitably not saying *us*, though they'd all played a role in the investigation so far. "I could have examined the dog earlier. Corpses have been stolen before, and I knew that. I could have put a guard on the laying out room."

"Up until this moment, that would have been silly," Saran said. "Beat yourself up about it if you want to, but the fact that someone hit Gwalchmai on the head and stole the dog's body puts us miles ahead of where we were even a half-hour ago. Someone has to have seen something. We have only to ask."

Gareth grumbled something under his breath that told Llelo he was still unhappy.

"I think I understand the problem, Father. We are used to coming into an investigation at the point someone has been killed and having to comfort family and friends in mourning. What's particularly awkward in this instance is that the survivors don't engender a great deal of sympathy. I don't like them. And yet, we have to protect them, while the dog, who should have been protected, is dead."

"Not to mention *missing*." Gareth had been pacing around the room, but like when Llelo and Cian had been there earlier, there wasn't much to see.

"I know!" Llelo still felt his own failure to examine it like a weight. "It's a dead dog. I shouldn't care more than if it were Nest or Deri—but I do."

Then Gareth's expression turned thoughtful. "Before, we were hampered by not knowing if this was even murder. Clearly, we had no notion of the right questions to ask. At least the questions are better now, and the window of opportunity both for poisoning the porridge and attacking Gwalchmai is very narrow."

Llelo perked up to hear the change in his father's tone. He was moving on from recriminations to assessing the crime. "Deri and Nest, for example, could have been responsible for the theft of the dog's corpse, but not the attack on Gwalchmai, so we should be able to eliminate them from the list of suspects. The same would hold true for Andreas and Manon."

"Similarly, unless those in the kitchen have a compelling motive that we haven't been able to discover, nothing says to me they are guilty." Saran shrugged. "I'm not sure that's wildly helpful."

"Cristina gets a reprieve as well," Gareth said, "if she ever was a suspect."

"It seems to me we need a list of everyone in the hall, because only they would have known you gave Gwalchmai the porridge," Llelo said.

"That's only a hundred people or so." Saran smiled. "Lots of people to interview."

Gareth looked at Llelo. "Didn't you say you sent Cynan and Madoc to the hall to see what they could learn? Let's see what they have to say."

"It's a place to start," Saran added, preparing to leave with Gareth.

Llelo, however, stayed where he was. "What if we can't dismiss all these people the way we have? What if there's more than one person at work here? For example, only Manon was in the hall initially. Andreas arrived later." He bit his lip. "They could be responsible if they were working together."

His elders turned back, eyes narrowing—not at him, but in thought.

"I realize that's nothing to be happy about," Llelo said, "but one could have done the poisoning while another attacked Gwalchmai."

"And then a third stole the dog's body? I truly hope not!" Saran let out a laugh.

Then Gwen appeared, walking quickly across the courtyard towards them. The rain was falling quite hard now, and she'd pulled her hood up over her head. Coming to a halt in the doorway, she took in the sacking on the table and the three of them standing around it, with no body in evidence, and grimaced. "I'm afraid we'll have to deal with this later. You must come with me, Gareth. We need you—" she cut herself off before adding, "It's just too awful."

"Of course." Gareth took one last look around the room and started towards Gwen. "You're making me ask what the trouble is. That isn't like you."

"I don't want to say it out loud." Gwen made a helpless gesture with one hand as she stepped back out of the doorway. While they'd been inside the laying out room, not only had the rain started falling harder but the temperature had dropped. It still wasn't a normal winter cold, but it was the kind of cold rain that would be miserable to be out in.

"Is it a new murder?" Llelo asked.

Gwen gave a little shake of her head. "It has to do with an old one."

They had all come outside by now, hoods up and cloaks tight around their shoulders, even Llelo, who for once wasn't feeling all that warm.

"Tell us the rest, Gwen," Saran said, "and then together we can deal with whatever this is."

Gwen's face had been hidden by her hood, but now she tipped back her head to look up at the sky. Rain fell on her cheeks, but she didn't seem to mind, because it was mixing with the tears Llelo had seen a moment earlier. With an angry motion, she wiped at the corners of her eyes and dropped her head again.

"Prince Cadwaladr is in the village church asking for asylum until the king accepts him back into Gwynedd."

15

Gwen

"It worked before, so he hopes it will work again?" Gareth's hood was thrown back too, as they were no longer worried about the rain, and he strode across the courtyard at Gwen's side. He'd been sick and angry all day, and now it was just as well the rain was falling on his head because it might serve to cool him off.

In the leadup to King Owain's marriage to Cristina (and Gwen's to Gareth), several people had been murdered and an attempt had been made on King Owain's life. Because Cadwaladr had been involved in intrigue before, it had been natural to suspect him, and he'd briefly taken refuge in the chapel at the palace at Aber before fleeing into the night. Eventually, he'd been exonerated, by Gareth of all people, and returned to King Owain's grace. In seeking refuge in Denbigh's church, likely he was hoping for a similar outcome.

Gwen herself was relieved Gareth's head hadn't burst into flames at her news. Anger could be a haven for a heart that was broken, but she found herself weepy instead. Maybe that was a woman's reaction, in part out of grief for herself, but more in empathy with those whose hearts were hurt more than hers.

Saran and Llelo had peeled off towards the great hall, tasked with finding Cynan and Madoc and keeping an eye on the wedding guests. Some might well be supporters of Cadwaladr, and Gareth wanted to know what they did when they discovered their lord was here.

"I didn't even tell you the other part of it." She was trotting to keep up with her husband's long legs. "Gareth." She touched his arm. "Cadwaladr specifically asked to talk to me."

Gareth stopped cold in the middle of the courtyard, so suddenly that Gwen walked a pace and a half beyond him before turning back. Fortunately, they'd come to rest on the flagstone path, so they weren't standing six inches deep in mud, made all the worse in the last quarter of an hour by the renewed rain.

"No. I forbid it."

The rain continued to pound down. They both ignored it.

She understood why he would feel the need to forbid her from accepting the task, and would even see it as his duty to do so. He loved her and wanted what was best for her. But the truth was, while as his wife it was her duty to obey him, it would be wrong for him to forbid her to speak to Cadwaladr—and when he was able to think clearly, she trusted he would see it too.

So she endeavored to be understanding and patient. She knew why he was being so protective, and she appreciated it.

"Last time this happened, Cadwaladr asked for Hywel and me. He knows better than to ask for Hywel today, or for you, which leaves me as his only option."

Gareth scoffed. "There are dozens of others: Cristina, perhaps, or Alice. She's his wife for heaven's sake. Why not ask for her?"

"You know very well that Cadwaladr and Cristina do not get along, since he is as much a rival for the throne of Gwynedd as Hywel. And Alice does not have King Owain's ear. I do, and Cadwaladr knows it."

"Then he should know better than to ask for you! He should have known better than to come here at all! Hywel was doing a little better this last week, and now it's all ruined."

Gareth's face was very pale. Gwen wanted to hug him, but she held herself back, since his hands were clenched into fists at his sides. Of the many benefits of being married to him for five years, one was an understanding of when and how to intercede in her husband's moods.

"He should," she said, "but he doesn't."

Gareth let out a sharp breath, and some of his anger seemed to leave him. "Has Hywel returned yet?"

"No."

Though they'd learned this morning from Cristina of Prince Hywel's absence from the palace, since then Gwen had spoken to Mari, Hywel's wife, and she'd reported that he'd left with the Dragons at first light in order to survey the state of the rivers and creeks in the countryside. The palace was safe, sitting as it did high on its plateau, but residents of the lower lands were likely to be experiencing flooding.

"Thank God for that." Gareth heaved a sigh.

Gwen was relieved to find her husband calming. Once the red haze of rage passed from his vision, his mind would begin to work.

"His absence makes it all the more important that you let me do as Cadwaladr asks. It would be better if this were over, one way or another, before Prince Hywel returns."

As she waited for Gareth's answer, Gwen endeavored to breathe evenly, hoping that her projected calm would cross the distance that had formed between them. The honest truth was that she didn't want to speak to Cadwaladr. Not at all. While Hywel had been her special friend growing up, she'd also known Rhun, who was two years older, and loved him and admired him. With his good looks and sunny smile, he'd been the object of her first infatuation as she'd grown into young womanhood, and for a brief period she'd dreamt that somehow their difference in stations could be overcome, and he would look at her as someone other than his brother's little friend and a bard's daughter.

She knew without entering the church and hearing Cadwaladr out that he was going to claim he never intended Rhun to die. He was going to say he was sorry. It might even be true, but only because being the hand behind Rhun's death, intentional or not, had meant he'd spent the last two years in exile. He would say whatever he needed to say to be accepted back into Gwynedd.

Finally, after a long count of ten, during which Gareth stared at the rain puddling in the dips in the stones at their feet, he nodded. "You are right, of course."

Now Gwen reached for him, and he pulled her close. They stayed that way, arms wrapped tightly around each other, her head to his chest and his cheek on her hair, until they both were breathing evenly. By now, they were both thoroughly soaked, but they cared not at all.

"*Cariad,*" Gareth said.

She tipped up her chin so their eyes could meet.

"You are stronger than I am."

"Only when you need me to be," she said.

It was at that point King Owain bellowed her name across the courtyard. "Gwen!"

It could have been worse; he might have summoned her before she'd completed her conversation with Gareth. Then again, the king wasn't without empathy himself—or understanding. He could have seen what was passing between them. Even a king hadn't the right to overrule the decision of a husband for his wife. Owain also needed Gareth to make the right one.

She shot her husband a rueful look, and they turned as one, arms still around each other, and hurried towards where King Owain waited at the gatehouse to the palace. Like them, he was standing in the rain, and though Gareth pulled Gwen's hood up for her to protect her head, late as that was, the king remained bareheaded.

Seeing them coming, he didn't wait for them to reach him before he turned and walked under the gatehouse. She feared he was going to take them straight to the church where Cadwaladr was waiting, but she did him a disservice to think so. Instead, he stood out of the rain, shaking the water from his hair and wiping down his face with a cloth his steward, Taran, handed him.

Gwen and Gareth had named their young son for this Taran, and since Taran the elder had no children of his own, the bond between them and him had grown stronger. Now he looked at Gwen with understanding tinged with pity. She smiled sadly back before turning directly to the king, having stopped in front of him and pushed back her hood again.

"My lord."

Normally, in the presence of the king, she and Gareth would not have stood so close together, but Gareth made no move to release her. He was telling King Owain that she was his, not Owain's, to do with as he wished, and if she agreed to see Cadwaladr, it was because Gareth had acquiesced.

King Owain didn't care one way or the other about the whys and wherefores, only that they did what he wanted. "Thank you for agreeing—" he stopped and shook his head.

"It's all right, my lord. Better me than almost anybody else, including, if I may say so, *you*."

Owain looked at her hard. "You don't have to do this. I could burn down the church with him inside."

"You could. Part of me thinks that's a splendid idea." That King Owain suggested it served to settle Gwen a bit more and make her think calmly about what she was facing. It also allowed her to add, in something of a jesting tone, "But you can always do that afterwards if you don't like what he has to say."

Owain growled. "I am *not* going to like what he has to say."

"No," Gwen said simply, "you're not."

Gareth had stopped vibrating like a harp string and managed to say in an equally reasonable voice, "My lord, you could send him away. Nobody would blame you."

The king pursed his lips in thought, but then he shook his head again. "To do so would be unbecoming of the King of Gwynedd. My station is bigger than the man who occupies the throne."

Gwen felt a swell of pride at her husband and her king. Both men had been furious a moment ago and undoubtedly would be again, but they also understood that politics sometimes needed to override personal feelings, and that emotion wasn't necessarily a good guide for how to run a kingdom. For all his temper, King Owain was a good king because he knew that simple truth.

Then the king bent his head and spoke words Gwen had never heard him say before: "I apologize, Gareth."

Gareth blinked. "My lord, you have no need to apologize to me!"

"I do. I should have spoken to you first about what I was requiring of your wife. The last time Gwen was so called upon, you and she were not married, but she is in your care now. I am her king, but you are her husband."

It had been a long while since Gareth and the king had conversed seriously over any matter. They'd been in each other's company a thousand times since Gareth and Gwen's wedding day, but

Gareth was Hywel's steward. Rarely did the king have a need to address him directly. Owain's intent look now, however, was full of respect and understanding.

Gareth bowed. "I did forbid Gwen to speak to Cadwaladr in the first moments after I learned what he wanted, but wiser heads prevailed."

"Gwen's, you mean?" Owain's mouth twitched.

"As you say." Gareth actually smiled. "If Gwen feels capable of speaking to him, I will not prevent it. I'm worried about her going in alone, however. Cadwaladr won't harm her, but she would make a good hostage, as she once did."

"I agree, my lord." Gwen nodded emphatically. "Not only do I not want to be alone, but I think it sends the wrong message. He asked for me, but he doesn't have a right to get whatever he wants."

"You know him well, don't you?" King Owain's expression turned musing. "I concur. The wrong message is definitely not what we want to send him in this moment, and it is always a bad idea to give my brother exactly what he wants anyway. Cadwaladr views any accommodation as a sign of weakness. You have to push back before you can give way—if we are going to give way, which I will not yet promise."

While Gwen was glad the king was behaving in a level-headed fashion, the mere fact that he'd broached the subject of giving way and implied it was possible meant he was thinking about it. Gwen herself was free to hate Cadwaladr, but King Owain's emotions had to be a great deal more complicated. He'd never been able to refuse his brother much of anything and had always protected him, even when doing so was damaging to Gwynedd. It occurred to her that these last two years had been painful for him not only because he'd lost his eldest son, but because he'd lost his brother too—made all the worse by the fact that Cadwaladr had arranged for Rhun's death, even if unintentionally.

It didn't help the situation either that Susanna, their sister, who was a capable woman in most respects, doted on Cadwaladr, against all reason. Gwen couldn't look past his bombast and treachery, but somehow both Cadwaladr's older siblings still thought of him as a little boy. To Gwen, it was disturbing to think that way about a middle-aged man.

"Excuse me." Abbot Rhys, their old friend and companion, edged closer from where he'd been standing with Father Adam, the village priest who'd brought the news of Cadwaladr's arrival to the royal court. "May I be of service?"

"Yes! You may! Thank you." Gwen barely restrained herself from leaping forward and hugging him, and some of the aching tension that had begun in her shoulders eased.

Rhys's monastery was all of six miles away, and he'd arrived the previous evening—before the thaw—at Iorwerth's request. Father Adam was perfectly capable of marrying the royal couple, but he lacked a certain gravity. What's more, Iorwerth didn't know him at all. Abbot Rhys was someone he trusted, and while it would be rude of Rhys to edge Adam out entirely, he could assist, even oversee, the ceremony.

Abbot Rhys also had long experience both with diplomacy in general *and* Gareth and Gwen's investigations. Really, if Gareth couldn't be beside her, there was nobody she would have preferred more.

She turned to her husband. "I can do this."

"Good girl," King Owain said.

But before Gwen could set off with Abbot Rhys, Gareth caught her hand and pulled her to him in another tight hug.

"Owain." A voice came from behind them, and they all turned to see Susanna, well-wrapped in a fetching blue cloak and with an expectant look on her face. "Is it true?"

Owain didn't have to ask her to elaborate on her question. "It is."

Gwen's heart sank to see how hopeful Susanna appeared. King Owain could never deny his sister anything either. Well into her forties, Susanna wasn't necessarily past childbearing age, but she was certainly past the time of looking forward to it. Having spent some months at a convent on Anglesey, she had returned to her husband and had been instrumental in planning Marared's wedding.

The king, however, didn't respond to his sister's emotion, and turned to Gwen one more time to give her a last instruction. "Don't argue with him or get yourself involved in whatever justification he tries to put forth to explain what he did or where he's been since. Hear him out and then report back to me."

"Yes, my lord." Gwen forcibly put aside all thoughts of what might happen *after* she talked to Cadwaladr. Right now, she needed to put one foot in front of the other.

Abbot Rhys held out his elbow to her, and she took it for the short walk to the church. This time, she found herself enjoying the pounding of the rain on her hood. Here was something *real*, as opposed to the unreality that faced her on the other side of the church door. To reach it was a matter of walking three hundred feet beyond the palace gate down the gently sloping hill.

The church was surrounded by its own little stone wall that Gwen herself was tall enough to climb over and wasn't intended to be defensible. With the palace so close, the entire village had a safe place to which to retreat were it ever attacked. Rather, the wall was designed to keep pigs from rooting through the gravestones and tearing up the soil, as they were prone to do. Abbot Rhys opened the gate for her, and they passed under the pretty archway that heralded the entrance to the grounds and walked up the path to the door.

Gwen stopped in the porch, glad to be out of the rain but at the same time reluctant to continue.

Rhys let her gather herself before putting a hand on the latch and asking, "Shall we?"

"I suppose so." She glanced back, unsurprised to see that a small crowd, amidst which were King Owain, Gareth, Susanna, and Father Adam, had followed them from the gatehouse. It was actually kind of surprising more people weren't there to watch, indicating the priest must have been discreet in spreading the news of Cadwaladr's arrival. But since King Owain was involved, as well as Susanna, people would start to wonder what was happening. Even with the rain falling hard, they would come to gawk. It was only a matter of time.

All the more reason to get this done quickly.

The great wooden door creaked with age as it swung inward, wafting genuinely cold air over Rhys and Gwen. Instinctively, Gwen sighed—not in dismay but as a further means of settling herself. She liked how churches smelled of stone, candles, and incense, and found comfort in knowing that anywhere she went, a church was the one place she could feel at home. No matter how large or small, their spirit was the same everywhere.

This church's main entrance was on the southwest side of the building, meaning they had to turn to the right to progress up the nave towards the altar. The church itself was not large, so it was impossible to miss where Prince Cadwaladr had set himself to greet them. Gwen had to think he'd heard them coming and prepared accordingly, because he was lying face down on the floor before the altar, his arms outstretched to make the shape of a cross.

The overt display of piety in someone as unholy as Cadwaladr shot a sharp spike of anger through Gwen, and she glanced at Abbot Rhys, not sure how to respond because anything she might think to say would reflect that anger. He was a priest and, while more worldly than most, by nature and vocation forgiving. She would hate for him to believe that Cadwaladr was—or could be—sincere.

She was relieved to see him frowning.

As if reading her thoughts, he said in a low voice, "God can redeem any man, my child."

"Not this one."

"Gwen—"

She shook her head. "Don't ask me to believe him, Father. I cannot. I couldn't even before—" she broke off, unable to complete the sentence with *he killed Rhun.*

As it was, with Cadwaladr lying on the floor before them, it was probably better not to say anything more anyway. The musician in her recognized the excellent acoustics in the church, and likely he could hear everything they said.

Shaking off her dismay and still determined to fulfill her commission as quickly as possible, Gwen strode down the nave towards Cadwaladr's inert form.

"I am here." She stopped abruptly a few yards from his feet. "Why are you here, and what do you want?"

16

Gareth

Gwen and Abbot Rhys had just disappeared inside the church when Hywel and the Dragons came into view, coming up the rise from the valley below. They were leading their horses rather than riding them—and moving slowly. As they got closer, they were also shown to be covered in mud from head to toe, and Gareth's initial assumption that they were exhausted was proven accurate.

Still, he sent up a prayer of thanks that they hadn't arrived even a quarter of an hour earlier. Gareth glanced at King Owain, a question in his eyes, and the king nodded gravely back, confirming Gareth's estimate that the best course of action would be to intercept Hywel before he reached the church.

To that end, he descended the hill to greet his lord, intending to be welcoming, but somehow the first thing out of his mouth was an accusation. "My lord, you should have woken me and told me where you were going."

"And a good day to you too!" Hywel laughed and didn't stop walking. His gait was slow enough to imply that if he stopped moving, he might not start again. Gareth had been that tired all day. Now that Hywel was here, the sick feeling in his stomach and his racing heart made him want to vomit. These were common reactions in him when a disaster struck about which nothing could be done. At least the arrival of Cadwaladr couldn't make his head ache more than it already did.

"I apologize, my lord." Gareth bent his head, accepting the admonition. "It was not my intent to be accusing or so abrupt."

"Wasn't it?" Hywel studied him with far too much perception. "What has put you so out of sorts?"

By now, they were only fifty yards from the church, and Hywel came to a halt in the road. His eyes weren't on Gareth but on the growing crowd gathered near the church gate. The rest of the Dragons stopped with him.

Gareth held his breath. The moment he told Hywel what was happening was the moment everything would change again. Up until now, he'd been able to pretend that this wasn't the case. But he could pretend no longer, and he allowed himself a moment's grief for his life as it had been.

King Owain remained in close conversation with Susanna, and his back was to them, set apart from the other onlookers by several paces. The moment the king turned around, he would have to acknowledge his son—and tell him what was transpiring in the church.

Since the whole point of walking down to meet Hywel was for Gareth to do it for him, he swallowed, still having trouble speaking. "My lord." He realized only now that he should have rehearsed what he was going to say, and he was behaving just as Gwen had when she'd come to tell him.

"Who died?" Hywel's words told Gareth he was already braced for disaster. Then their eyes met, and Hywel said more gently, "Just tell me. It can't be worse than what I'm feeling now, not knowing."

"Unfortunately, it can." Unbelievably, Gareth found laughter in his throat. He supposed that was better than tears.

Hywel responded with a ghost of a smile, recognizing, as he would, what Gareth was trying to do.

At this point, Gareth had no choice but to plow ahead. "Nobody died." He paused, rethinking what he'd been about to say. "Well … a dog died, but that has nothing to do with what's happening at the church."

Hywel was still smiling slightly. "You intrigue me."

"I'm sorry. I don't mean to." Gareth took another breath before blurting out, "Your uncle has returned."

He spoke in a rush, and the speed of his words meant it took a heartbeat or two for Hywel to catch up. In fact, if Hywel hadn't been looking directly at Gareth, he might have thought his prince hadn't heard him.

Gruffydd, the captain of the Dragons, who'd been listening from a pace away, processed the news first. "By the bones of St. Gwenffrewi, why?" He had been the captain of Rhun's guard before he'd captained the Dragons, and his grief had been as great as Hywel's.

"We don't yet know what he wants," Gareth said, "though we all know he wants something."

"Is everyone outside because he's in the church?" Hywel started forward. "Again?"

"Yes." Gareth put out a hand to arrest Hywel's forward progress. "Cadwaladr sought sanctuary and asked to speak to Gwen." He searched Hywel's face, wanting to adjust his words to what Hywel was feeling. "Again."

While Hywel did stop walking, he was nowhere near as upset as Gareth had expected. In fact, he was far less so than Gruffydd, who was still cursing long and loud while staring at the church with such ferocity, it was as if he could have speared right through the stones and skewered Cadwaladr in the chest.

The rest of the Dragons stood silently by, waiting for a sign from Hywel as to what he wanted them to do next. Any one of them would have happily mounted his horse, ridden straight into the church, and murdered Cadwaladr before the altar. Hywel had only to give the word. Their loyalty to their prince, to a man, including Gareth's son Dai, was absolute.

Hywel's expression, however, other than a certain whiteness around his mouth that hadn't been there before, remained entirely calm. "My father will take him back, of course."

Gareth swept a hand through his hair, flicking the rainwater off the short ends. He truly had nothing to say. From the moment Gwen had told him Cadwaladr was in the church and that he had asked for her, he'd assumed Owain would give way. It was part of the reason Gareth initially had forbidden Gwen to go at all. If they could refuse Cadwaladr his first request, perhaps it would be possible to refuse the rest.

And even if King Owain's initial response hadn't immediately opened a door for taking Cadwaladr back, Susanna's bright eyes had told Gareth she would force the issue. King Owain would never be able to stand against both his brother *and* his sister.

And so Gareth didn't argue with Hywel's assessment. Rhun had been a *good* man in a way that some in this day and age derided as hopelessly naïve—or outright denied could exist at all. And yet, not only had Rhun existed, but he'd been as honest, honorable, and upright as any man Gareth had ever met.

Cadwaladr was none of those things, even as he proclaimed himself to have nothing but good intentions, and that any evidence against him was misguided or twisted or just plain wrong. In all the years Gareth had known him, he had forever been one to make excuses for himself, to tell himself that whatever lie he'd just told was for the greater good. Or worse, he'd been perfectly capable of convincing himself that what he believed wasn't a lie. When Gareth had served Cadwaladr after the war in Ceredigion, he'd known the kind of man Cadwaladr was, as had all of Cadwaladr's men, and Gareth had ultimately decided that honor demanded he refuse to serve him anymore. To this day, certain men despised Gareth for making that choice.

To Gareth, however, by the end, leaving Cadwaladr's service hadn't been a choice. And when he'd left, he hadn't slipped out in the night, but had spoken to Cadwaladr's face the truth as he knew it.

That, naturally, had been an unforgivable sin in Cadwaladr's eyes, and it wasn't any wonder that today he'd asked for Gwen rather than Gareth. Cadwaladr *hated* Gareth. At times, Gareth liked to think his own hatred for Cadwaladr had turned to pity, but if he was being honest, he hadn't matured that much.

Hywel met Gareth's gaze again, and Gareth saw everything going through his own mind reflected in Hywel's face. Their mutual understanding settled Gareth a bit more, and maybe Hywel as well, because he said, "My father loves his brother, and he forgave him every transgression that came before Rhun's death. Cadwaladr will tell my father he never meant to harm Rhun, which is probably even true."

"Right." Gruffydd snorted derisively, so caught up in his own emotions that he wasn't respectful, even of his prince. "It was Gareth he meant to murder."

Hywel didn't censure his captain, instead maintaining his preternatural calm. "My father knows this too." He began walking up the road towards the church. "I suppose we should find out what my uncle has to say."

Gareth fell into step beside Hywel, respecting his measured response, even as he swallowed down his own far more childish and violent one. As he'd been just five yeears old when his own parents had died, Gareth had been too young to understand his grief. When the uncle who raised him afterwards had been killed in battle when

Gareth was sixteen, he'd known true grief for the first time: the kind that left a man writhing on the floor, overcome by pain too great to bear.

Rhun's loss had been like that for Hywel. Gareth had held him as he'd cried. While Gareth didn't ever want to become numb to death (and certainly never wanted to feel that kind of pain again), he understood it better now. What he saw in Hywel, however, was a numbness that frightened him. When a man turned off all emotion, as Hywel was doing now, he was capable of anything. And Hywel had been quite capable of a great many things before. They'd openly talked about hunting down Cadwaladr and murdering him them-selves. In Hywel's present mood, he seemed entirely capable of such a deed.

God help him, if that was the course of action Hywel chose to follow, Gareth would be right there with him, come what may.

It was easier to deal with Gruffydd's anger. They knew what he wanted and that if he wasn't held back, he would kill Cadwaladr and accept the punishment. For now, they couldn't let him. Though Cadwaladr had gotten away with murdering the King of Deheubarth as well as the heir to the throne of Gwynedd, anyone of less stature than a prince of Gwynedd would not be so fortunate.

As it was, Hywel wasn't sharing what was truly in his mind, and Gareth had no right to pry, not here, not now, so there was no help for it but to walk beside him and face what came. Dai, who'd ridden out with the Dragons today and was nearly a full-fledged member by now, silently took the leading reins of Hywel's horse. Dai had lost both of his birth parents too. Truthfully, it was a rare man who didn't know horrific loss.

Hywel came to a halt in front of his father, who had turned to see him coming. In the interim, Susanna had retreated to the shelter of the gatehouse, and Gareth had a moment's pang she'd already achieved what she wanted.

"Sir." Hywel chose the more formal greeting, rather than saying *Father*.

King Owain pressed his lips together as he studied his son. Hywel was covered in mud from his ride, but the rain that was still coming down was washing clean his face. Gareth wished the troubles of the day could be cleansed as easily.

"Gareth told you?"

"Yes."

The word held such weight that Gareth felt it in his own chest.

King Owain recognized it too. "Son—" he stopped. "I'm sorry."

"I know you are, Father. I am too."

"I won't forgive him this time."

Hywel shook his head. "Don't promise me that. It isn't necessary and likely isn't true. Cadwaladr is here because he has something to trade, and it has to be something so momentous that he knows already you won't be able to refuse him."

Even though it was Gareth's job as Hywel's steward to advise him and present competing ideas for any situation, he hadn't quite reached that point in his own assessment. He'd been falling short all day, but this time he didn't berate himself for his failing. Hywel was cleverer than any man he knew. Gareth had long since accepted that his job wasn't to outthink Hywel, but to stand at his side, and to advise, and to occasionally be his conscience.

King Owain looked long at his son, his expression giving nothing away.

Though what their eyes had said to one another wasn't clear to Gareth, Hywel must have seen some kind of response, because he added, "The needs of Gwynedd come first, Father. You are right to think so, and you should not regret it. Rhun knew it when he was the *edling*. It took me longer to see it, but the two of you, and time, taught me."

"We'll see." The king returned his gaze to the church.

"I suppose we will, provided Cadwaladr doesn't eat Gwen first."

It was a jest, one entirely in character if they'd been discussing anything or anyone else, but a bit shocking when the topic was Cadwaladr. King Owain swung his attention back to Hywel, a bark of a laugh on his lips, which matched the smile on Hywel's own.

"Stay beside me son. We will face what comes together."

17

Gwen

Cadwaladr as a prince and a personality had always been larger than life. Expansive. He filled any room he entered. He had a way of being that drew people to him. They *wanted* to serve him, up until the point they realized the eyes looking back at them were of the devil rather than the angel they thought they were committing themselves to.

By then it was usually too late.

Cadwaladr had learned nothing to make him any different in the two years since Gwen had watched him flee the scene of Rhun's death. Looking down on him now as he lay in the shape of a cross, Gwen saw him as he was and had always been: a twisted, treacherous, greedy, privileged prince who cared only about himself.

God help her, but she could see nothing redeeming in this man.

Abbot Rhys put a hand on her arm. "Let me speak to him first."

It was good of the abbot to offer and just as well, since the only words welling up in Gwen's throat were full of invective. She had tried to let go of her anger, because hating hurt her far more than the object of her hatred—this man who hadn't even been in Wales for the last two years. She could waste away with that emotion eating her up inside, and then she wouldn't be good for anyone, least of all her children or Gareth, who mattered far more than the loathsome prince before her. Even more, her anger at Cadwaladr gave *him* power over *her*, which she hated almost as much as she hated him.

Telling herself that he was pathetic and pitiful, she turned away to face the door by which they'd entered the church and released a breath she hadn't realized she'd been holding. With it, a sense of calm seeped through her like warm water in a bath, and the quiet in the pretty little church settled around her once again. Though Abbot Rhys would urge her to forget and forgive, she didn't have to do either to be honest with herself. Her feelings were her own, and the less she allowed them to control her, the less control over her Cadwaladr would have. *That* was certainly a goal worth striving for.

With a sternly worded internal admonition, she told herself that she was a big girl now, and she could do this.

Behind her, Abbot Rhys said, "Gwen is here, Prince Cadwaladr. I am Rhys, Abbot of St. Kentigern's monastery in St. Asaph. We met several years ago."

Gwen noted the absence of the honorific, *my lord,* in Abbot's Rhys's address. Gwen wouldn't have even called Cadwaladr *prince.*

Cadwaladr remained face down on the floor. As a result, when his reply came, it was slightly muffled. "I have come to ask forgiveness, Father. Forgive me, for I have sinned."

Cadwaladr's words snapped Gwen back to complete consciousness, her moment of peace swept away by his *arrogance*. He genuinely believed he would be forgiven—that he *deserved* to be forgiven. All of a sudden, the church didn't feel so peaceful anymore, and instead was cold and unfamiliar, as if the wind whistling through the space between the frame and the door was really the ghosts of all those people Cadwaladr had wronged—or killed.

She shivered, pulling her cloak closer around herself, and then swung around, her eyes flashing—and met the calm and knowing gaze of Abbot Rhys, who put up a hand to stop whatever words she was going to say. Even she didn't know what those words would have been.

Abbot Rhys was right that, whatever they were, they would have been said in anger, which had no place in this church today, even if they were exactly what Cadwaladr deserved. She reminded herself again to breathe and to look beyond the shape of Cadwaladr to the soul within, as Abbot Rhys was attempting to do. For an instant, she was flooded with pity, and it was a relief to feel something besides anger. But then she pulled back that emotion too in order to protect herself. If Cadwaladr saw pity for him in her face, he would exploit it as surely as the morning lark would sing.

"Absolution is for the confessional and is a matter between you and your priest," Abbot Rhys said. "It isn't what Gwen and I came for today. We are here, as you requested, to listen. Was your intent in coming to Denbigh simply to ask forgiveness from God and your brother, or do you have a larger purpose?"

His words were calmly said but, for all that, uncompromising. If Cadwaladr had hoped for a sympathetic ear, Abbot Rhys was signaling he wasn't necessarily going to get it. Forgiveness might be something for which Cadwaladr had already asked a priest, but absolution was granted only to those sinners who regretted the sin and pledged never to repeat it. Gwen supposed even that was something Cadwaladr could do—provided the sin he confessed to was arranging for the murder of Rhun, accident or not. Rhun was gone. He couldn't be killed twice. If the sin was that of lying or another form of deception, the priest would be a fool to absolve him. It was a sin Cadwaladr committed as easily as he breathed.

But that was the same bad road she'd been going down earlier, and she disciplined herself once more, folding her arms across her chest, as a physical manifestation of what she was trying to do emotionally. The motion even brought a moment of levity to her heart, because only that morning Tangwen had stood the same way, accompanied by a vigorous refusal to have her hair tamed. Gwen kept an image of her daughter's bright face at the forefront of her mind, as a reminder of why she was here.

Finally deciding his posture of submission and penitence truly was lost on Gwen and Rhys, Cadwaladr brought in his arms and pushed himself up off the floor. Standing before the altar, he brushed at the front of his tunic and jerked it straight, before making the sign of the cross and backing away. Then he turned and came halfway down the nave until he reached the spot where Gwen had chosen to stand.

At that point, he spread his arms wide. "Thank you for being willing to hear me out."

That he would say *thank you* was almost worse than hearing he wanted forgiveness. Gwen was aware, however, that he couldn't say *anything* that wouldn't irk her. He had a relatively nice voice in the middle range, but it nauseated her to hear it.

Upon closer inspection, Cadwaladr wasn't quite his usual self either, in that his clothes were worse for wear, his hair was overlong and mussed, and he had a smudge on the end of his nose. Since the floor of the chapel was spotless, the dirt on his tunic wasn't from lying on it. He'd made an attempt to polish his boots, but he was otherwise disheveled, and a quick glance at the cloak he'd hung over the back of the altar rail revealed it to be also filthy with mud to a depth of those six inches Gwen had been glad she hadn't experienced earlier in the courtyard with Gareth.

Cadwaladr had come a long way through terrible weather to reach Denbigh. The effort involved would have been impressive in someone Gwen loved, but coming from Cadwaladr, it made her distrust him all the more, and she battled internally as to what point she should or should not give him the benefit of the doubt. A grand gesture of sacrifice would be just like him. Even after everything he'd done, he still had his supporters in Gwynedd, who believed the law of inheritance, which said all sons should inherit equally from their father, should be rigidly adhered to, even with royal sons. They would have him sharing power with King Owain.

A throne could not be split in two, however, even though, over the years throughout Wales, sons of dead kings had attempted to do exactly that. In Gwynedd, one solution, occasionally implemented, designated one son to rule east of the River Conwy while another ruled in the west. Perhaps when Owain and Cadwaladr's father had died, Cadwaladr had expected an inheritance along those lines, only to be disappointed when Owain, as *edling,* had claimed all of Gwynedd and bestowed only Merionnydd, parts of Anglesey, and the newly-won Ceredigion on him. That had been in 1137. Gwen could easily see how a simmering resentment could have bubbled over into the murder of Anarawd six years later and set Cadwaladr's feet on a path that had brought him here today.

Then Cadwaladr looked directly at her for the first time. "It is nice to see you, Gwen. You look well."

She wasn't going to be drawn in by a polite opening, but she was nonetheless surprised to find her tone normal. "Why did you come?"

Obviously, one reason was because Cadwaladr very badly wanted back in Owain's good graces, though she was willing to be pleasantly surprised otherwise. She genuinely did wonder *why* he wanted back in. Last she'd heard, he had been living well as a noble companion in the royal court in France. Before that he'd been a lackey to King Stephen.

"I bring a message to my brother from Prince Henry."

Prince Henry, in whose court Cadwaladr had been living, was the son of Empress Maud, King Stephen's rival for the throne of England. Gareth and Gwen had met Henry years ago, before Tangwen's birth, and saved his life. When Taran was an infant, they'd answered Henry's call to investigate the death of his uncle, Robert of Gloucester—and saved his life again. Cadwaladr had been a messenger for King Stephen that day.

Nobody said anything for a moment, and Gwen didn't give herself away by glancing at Abbot Rhys, who seemed content to let her take the lead.

After a moment's pause, she said, "Are you going to tell us what that message is?"

"Prince Henry meant it for my brother's ears alone."

"Then why ask for me?" Gwen just managed not to snort her disgust.

"Because you are an honest, kind person, and I knew you would carry my message to my brother without prejudice."

Gwen stared at him, stunned to her very core. It suddenly came to her that, while he might accept that she had some reason to be mildly out of sorts with him, he had no idea how much she hated him. He might not even be able to imagine she *could* hate him. Or that *anyone* could hate him. And then, even worse, she realized the extent of the problem: he was incapable of seeing his culpability in Rhun's death. To him, it was an accident, an honest mistake anyone could have made, never mind that the ambush of Rhun had been set up to murder Gareth, *Gwen's husband*.

None of that, even after two years in exile, had penetrated Cadwaladr's surety of himself. For the first time, she began to wonder if he was genuinely incapable of understanding it, and that he was, truly, mentally deficient. He was certainly emotionally crippled. As a king's son, he had been catered to and protected throughout his childhood, and King Owain and Susanna had continued to shelter him into adulthood, long past the point it was reasonable or seemly to do so. He was a middle-aged man! It seemed impossible for him not to know how she felt. But how else to explain the patient, somewhat supercilious smile on his face?

And with that new clarity, Gwen accepted that her anger and disdain for him over the years had entirely passed him by. Even if she conveyed how she felt in word or deed, he still wouldn't believe she could truly despise him or that he, in any way, deserved her ire. She had thought he was willfully ignorant. Instead, he was oblivious.

And just like that, her own anger, which had been playing hide-and-seek with pity for the last quarter of an hour, disappeared like a popped soap bubble in Taran's bath. Cadwaladr was a charlatan, a fool, and a traitor, but he was also so deeply enmeshed in his own myth of himself, which he'd created for himself, that he no longer saw that myth for the lie it was, if he'd ever known it. She wasn't excusing him by any means, but she wouldn't waste another thought on him. Whether or not she showed how she felt about him, he wasn't going to change. Better to save her feelings, to keep them to herself, so he couldn't use them against her.

Abbot Rhys, being a far more perceptive man than Cadwaladr, not to mention a good friend, was able to recognize Gwen's expression for what it was when she didn't answer right away, and he stepped into the silence. "You are going to have to give us something more than that. Your brother is not inclined to speak to you at all."

"I heard his voice outside just now. He's there." Cadwaladr scoffed, reverting in that instant to his usual self. "Open the door and tell him he needs to hear me out."

It was a demand. Gwen was honestly surprised it had taken him this long to assert what he perceived as his rights. By way of a reply, she turned on her heel and strode for the door. Part of her was made almost gleeful at Cadwaladr's choice of words, because she was going to repeat them word for word to Owain, exactly as Cadwaladr requested.

"No, no, no, no, no." Cadwaladr hustled forward and got in front of her before she could reach for the latch. "Wait." He moved a hand to touch her arm, and she jerked backwards, away from him, as if she'd just been spattered with hot oil.

"Don't touch me."

"Fine." He put up both hands in a manner that implied her request was unreasonable but *he* was such a reasonable man he was going along with it anyway. "Whatever you want."

She hated being humored. For all her intermittent resolve, she was doing a terrible job of not showing how she felt. With an effort, she mastered her distaste for him and wrestled her expression back to something approximating neutral.

For his part, Cadwaladr put his heels together and gave her a short bow. "This is what I would like you to say to my brother, if you will: *With penitence in his heart, Prince Cadwaladr requests the opportunity to speak to you about matters that are urgent.*" He paused, thinking.

"Is that all?" Gwen would have brushed past him if it hadn't meant touching him. He was steadfastly blocking the door.

He put up one finger. "Not quite." Then he continued, "*He brings a message from Henry, rightful prince of the English. If you will listen, I assure you it will be worth your while.*"

"Fine." Gwen mocked herself for thinking for even a moment that he was truly repentant. He couldn't just say, *I'm sorry. I was wrong. Please forgive me*. With him it was all excuses or carrots to dangle before Owain's face. It was a wonder he hadn't already brought out the stick.

She still didn't have enough control over her expression that what she was thinking shouldn't have been obvious to anyone who actually *cared* what she was thinking. Cadwaladr, as always, was focused entirely on his own thoughts and desires. For him, everything was a *need*.

Thus, still oblivious and ignorant of what he had wrought in her, Cadwaladr stepped back and bowed again, this time with a flourish. "If you will. Please." Then he opened the door and held it wide.

Unable to conceive of an immediate alternative, she stepped out—and came to a dead halt at the sight of Hywel standing in the rain beside his father on the other side of the church's gate, his back to her.

Worse and worse.

She had no time to plan an alternate strategy because, a heartbeat later, having heard the creaking of the door, both Hywel and Owain turned to look. Owain remained bare-headed as before.

Maybe he liked the rain on his head and face. If so, she could understand.

Abbot Rhys called from behind her. "I'll stay here, Gwen, for now."

She nodded without looking around, which Rhys must have seen because she heard the door close with a thud.

She walked through the rain. She couldn't cry, even though her throat was clogged with tears. It was somehow comforting that her cheeks were wet anyway.

Gareth stood at Hywel's elbow, and she didn't dare look at either of them in case the tears fell before she did her duty. When she reached King Owain, she halted a few paces away and, in a stony voice, repeated to the king exactly what Cadwaladr had instructed her to say.

Having finished the assigned task, she let out a breath and then, pressing her palms together, brought them up to her lips and looked at the king over the top of them. "Do you have an immediate reply?"

"Is there anything more I should know? Anything else he said that would be relevant to my decision?"

Gwen thought about the way Cadwaladr had laid himself before the altar in a posture of penitence, how he'd initially asked for forgiveness and then his contrition had turned abruptly to his usual demands, and how he'd carefully thought through what he wanted Gwen to say.

"No, my lord. You have all the information you need."

Owain eyed her. "You're telling me he is unchanged?"

She managed a nod.

"Then, to answer your question: I have no immediate reply. Let him stew a while. Hywel and I need to think of what to say and how to say it." He looked at Hywel. "Come, son. Walk with me."

18

Hywel

This had always been Rhun's role.

As Hywel walked back through the palace gatehouse beside his father, he couldn't help thinking about his brother, trying to put himself in Rhun's shoes, as well as decide what he would want done.

In the first weeks and months after Rhun died, even in the midst of his grief, Hywel would occasionally forget he was dead. Usually this happened first thing in the morning, before he was properly awake, or when something happened he knew Rhun would have enjoyed hearing about. Then, Hywel would say to himself, "Don't forget to tell Rhun—"

The very thought, however, was always enough to remind him that he was alone. His loss these days was never more acute than when Hywel had something he wanted to share and couldn't.

When it came to Cadwaladr, Rhun had always been more forgiving than Hywel. It was probably true that Hywel was cleverer, but he'd come to realize, thankfully *before* Rhun died, that he wasn't

"

smarter than his brother. Just because a man met the world with open arms didn't make him a fool, ignorant, or stupid. Rhun had known the truth of people and loved them anyway. It might even have been that he loved them for their faults. Rhun had been beautiful that way.

But even Rhun had understood the truth of Cadwaladr. Loving Cadwaladr meant being betrayed time and again, as they'd all experienced time and again. Forgiving Cadwaladr meant letting him back into one's life only to watch him hurt everyone—and oneself—again. If Hywel's father allowed Cadwaladr to return to Gwynedd, he would do so knowing in advance what the outcome was going to be and going ahead with it nonetheless.

Hywel warned himself that knowing the future as if he were a parent and his father a toddler taking his first steps along an uneven path didn't mean his father wasn't going down it anyway. Just because Owain was asking for Hywel's thoughts didn't mean the outcome was going to be any different, and they all weren't going to fall on their faces and end up crying.

They bypassed the great hall and the adjacent receiving room, deeming neither private enough, and went straight to the king's bedchamber in the next building over. This was to be so private, in fact, that neither Gareth nor Taran were invited. If nothing else, Hywel warmed to the measure of trust his father was placing in him.

In this palace, Cristina had a room of her own, which she shared with her small boys. That was probably the only reason she wasn't present at this moment. Many Norman noblewomen had little to do with their children, but Cristina had a very clear vision of how she wanted her sons to be and had discovered that raising them, as with most things, wouldn't be done right unless she did it primarily herself.

That said, she had to have realized there was a commotion going on at the church. She had enough spies and lackeys for one of them to have run straight to her. *So where was she?*

Not here, obviously, and Hywel supposed now wasn't the time to worry about what Cristina was doing. She was a snake too. Gareth had reported that she'd been cooperative, even *nice,* today. It was unprecedented and, to Hywel, suspicious, but Cadwaladr's request was right in front of them. Maybe one day her crimes would rise to the level of Cadwaladr's. For now, they paled in comparison.

Owain strode to the table and poured both himself and Hywel a cup of wine. After they'd each taken a swig, he gestured to Hywel with his cup. "I should send my brother on his way."

"You most definitely should, but you can't," Hywel said flatly, surprising himself with how sure he was of this. Deep in his chest, rage was boiling, but he swallowed it down before it could clog his throat. "Prince Henry may well be King of England someday. If Cadwaladr really has brought a message from him, Gwynedd is not so powerful that it can ignore what he has to say."

"*If.*" Owain snorted in disgust.

"Oh, his message is real, Father. I have no doubt that Cadwaladr has convinced himself he did nothing wrong, but he knows better than to come home empty-handed. He possesses a very strong instinct for his own survival, and it would have told him the necessity of bringing you something worthwhile." It felt odd to be playing the role of reason in this. He wasn't even at war with himself. He was detached, and it allowed him to see the truth. "I wouldn't be at all surprised if we eventually learn that whatever Henry is offering was first suggested to him by Cadwaladr."

Owain began pacing back and forth in front of the hearth, unable to settle. "My guess, Henry is tired of his company and is seeking a way to get rid of him."

"Henry may be even smarter than that," Hywel said. "He knows at least something of Cadwaladr's past because Gareth told him of it. He knows the turmoil sending Cadwaladr to you will engender in Gwynedd. And yet he does it anyway? My guess: Henry believes now, more than ever, that he will be King of England one day, at which point what to do with you and Gwynedd will become a pressing question. Ranulf of Chester, uncle to Cadwaladr's wife, looks covetously on Gwynedd, and Henry might be persuaded to reward him with it."

"That would be an undesirable outcome."

"It would indeed. And it could be an outcome if Cadwaladr is in Henry's court for the next few years, agitating for his birthright."

At his father's grunt of understanding, Hywel continued, "As I said, Henry is probably smarter than I would like. While he would prefer to have you on his side, perhaps to the point of becoming a thorn in King Stephen's side, he will take what he can get. At a minimum, if you accept Cadwaladr back, he will have an ally in your court."

"And one who can be relied on to sow dissension with every breath." Owain stopped his pacing as he reached the window. "I would have been happy never to see him again."

Hywel thought it was kind of his father to say, but didn't believe him. "I feel the same way, Father, as well you know, but we both knew it would never be possible, short of Cadwaladr's death. Or ours. He is a millstone around your neck, made all the worse because you do love him. Even still."

Owain swung around to look at Hywel. "Not more than Rhun."

"No, but that isn't a requirement, nor what love is about." He met his father's gaze. "Love doesn't have to be weighed and apportioned frugally like silver."

They'd had frank conversations before, and they'd been rubbing along well as the months had gone on. But, for the first time in his life, Hywel felt an actual camaraderie with his father that filled his heart. He'd been the *edling* for two years, but with the arrival of Cadwaladr, Hywel and his father were suddenly equals—or as equal as a father and son could be. They were united in their fears and hopes for their country—and in their love for each other.

In that moment, Hywel knew he would walk through fire and brimstone, to hell and back if need be, for his father. And maybe, just maybe, his father was realizing that he would do the same for Hywel.

"So we talk to him?" King Owain asked.

"We do."

Owain canted his head. "Where?"

"In the church. It's neutral ground."

"Wouldn't it be better to have him on his knees before me in my hall with everyone watching?"

"While it might provide us both with a momentary satisfaction, Cadwaladr loves nothing more than an audience. He would spread his arms wide, protest his love for you, and beg forgiveness for whatever it was he might have done, which truly he does not understand. Your people would fall at his feet, like they always do, telling themselves that he couldn't possibly be the villain responsible for Rhun's death and that he was wronged. Worse, in their adulation, Cadwaladr would believe it too."

Owain had been watching Hywel during this recitation, and now he cocked an eyebrow. "You and Gwen. You do know him well."

"I don't have to know him well to know this. We've all seen him do it."

"More times than I should have let him." For a moment, the king's grimness gave Hywel hope that *this time* his father's resolve wouldn't dissipate the moment he saw his brother. It was probably unwise to get his hopes up.

In accord, they headed back to the church, on the way collecting Gareth and Taran, who'd been waiting patiently for them to return, talking quietly together in the guardroom of the gatehouse with Gwen. Someone had found her a dry cloak, and she was wrapped to her ears, and her face wasn't quite as pale as before. While a full audience was a terrible idea, witnesses were vital when talking to Cadwaladr about anything important. With the presence of Abbot Rhys, who'd remained behind in the church, Cadwaladr couldn't protest after the fact that what had transpired between him and his brother was being misrepresented.

Which was how, sooner than Hywel was probably ready for, he found himself on the church porch.

Before Gareth could open the door, Gwen put out a hand. "Just so you know, when we arrived before, Cadwaladr was lying before the altar on his stomach in the shape of a cross."

Hywel made a face, and King Owain snorted under his breath—though when Hywel looked at his father, he saw that the snort wasn't so much in disdain but in laughter. "That's my brother for you. He will do anything to make himself look good."

"My father asked before if there was anything else we needed to know, and you said there wasn't," Hywel said, realizing he shouldn't have taken Gwen's calm demeanor as the truth, because of course it couldn't have been.

"I know that's what I said, and maybe I should have said more, but I was being careful not to insert my own prejudices into the situation, and anything I would have told you would have come through that reflection."

The king put an arm around Gwen's shoulders and squeezed. "Never fear your thoughts are unwanted, Gwen. You should know that by now."

"Yes, my lord." Gwen's expression, however, when she met Hywel's eyes a moment later, was somewhat sardonic.

"Right." King Owain drew himself up to his full height. "Let's get this done."

Gareth opened the door, and they trooped inside.

Thankfully, Cadwaladr wasn't back on the floor, but stood instead with legs spread and his hands clasped behind his back, turned away from the altar. At the sight of Owain walking towards him, he didn't wait for his brother to greet him but hurried forward, grabbed Owain's hand, and knelt before him.

"Brother, brother, I am so sorry for all that I have done. Please forgive me."

Beside Hywel, Gwen tsked under her breath. "Finally, a real apology."

But then, typically, Cadwaladr corrupted it with excuses. "I wasn't thinking straight and took bad advice from people I thought were my friends. I'm sure this is all a big misunderstanding that will be sorted shortly. I never intended to hurt Rhun—"

The look on Cadwaladr's face as he gazed up at his brother was one of sheer anguish. If Hywel hadn't known him as well as he did, he might have thought it was a true emotion. Instead, he hardened his heart, determined never to be drawn in again.

The expression on Owain's face was equally intense.

Cadwaladr saw it and immediately snapped his lips together, smoothing his expression an instant later.

"Don't say his name." King Owain would have been within his rights to shout, seeing as how the so-called apology was long overdue. But instead, his voice came out hard and cold—enough to penetrate even Cadwaladr's bluster.

Cadwaladr stood up and bent his head in a brief obeisance. "My apologies, my king."

Nothing Cadwaladr could do would ever make Hywel trust him again—or love him, for that matter, if he ever had. Cadwaladr could apologize, but it would serve only to make Hywel angry. Cadwaladr could be matter-of-fact, as he had suddenly become, and Hywel would despise him for it equally.

But, at least, with the latter demeanor, emotion could be put aside for a time.

"Say what you came here to say," Owain said.

And then you can go, would have been the next words out of Hywel's mouth, but his father didn't speak them. The cold feeling in Hywel's belly hardened into a lump, not so much like a stone but more like cold porridge, a meal that tasted like nothing going down and was impossible to digest.

Cadwaladr put his heels together and did as he was bid. For once. Even he seemed to realize it was now or never. "Prince Henry has a proposal for you." He stopped, looking expectant.

"Thus Gwen told me," Owain said. "What is it?"

Cadwaladr's expression turned dubious as he looked around the interior of the church. "You want me to blurt it out here?"

"This is a place of God," Owain said. "Where better?"

Hywel had never known Cadwaladr to be as expressive in his features as he was today. Perhaps the fact that this was so indicated a true desperation. Regardless, now Cadwaladr looked as if he thought any place would have been better than this, especially one that included a fire and a cup of warm mead.

But when Owain didn't waver, Cadwaladr bent his head again and gave way with a modicum of grace.

"Prince Henry intends to invade England in the spring in order to overthrow King Stephen once and for all. He has made an alliance—a pact, if you will— with his uncle, King David of Scotland, and Earl Ranulf of Chester. They intend to split England among themselves. They invite you to join them and propose, if your help results in victory, to have you ruling all of Wales in the bargain."

19

Gwen

Gwen had been standing with her hands clasped before her lips, and now pressed her fingers against them, trying very hard not to show how stunned she was at the news Cadwaladr had brought.

The surprise wasn't because the idea of Henry attacking King Stephen's forces was in any way unexpected. They'd known his return to France earlier that year had been temporary. Nor was it news that Henry would ally with King David and Earl Ranulf and make a pact to split the lands they conquered among themselves.

The message Cadwaladr brought was shocking because it was King Owain Gwynedd to whom Prince Henry was turning, and because he was admitting to the plan before he'd received any assurances of support. There was nothing to prevent Owain from going immediately to King Stephen and laying the entire plot at his feet.

King Owain himself was aware of these issues as much or more than Gwen, and though he was normally a demonstrative person, he managed not to show what he was thinking. Instead, he eased himself onto a nearby bench and settled his back against the wall. All the while, his gaze remained steady on Cadwaladr's face.

The brothers looked at each other for another long moment before Owain asked his first question: "Why me?"

Cadwaladr's reply was immediate. "Why not you?"

Owain spread his hands wide. "You know very well why not. Both Madog of Powys and Cadell of Deheubarth are far more natural allies of Henry than I am."

Cadwaladr had a ready answer for that too, one that was objectively true, but sounded strangely complimentary coming from him. "Neither of them have your power, range, and influence. Nor your honor. They are also both hemmed in by Marcher lords, and have already switched sides multiple times in the war between Stephen and Maud. You have refused to take sides. Ranulf himself says you cannot be bought."

King Owain rubbed his chin as he studied his brother, and then broached the next issue. "Henry is taking a risk in telling me about his plan. What's to stop me from running straight to Stephen?"

"Why would you do that?"

"Stephen is the King of England. Henry remains a pretender to the throne. Which one really has more to offer me?"

Cadwaladr snorted. "Henry will be king one day."

"Stephen's son Eustace is a perfectly worthy heir to the throne."

"Many English barons prefer Henry to Eustace. They just haven't said so yet. Would you really risk Henry's wrath on the chance of getting more than he has just offered you? What more could you want than to rule all of Wales?"

For once, Cadwaladr had a point, and Owain canted his head in tacit admission. "What about Madog?"

"What about him?"

"Well, for starters, he's here. This is the long-awaited wedding of Iorwerth and Marared. You're telling me King Henry is genuinely offering to elevate me above Madog?"

"Henry doesn't trust Madog."

"And he trusts me?" Owain laughed.

Cadwaladr didn't laugh with him, but remained very serious. "Yes."

Owain sobered. "Be that as it may, Madog is *your* friend. How do you feel about Henry offering me this chance when you would have preferred it had gone to Madog?"

"Who says I would have preferred it? My lands are not in Powys," Cadwaladr said, "and my feelings don't come into it."

Gwen barely managed to swallow down her gasping laughter. Never before had Cadwaladr's feelings *not* come into it. If Madog were here, he should also have taken heed: Cadwaladr's loyalty was exactly that thin.

"You have been Madog's ally in the past."

"I have been your ally in the past."

"Yes, you have." Owain laughed again. "Then, if not Madog, what of King Cadell of Deheubarth?"

"Prince Henry sees in you an ability to lead that none of these other kings have. Cadell controls a small area, he has never truly been a king in the sense you are, and doesn't have the head you have for leadership anyway."

Cadwaladr seemed to have an answer for everything. He was too smooth and yet, what he was saying made sense. It was very disconcerting.

Owain still looked disbelieving. "What about Richard de Clare? He allies with Henry now, but how long would that last once he discovers that I, rather than he, will be elevated to King of Wales?"

"Richard de Clare is too young to be accepted beyond his borders and couldn't rule Wales without additional bloodshed. What's more, neither you nor Madog would submit to him. Anyway, haven't you heard? Before Richard's father died, the Clares reconciled with King Stephen. That means Cadell is wavering too. Henry will not look to either for support again."

Gwen had met Richard de Clare the previous year in Deheubarth when his father was still alive. He had come to fight against King Stephen then, in alliance with King Cadell. Now, as Earl of Pembroke, at all of eighteen years old, despite Cadwaladr's naysaying, he was already a force to be reckoned with. He had been on friendly terms with Gareth, but that likely wouldn't translate into submitting willingly to King Owain, should Owain take this bargain.

The King of Gwynedd studied Cadwaladr for so long, Gwen's legs began falling asleep. She wavered slightly, and Abbot Rhys took a tiny step towards her to bolster her left side while Gareth's shoulder brushed hers on the right.

That small motion stirred Owain, and he finally replied, "You have been frank with me, and I will do you the same favor. You have allied with both Ranulf and Madog in the past, with the intent of murdering me and placing yourself on the throne of Gwynedd. Why should I believe this isn't your plan now, with Henry as your pawn this time?"

For once, Cadwaladr didn't answer right away, instead staring up at the plain wooden beams that supported the roof of the church. They were not interesting, but they seemed to be allowing him to gather his thoughts. Gwen could almost see his mind working furiously as he decided what to say—or maybe how to say it. His entire being was invested in getting King Owain to accept this deal. For that prize, it was worth being logical and reasonable.

"King Henry told me outright that if I were King of Gwynedd, upon your death or otherwise, he would not be making this offer."

And maybe, truthful.

"He doesn't trust you!" Taran was the first to respond, and he barked a laugh.

It wasn't really like Taran to intervene between the two brothers, but he had been at Owain's side since they were young men, and it had been Taran, as well as Hywel, to whom Owain had turned at Rhun's death. He had earned the right to mock.

Hywel, meanwhile, paced away towards the shrine of the Virgin Mary, inset against the northern wall. Looking up at her face, he dipped his fingers into the font, crossed himself, and then paced back, to come to a halt three feet away from Cadwaladr himself rather than returning to his former position off to one side.

"Now we need to hear the price."

Because, of course, there would be one. There always was one.

Gwen knew what the price was going to be, and she was quite sure that Hywel knew too. *Everyone* in the church knew what Owain would have to pay, so nobody blinked when Cadwaladr said, "My brother will restore me to my lands in Merionnydd and Anglesey, and return to me the right to stand at his side, as his brother and a prince of Gwynedd."

He hadn't asked for Ceredigion back. Looking into Hywel's face, he knew better.

The pause this time went on for longer, perhaps a count of twenty as Hywel gazed steadily back at his uncle. Uncle and nephew looked very little alike on the surface: Cadwaladr, like Owain, was tall and blond, with the bulk of middle age around his waist, while Hywel was shorter and darker, and more lean now than before Rhun's death. But something about their expressions and the way they held their heads made it clear they were joined by blood, even if both wished otherwise.

And then Hywel gave a sharp nod. "Done."

20

Gwen

Having emitted that single word, Hywel turned smartly on his heel and strode down the nave towards the door.

Gwen's instinct was to run after him, but Gareth was already on his way. She let them go, knowing comfort from her might well not be what Hywel wanted, and if he did want it, these days it was Mari's place to offer it, not Gwen's.

Cadwaladr appeared taken aback, both at what Hywel had said and the suddenness of his departure. He turned to King Owain, who'd risen from the bench upon which he'd been sitting to watch his son go. "Does he speak for you?"

"He does." To his credit, Owain didn't hesitate.

Cadwaladr stared at his brother—gaped even—visibly rocked back on his heels. Then, between one heartbeat and the next, his expression shuttered, and if Gwen hadn't been looking closely, she might not have known how surprised he was.

He knew better than to make a comment. Even Cadwaladr wasn't so unaware and insensitive that he didn't understand what he could and could not say to his brother in this moment. King Owain had made it clear earlier that Cadwaladr wasn't to speak Rhun's name, and now any criticism, implied or otherwise, directed towards the son who'd stepped into Rhun's shoes was forbidden. Cadwaladr had enough of a sense of self-preservation to realize that to do so would destroy whatever accord the last few moments had achieved.

So instead of approving, disapproving, or apologizing again, Cadwaladr bowed. "Then, if you will excuse me, I would like to see my wife, whom I understand is here. It has been too long."

"She is here." Owain nodded to Gwen, who realized he meant for her to escort Cadwaladr to wherever Alice could be found, likely the same guesthouse where Gwen herself was staying.

Everyone so far, other than Taran with his mocking remark, had been perfectly diplomatic and civilized. That, in and of itself, was disconcerting, given the anguish and sorrow Cadwaladr had caused. Gwen herself was uncomfortable with what King Owain was asking of her. Cadwaladr was a loathsome human being, and she'd spoken to him at all today only because it was her duty.

But Hywel had set the stage for how they were going to treat Cadwaladr, and since Hywel was her liege lord, she could not gainsay him. Who was she to say that the path he was charting was wrong? It had been she herself, moments ago, who'd resolved not to hate Cadwaladr anymore.

They needed to have a conversation, however, either just the few of them or with King Owain, about what accepting Cadwaladr back into Gwynedd *meant*. Was he truly to be welcomed? Was everyone to pretend he hadn't done what he'd done? Were *those* the real conditions of the deal King Owain was striking with Prince Henry?

Gwen managed to walk from the church to the gatehouse and then across the courtyard to the guesthouse without saying a single word to Cadwaladr. He seemed content enough with what he'd achieved that he didn't press her, just strolled along in her wake in an irritatingly cheery fashion. At one point, it seemed he might even have been whistling.

The fact that the wind was still blowing hard, though the rain had ceased while they were in the church, was all the excuse Gwen needed to keep her hood up and her head down.

Regardless, the end result was that they blew into the guest-house common room with something of a gasp, and Cadwaladr caught the door before it banged so hard against the wall it broke its hinges. Gwen's family had dispersed, but Alice was standing before the hearth, speaking to Manon, wife to Andreas, Deri and Nest's steward.

After Gwen entered, she stepped to one side, both to get out of Cadwaladr's way and to orient herself to her new reality. It turned her stomach that Cadwaladr would be sleeping in a room in the same building as Gwen herself. Not to mention Hywel and his family.

On top of which, the drama of Cadwaladr's arrival had put the murder investigation entirely from her mind, and the presence of Manon reminded her of how much they still had to learn. She had a moment's pang for the welfare of her brother, for whom she hadn't spared a single thought in the last hour, not even when the discussion had turned to Richard de Clare and Cadell of Deheubarth, at whose behest Gwen and Gareth had been at Dinefwr when the revelers in the great hall had been poisoned.

At their arrival, Alice and Manon both turned towards the doorway. Manon took one, wide-eyed look at Cadwaladr and dropped a curtsey. Then, head down, she hurried away, passing Gwen without a glance. Gwen had no idea how Manon and Alice had become acquainted, and it was something about which she needed to ask—though not of Alice right now, since the whole point of coming here was to bring Cadwaladr to her.

At the sight of her husband, Alice's eyes lit in a way that told Gwen she was either very glad to see him or was doing a remarkable job of feigning it. Heedless of the fact that Gwen was watching, the couple met in the center of the room and embraced. They did not yet speak, however, and Cadwaladr turned slightly to look meaningfully at Gwen.

Although she very much would have liked to hear what they had to say to each other, Gwen gave him a brief nod in acknowledgement and backed out the door. Although she was tempted to eavesdrop, the consequences of being caught were a little too dire, and she left the vicinity entirely, head high and counting her blessings that the first interactions were over. Everything would become easier after this, if only because familiarity could renew contempt.

For her part, Manon had stopped in the middle of the courtyard and was now talking to her husband, their heads close together. The clouds had dispersed enough that a weak sun was peeking through a gap for the first time in two days. It was enough to prompt Gwen to push back her hood and march right up to them, taking what felt like the perfect opportunity to question them about the dead dog.

Cadwaladr's arrival could have encouraged Gwen to put the entire investigation aside, faltering for lack of suspects and clues, but the attack on Gwalchmai and the theft of the dog's corpse had thrown into sharp relief the necessity of continuing. Gareth was going to be busy with Hywel for some time, so for the moment, it was up to her.

"Excuse me." She stopped a few feet from the couple, who hadn't noticed her approach. "I was hoping we could speak."

"Of course." In a smooth motion, Andreas put an arm around his wife's shoulders, and the pair turned to face Gwen, expressions serene and eyes shuttered. Although Welsh by birth, Andreas had the hair, pale skin, and blue eyes of a Saxon, much like Nest. As if to make up for his lack of overt Welshness, he wore a flamboyant mustache that curled at the ends. "What would you like to know?"

Their calm demeanor made Gwen more settled too. Of course, they would have no way of knowing how much Cadwaladr had upset her world and her equilibrium. From now on, she might admit it only to Gareth—and even then only in the privacy of their bedchamber. "What were you doing with Lady Alice just now, Manon?"

"My father sang at her wedding to Prince Cadwaladr." Manon replied without a falter. "She was renewing our acquaintance."

Gwen had forgotten that. Gwen's father should have been the one to sing at that wedding, but he'd had his falling out with Owain by then.

"It seems like an odd time to do so."

"She was waiting for King Owain to welcome her husband back into his court. What better time could there be? I was happy to provide her with the distraction."

Gwen frowned. "How did she know Cadwaladr was here?"

"Queen Susanna told her."

Of course she did. Gwen had needed to ask, even though the answer should have been obvious.

The smoothness of Manon's answer and the ease of her replies was putting Gwen off a bit, but she continued anyway: "The investigation into the death of Nest's dog is continuing. I was hoping you could help me discover who might have had a hand in it?"

Andreas's reply came as quickly as his wife's had done earlier. "As I told your husband, I haven't the slightest idea."

Gwen pinned her gaze on Manon, not yet ready to let it go. "Do you have any thoughts?"

"I wouldn't know." Manon's eyes were wide and innocent. Gwen knew her to be roughly thirty years of age, the same as Nest, but she looked much older. Gwen had always thought of her as pretty, though not in the class of Nest. This week, however, she'd been pale and drooping, and she had frown lines around her mouth that would become permanent if she wasn't careful. She was very slender too, almost skin and bones.

Her drab appearance made Gwen very aware of her own manner, and she put a bit more sunshine into her voice. "I was sorry not to see you on the dais this week. Can I look forward to it later?"

"Oh no." Manon shook her head vehemently. "I have no interest. I never liked it much, in truth."

"I wouldn't have said that was the case." Gwen looked at her curiously. "You seemed to enjoy it very much once upon a time."

Andreas tightened his grip on his wife. "Manon has other interests now."

Gwen met Manon's eyes, unsure how to respond. Manon merely looked blank, and Gwen couldn't tell if she agreed with her husband or was afraid to contradict him. Gwen resolved to speak to her again when she could get her alone.

"Did you go to the kitchen this morning, either of you?"

"Again, as I told your husband, I did not." That was from Andreas and his tone implied he resented being asked again.

"That was unusual for you, I understand," Gwen said.

"Yes. Sadly, I wasn't there to oversee the porridge."

"That's unfortunate, today of all days."

Andreas's eyes narrowed. "Are you accusing me of something?"

"No, just asking questions."

Manon's face had taken on something of a pinched look as Gwen had been talking to Andreas, prompting Gwen to turn to her again. "Manon?"

"I do not remember entering the kitchen."

That was an odd way to phrase it. It might even be true, though the kitchen staff had reported to Llelo that she'd been there. "Do you often not remember what you did in a morning?" Gwen was genuinely curious.

"Of course not." Manon shook her head. "I might have done. I don't know."

Gwen decided to let it go for now, if only because Manon herself was looking more and more uncertain, if not to the point of being frightened. *Something* was going on here. "You were in the hall, though. Did you see anything unusual?"

"Not that I recall," Manon said.

Andreas gave a tsk of disgust. "We don't know anything that can help. I'm sorry."

Their joint attitude had gone from unhelpful to obstructionist. Manon seemed to realize the impression they were making, and her expression softened. "I really liked the dog. I'm very sad she's gone."

For a moment, the woman looked almost normal, and Gwen's heart warmed to her a bit. "May I ask, just to clarify, where you have spent your morning since?"

Manon put her hand on her belly. "I felt unwell most of the morning and spent it in my wagon."

"You didn't touch the porridge did you?" Gwen took a step closer, more than a little alarmed.

"No."

Then Gwen's eyes went to Manon's hand. "Are you—" she took another step, "—with child?" Given the number of years the pair had been married without having children, sometimes that was an unkind subject to bring up, but it seemed obviously true now, even before Manon's expression filled with happiness.

"Yes! I became sure of it a few days ago. Of late, I have been ill most mornings."

Andreas appeared genuinely happy too. "We never thought it would happen."

The subject was cheering, but Gwen wasn't done with Andreas. "Given your employment as their steward, do you have any thoughts as to who might want either Deri or Nest dead?"

"The idea is ridiculous." He scoffed. "What has either of them ever done to anyone besides sing?" Then his lip twitched. "Jealousy is a motive, I suppose." He looked meaningfully at Gwen.

She sighed. "Are you suggesting that my father might have had a hand in this because he has been barred from singing?"

"The purse is quite large."

Gwen acknowledged the truth of that with a nod, and deliberated if it was politic to tell him Meilyr was getting paid anyway. Deciding it was better than Andreas spreading rumors that her father had it in for Deri and Nest, she said, "My father is well-content in King Owain's service. Besides, Gwalchmai was attacked this morning and left for dead by whoever stole the porridge, so we couldn't discover what poison was used. Meilyr would never attack his own son."

Andreas's mouth fell open.

"You didn't know?" Gwen asked. "For hours, he lay hidden in the grass by the herb hut. Thankfully, the weather is unusually warm and he wore his cloak, else he really might have died."

This news caused Manon to sway slightly, her hand to her heart. "But he's going to be all right?"

"We think so." Gwen had had enough of them, and they clearly had had enough of her because they turned as if to move on. She had one more question, however. "If you are acquainted enough with

Alice to speak to her in the common room, Manon, you must also know Prince Cadwaladr. Did you know he was coming today before Susanna told Alice?"

"Of course not." Manon shook her head forcefully.

"Why on earth would you think so?" Andreas added before turning Manon fully around and striding off in the opposite direction.

Gwen watched them go, uncertain what she'd missed that had prompted the abrupt departure. She thought back to the brief exchange she'd witnessed between Alice and Manon, and then again when Manon and Andreas had been talking in the middle of the courtyard. In both cases, they'd been standing with heads together, their faces very serious, implying something quite different than casual conversation or joy over a baby. To Gwen's eyes, it had looked more like conspiracy.

21

Gareth

"Spit it out," Hywel said when they had achieved a safe distance from the church. "Whatever you feel the need to say, say it now."

"I am not here to say anything, only to be whatever you need me to be."

Hywel shot a sardonic glance at Gareth. "You don't need to handle me like I'm a hot poker, Gareth. I'm fine. Really. I have known from the moment we learned Cadwaladr was behind Rhun's death that today was coming."

Hywel had come out of the front door of the church and walked right by where everyone continued to wait, hovering under trees or in the lychgate of the church. Gareth had followed immediately after, not going so far as to fall into step beside him, but he had stayed close enough for Hywel to know he was there. He'd expected to find Hywel with his own personal thundercloud hovering over his head, and was now almost more disconcerted to see the prince perfectly calm.

Hywel moved another few paces beyond where the bulk of the people had gathered. "Truly, all is well. You don't have to stay with me. I have my Dragons." He motioned to where they waited, another fifteen yards away, though Gareth noted Hywel hadn't actually joined them.

"Is that an order, my lord?"

Hywel scoffed. "Heaven forbid."

"Then may I ask how it is that you are—" Gareth hesitated, thinking better of articulating his thoughts, not wanting to upset Hywel's equilibrium.

"How am I what—so calm? Not tearing out my hair with every step?" Hywel laughed mockingly. "You think I'm not?"

"You do not appear angry."

"I do not appear angry for the simple reason that I am not angry." The prince canted his head, his brow furrowing. "How strange. Earlier, when my father and I conferenced, I could feel rage building inside me, even as I did everything in my power to suppress it. But by the time we returned to the chapel and I saw Cadwaladr in person, it was gone." Now he bit his lower lip. "Could it be that I am becoming a better person?"

Gareth laughed before he could stop himself. Hywel didn't join in, prompting Gareth to immediately sober. "My apologies, my lord."

"You don't have to apologize to me, Gareth. I know you are with me in all things, but I also know that I am not the same person I was when Rhun died. I have become more like him in many ways, but I have also become more *myself*. I will never forget or forgive

Cadwaladr for what he did. I will never trust him. But anger gets in the way of clear thinking."

"You speak the truth, my lord." Gareth bent his head. "It is as Abbot Rhys has counseled many times."

"That isn't to say Cadwaladr isn't still a treacherous rat." Hywel's face blossomed into a genuine smile. "There's the anger." The smile broadened. "No need to worry that I've suddenly become someone else entirely."

Then he frowned, his attention returning to the Dragons. "What happened to the horses?"

"I expect Dai took them." The Dragons were still filthy, but all their horses were gone, along with Gareth's son, Dai.

Hywel nodded. "He's a good lad. He will make a fine Dragon."

Gareth was astounded Hywel could be thinking about anyone or anything other than Cadwaladr right now.

Then Hywel turned the other way, reversing course to move towards the onlookers while making shooing motions with his hands. "My friends, it's over. Go on. Get out of this weather. There's nothing to see here. All is well."

It was essentially what he'd said to Gareth, and Gareth no more believed his prince now than he had a moment ago. The people, however, were used to obeying, and they began to move away, even if many showed reluctance.

Hywel watched them for a moment, to make sure they were really going to disperse, and then he jerked his head at the Dragons. He didn't have to say, "Come!" for them to know what he meant.

Then he nudged Gareth's elbow and said under his breath, "I don't want to still be standing here when Cadwaladr comes out."

That too was more like the Hywel Gareth knew, and they walked back to the palace, matching stride for stride. The Dragons followed, ultimately picking up their pace to a quick trot, such that by the time Gareth and Hywel passed through the gatehouse, they were a few paces behind. Without asking where Hywel intended to hide, Gareth steered him to the stables, and, once there, the Dragons ranged around their prince.

As Gareth had presumed, Dai had stabled the horses, and they whickered happily in the company of their brethren. With a wave of his hand, Gareth sent the other stable lads away, leaving only Dai, brushing Hywel's horse, close enough to listen.

When Hywel was done relating the outcome of the meeting with Cadwaladr, Gruffydd gazed at his prince with something like horror in his face. "My lord—"

Gareth stopped him with a gesture before he could protest openly at the apparent easy acceptance of Cadwaladr's return. "What's done is done."

For his part, Hywel stood with his hands behind his back and his feet spread. "This is a storm we will weather together. I am trusting you to have my back, as you always have." It was as clear an indication as Hywel had given so far that he was not in the mood to discuss the whys and wherefores, but wanted to be obeyed.

"Yes, my lord. Always." Gruffydd swallowed down any objection.

"It's past noon now." Gareth nodded at the circle of men. He wasn't their captain, but he was Hywel's right-hand man, and they accepted him as such. "If we are to present a united front to the world, Prince Hywel needs to be seen in the hall for the meal. Dai, Steffan, and Iago, please escort him," he turned to Hywel, "if it pleases you, my lord." And then in a low voice, he added. "We do need to think, and to plan for the inevitable. But perhaps you shouldn't be a part of this right now."

Hywel's eyes were thoughtful as he looked at Gareth. "You do understand." He gave a sharp nod. "Keep me informed. You have my complete trust." Then he looked past Gareth to Gruffydd. "As do you, Gruffydd."

"Thank you, my lord." Gruffydd bent his head.

Hywel and the others left the barn, leaving Gareth alone with Gruffydd, Cadoc, and Aron.

With Hywel's departure, however, Gruffydd threw off his polite mask and leaned in, his eyes deep pools of rage. "What. Is. Happening?" The precise enunciation of his words gave his speech an almost English clippedness.

"You heard the prince. Cadwaladr is back. I saw it with my own eyes." At that moment, loud talking came from the bailey, and Gareth turned to see Gwen leading Cadwaladr across the courtyard, followed by five of his men, who had come out of wherever they'd been hiding. That he still had followers at all was astounding. Or not. The man could talk the bark off a tree.

Gruffydd had no thought in his head for anything but hatred and anger. He started forward, even as Aron put out a placating arm.

Gareth moved in the same moment as Cadoc, blocking Gruffydd's exit from the stables. "Your lord has made a decree, one that you must either follow or abandon him forever."

Gruffydd didn't even hear him—or if he heard, he didn't comprehend. "Let me through!" He appeared to be about to draw his sword.

"You cannot." Cadoc got there first, gripping Gruffydd's wrist tightly. He was no larger than Gruffydd, but Gruffydd could not overcome him. Cadwaladr had moved on before Gruffydd had called out, so presumably he hadn't heard either, or if he had, he hadn't thought anything of it. Cadwaladr, of all of them, was serene in his misunderstanding of the world.

With Gruffydd contained, at least for now, Gareth closed the door to the stables. A gray darkness encompassed them, relieved only by the thin daylight coming through a second door at the far end.

"He *murdered* Prince Rhun!" Gruffydd was still raging, fighting his friends for freedom.

"Yes, he did," Gareth said, in a completely flat tone.

The fight in Gruffydd went out as if Gareth had thrown water on a campfire. His shoulders sagged, and he almost hung between his fellow Dragons.

Gareth pressed home his point. "Prince Hywel himself has declared Cadwaladr returned to the fold, and *Hywel* is your lord now."

"How *could* he?" The words came out a moan. "Rhun was his brother!"

While Hywel had seemed far too content for a man who'd just welcomed his brother's killer into his home, Gareth didn't think it was entirely a false front. Truly, Gareth preferred facing Gruffydd's pain over Hywel's. With a flash of insight, he knew what to say and stepped right up to Gruffydd, so their noses were a handspan apart.

"He knows."

Gruffydd gaped at Gareth, gasping a bit as his rational mind returned. "What-what are you saying?"

"Prince Hywel knows what he is doing. You have to trust him. While I expected him to be raging like you, and perhaps he will in the future in the same way he has raged against Rhun's death in the past, we should be happy he isn't."

"Should we?" Gruffydd said.

"He was disturbingly calm just now," Cadoc put in.

"Almost happy, I would even say." This was from Aron.

"I don't know about happy, but content?" Gareth said. "Yes."

"Why?" Gruffydd was still in too much pain to comprehend.

"It shouldn't be so strange if you think about it," Gareth said. "For two years, he has been dreading Cadwaladr's return and wondering how he would respond when it happened. He feared the test but, even more, he feared being found wanting."

"He stood up to it, though." Aron tapped a finger to his lips. "He had already experienced Rhun's death, which was the worst thing that had ever happened to him. It was the worst thing he could imagine happening to him. Now, Cadwaladr has returned, and my lord Hywel has discovered he can encompass that pain too, and it's less of a burden than he feared. The face he is showing us may be his true one."

"*Anger gets in the way of clear thinking,*" Gareth quoted, "and we want our lord thinking clearly about now."

Gruffydd swallowed hard. "I have not been. Forgive me."

They all made the same dismissive gesture, though it was Gareth who said, "There is nothing to forgive. You expressed only what we were all feeling."

"I am the captain of the Dragons." Gruffydd mumbled under his breath. "I should do better."

Cadoc clapped Gruffydd on the shoulder. "Because you couldn't, we did."

Gruffydd let out a breath, and the four of them stood silent for a moment, at first with their heads down, thinking. Then, as one, their heads came up.

Cadoc spoke first, again somewhat musingly. "Our lord has always been the cleverest of us. He would know it isn't easy to rob a thief."

"Or lie to the routinely deceitful." Aron looked at Gareth. "How do we do this? How do we pretend that all is well when it isn't?"

"I do not know if I can, only that I must. *We* must, and it is our task now to navigate the aftermath of Cadwaladr's arrival. A moment ago, when I saw Cadwaladr walk through the courtyard, he had five men with him—men who remain loyal even after everything he's done and throughout everything he *is*. It reminded me that the people of Merionnydd and Aberffraw, through no fault of their own, will be coming directly under his control once again. Many of our lesser nobles, whose lands fall within his domains, have no choice but to follow him."

Aron grimaced. "It is yet another consequence of today, both unintended and unfortunate."

"Certainly, but that wasn't my point. Hywel would have agreed to this only *if he thought the alternative was worse.*"

"I don't know what you mean by that," Gruffydd said. "How could it be worse?"

As usual, Aron understood before the rest. He put a hand on Gruffydd's shoulder and shook him a little. "He means that leaving Cadwaladr to run amok in Prince Henry's court could have dire, unintended consequences. He is asking us to imagine the opposite of what did occur. What would happen if King Owain rejected Cadwaladr's overtures? In so doing, he would have rejected the treaty Prince Henry was offering as well. If it didn't go to Owain, to whom would he then give it?"

"Madog," Gruffydd said.

"Cadwaladr says no. If Henry never becomes king, then we might have gotten off easy. But if he does become king, and Owain had spurned his offer? We might find ourselves without any ally in England." Gareth looked at Aron. "But that isn't even the worst outcome. I'm more concerned about what would happen with Cadwaladr himself. Up until now, Cadwaladr had hope that he could be restored to favor. Whatever havoc he has wreaked in England in the courts of both Stephen and Maud has been for his own benefit, but not directed against Owain."

Cadoc was nodding now. "But with the finality of being sent back with his tail between his legs, he would spend the rest of his days inciting rebellion and resentment against Gwynedd in Wales and England."

"It is only a matter of time before Cadwaladr commits some atrocity that can't be forgiven," Aron said. "We may be simply postponing the inevitable."

"I actually assume we are," Gareth said.

Cadoc nodded. "We aren't going anywhere. We must remain vigilant."

"We thought that way before," Gruffydd was frowning, "and look what it cost us."

"Apologies, Gruffydd." Cadoc put out a hand. "You have the right of it, but you can see why Prince Hywel prefers at this moment to keep his uncle where he can see him."

"If we are to stop Cadwaladr, we must be clever—more clever than I feel myself now to be," Aron said.

"I feel the same," Gareth said. "Maybe Hywel does too. But as my father-in-law might say, *you can't play a harp with an axe.* We must be very gentle on the strings until we're sure of our tune."

Gruffydd turned to where his saddle bags had been laid, once they'd been removed from his horse, and detached his wineskin. He took a long drink and then wiped his mouth with the back of his hand, calmer than he'd been since the moment he'd learned of Cadwaladr's arrival.

"Whatever we do," he finally said, "it won't be done here, and it won't be done today. While we are speaking in aphorisms, *the suc-*

cessful hunter is one who has the patience to lie in wait. This time, Cadwaladr, not we few, must be the prey."

22

Gwen

With the palace packed to the rafters and the great hall unable to accommodate even half the wedding guests, King Owain had ordered another pavilion set up. The ground was wet with rain, but the benign weather meant the air temperature was not uncomfortable, especially with two hundred people pressed closely and ringing with excitement—not only about the wedding, but also about Cadwaladr's arrival and apparent reinstatement.

It was a day nobody had seen coming when they had woken that morning. Winter was always a time for gatherings and gossip, and the news coming out of Denbigh this year would keep tongues wagging from Holyhead to Aberystwyth for months to come.

The Dragons and Gwen's family were clustered together at several tables at one end of the pavilion. Hywel had sat with his uncle for most of the afternoon, but by evening had decided he'd done his duty. As heir to the throne of Gwynedd, he was holding court on his own in the pavilion, almost as if he were in his own castle.

They had one more full day before the wedding. As far as the Gwynedd contingent was concerned, the ceremony couldn't come too soon. They just wanted to get through the week in one piece. By the amount of food and mead they were consuming, the Dragons were treating this meal as if it might be their last one.

Gwen herself had no appetite, but she watched her daughter chew through a giant piece of mutton without stopping to breathe. Then Gwen nudged Mari, Hywel's wife, who sat on Gwen's other side. "We thought today was a long day, but I fear tomorrow."

Gareth was several paces away, ensconced next to Hywel, who was also buffered by Gwen's two elder sons and the Dragons. Mari hadn't done any investigating so far, but she knew all about what had transpired. She wasn't sitting with her husband either, in large part because her two children, Gruffydd and Cadwallon, were no more containable than Gwen's.

At the moment, Mari's boys were gamboling gleefully through the wet grass just outside the pavilion, under the watchful eyes of their respective nannies, playing with Taran, who was some nine months younger than Cadwallon. The pavilion had been set up high enough on the crag upon which the palace had been built that the river running high below them couldn't touch them. As Hywel and the Dragons had discovered in their scouting that morning, theirs wasn't the only river in danger of jumping its banks.

Conall, who was sitting across from the two women, put down his knife, having consumed the onion he'd speared upon it. "So much trouble caused by a dead dog." He gave a low laugh. "And I don't mean Cadwaladr."

Gwen put a finger to her lips and leaned across the table. "We don't speak of these things out loud." But then she resumed her place and spoke in a more normal tone. "It's a dog that died eating food meant for a person, who is still alive, thanks only to that dead dog. And that's putting aside the attack on my brother as if it's unrelated."

"Not something that should be put aside. Though—" he made a gesture to indicate the guests in the pavilion, or maybe to encompass the world at large, "—we possibly have greater concerns."

"Maybe not. Cadwaladr isn't going anywhere, more's the pity," Mari said. "For now, we need this wedding to go forward with as little fuss as possible."

Gwen eyed her friend. "Is your mother-in-law getting on your nerves?"

"Step-mother-in-law," Mari corrected, "and yes. She was wound up tightly before the dog died. Now, she's intolerable. Though, I'm glad she has apparently come to a truce with Gareth."

"For now," Gwen said.

"I can understand Gareth's preoccupation with the events of the afternoon unrelated to the investigation," Mari said, "but the rest of us—or, I'm sorry, the rest of *you* because I don't know what kind of help I can be—can't be waiting to pursue the truth of what happened. We have to put Cadwaladr, not the investigation, aside."

"What if he can't be put aside?" Conall slathered a thick layer of butter, followed by a drizzle of honey, on a piece of bread. The arrival of Cadwaladr certainly hadn't put him off his food either. "How farfetched is the idea that the person who poisoned the porridge knew Prince Cadwaladr was coming?"

Mari's brow furrowed. "Are you saying that someone wanted Deri or Nest dead and used Cadwaladr's arrival as a cover for murder—or rather, attempted murder as it turned out to be?"

"Or maybe I'm saying that Cadwaladr had something to do with the poisoning," Conall said.

"Knowing Cadwaladr, that sounds more likely than not," Gwen said. "We have no motive, of course."

Conall swallowed another bite before speaking. "I'm simply trying to look at it from all angles."

"As we should be," Gwen said. "Unfortunately, even after a morning of questioning suspects and victims, I don't know enough yet about what happened to know if your suggestion is reasonable. I do know enough about Cadwaladr to worry you could be right."

Gwen looked into the distance, towards the palace, envisioning him seated at the high table next to the king. King Owain had assured his son that Cadwaladr's crimes were neither forgotten nor forgiven, but Cadwaladr wouldn't see it that way. Admitting him into the hall implied not only a tacit acceptance, but absolution.

"Don't say anything to Gareth about this yet, Conall. He sees red every time Cadwaladr's name is mentioned, even more when faced with his presence. But given the events of the day, how surprising would it be if Cadwaladr had a spy or two here before he came?"

"You are so right to think so! Of course he would." Mari gave a low laugh. "But who?"

Again, Conall gestured to the people around them. "There are too many people at Denbigh to even make a guess."

"Maybe," Mari said, "but for a spy to do him any good, he or she would have to be highly placed. A servant could eavesdrop and tell him some things. Alice herself could tell him some things, but maybe not enough of what he wants to hear."

"I should have thought of this before," Gwen said. "Do you think Hywel has and hasn't said?"

Mari tsked. "Of course he has."

"My vote would be for one of Madog's people or one of the lesser lords who are here for the wedding," Gwen said, "rather than someone close to Owain or Hywel. Now that I think about it, I'd be more surprised if Cadwaladr *didn't* have someone."

"At a minimum, he has Queen Susanna." Conall made the comment without rancor, more as an observation.

"Susanna has proven already that she will never betray either Madog or Owain—and if forced to choose between the two she chooses neither." Mari canted her head. As the daughter of a spy, and Hywel's wife, intrigue was not new to her. "Cadwaladr, meanwhile, can rely on her to love him and spoil him, but to expect her to inform on the doings of Gwynedd and Powys, news her husband might not want him to know—and King Owain would definitely not want him to know—might be a bridge too far."

Gwen bit her lip as she looked at Conall. "We are going to have to start anew."

"We?" Conall looked dubious. "People don't want to talk to me. I am not one of you, and my Welsh might not be up to the task."

"You are too modest," Gwen protested.

"As I'm sure you learned in Ireland, when a man comes late to a language, native speakers tend to treat him as if there's something wrong with his mind, as if he is not quite capable."

Gwen spread her hands wide. "I grant you that, but perhaps you can use it to your advantage. Let others instruct *you*. Let loose some of that stored-up charm."

"You realize what you're asking, don't you?" Conall laughed out loud. "You want me to play the innocent? Though truly, given the number of people in this castle who think very highly of themselves and spare no thought for others, perhaps it won't be as difficult as all that."

Gwen laughed too, but then sobered and drew his attention to Queen Susanna, who'd just arrived in the pavilion. "And there's your first target."

While the queen was stopping every few feet to speak to guests who put out a hand to her or rose to bow and offer their greetings and congratulations, she was clearly on a quest.

"You're enjoying this aren't you?" Conall glanced down at Gwen, who grinned back at him.

"Very much. Shall I send one of the Dragons with you for protection?"

23

Conall

Protection from Susanna wasn't necessary, and certainly Conall had no interest in having a Dragon by his side, particularly if the one Gwen chose was one of the more perceptive, like Aron or Cadoc. Conall had carried a torch for Susanna all these years, and likely Gwen knew it—thus the subtle teasing that was just polite enough for Conall to ignore. A Dragon would have no such restraint.

He'd seen Susanna for the first time in more than twenty years in the aftermath of Rhun's death at the conference at St. Asaph, which was also the last time the kings of Gwynedd and Powys had met in person. Conall had been struck at the time both by Susanna's beauty, which had only increased with age, and by the insurmountable difference in their stations. He'd known about that difference back in Ireland, of course. When they'd met, Conall had been barely a man and merely the nephew to the King of Leinster. She was a king's daughter. At the time, she was being considered for Diarmait, a prince and the future king.

The two of them had exchanged pleasantries a week ago when each had arrived in Denbigh, and she'd made sure he knew she remembered him, but Susanna was a woman with a clear vision of who she was and what she wanted. Fraternizing with a friend she'd made twenty years earlier, especially a male one, held no interest for her.

At the sight of Susanna moving purposefully through the crowd, he'd risen from his seat immediately, but she didn't see him, instead steering towards the edge of the pavilion.

Conall trailed after her until she reached Deri, her apparent destination. The bard had been sitting alone with his instruments on the far side of Hywel's table. He'd spent the meal walking around the grass in the dark, playing one tune or another, sometimes with an instrument and sometimes using just his voice. Conall had seen similar behavior in Meilyr and Gwalchmai before a performance. As with old soldiers like Conall, musicians needed to warm up before they could be at their best.

Susanna's subsequent close conversation with the bard made Conall reluctant to approach, though he did move closer and lounge casually against the edge of one of the tables, which diners had recently abandoned.

As of yet, there was no sign of Nest, and Conall was close enough now that he could hear the queen assuring Deri that his sister was coming. Last Conall had heard, the compromise reached between the bards and King Madog was that initially Deri would sing alone in the great hall, as he appeared to have done, and then Nest would join him outside in the pavilion, sparing her for one day, out of respect for her grief, the need to perform in the great hall.

Likely if Gwen hadn't been convincing enough with Nest earlier to get her to revisit her refusal to sing, Susanna, who was a force to be reckoned with in her own right, would have been the one to finish the job.

Conall took a few steps closer and came to a halt a respectful six feet away, trying to convey, without interfering with Susanna's conversation with Deri, that he would like to speak to the queen. The pair were talking a little more loudly than usual, such that Conall could hear them from where he stood. Even with their higher volume, Deri had his hand to his ear and seemed to be having trouble hearing. Conall himself didn't hear as well as he had in his youth, and he moved outside the loud and crowded pavilion to wait for Susanna in order to lessen the overload on his own ears.

After another few sentences, which Conall couldn't overhear, Susanna nodded at the bard and walked out of the pavilion into the grass. Conall moved to intercept her, angling so he would come into her line of sight before he reached her.

Once that happened, some fifteen feet from the edge of the pavilion, just outside the ring of light thrown out by the torches that surrounded it, Susanna lifted a hand in acknowledgement that she'd seen him, and her face lit up with a smile.

"Hello, Conall! I was so pleased to know you'd come to Marared's wedding. How has this week been for you?" Her voice was bright and cheery, and he kicked himself for half-hoping she felt about him as he felt about her. In his head, her unrequited love had explained her reluctance to speak to him beyond a few words. It turned out, she wasn't reluctant at all—just busy—and had no idea of his true thoughts. He was an idiot, always had been.

Then she held out a hand as the first raindrops of what might be another deluge began to fall. "We are in for it, I think."

Conall immediately whipped off his cloak, so he could hold it above both their heads, and tried not to think how close to her that put him. It would have been unseemly under any other circumstances. Her scent wafted up to him—roses, he thought—and he struggled to focus on why he was there.

"For me, as the ambassador from Leinster to the court of Gwynedd, this is a wedding not to miss."

"Circumstances have changed a great deal since I saw you last, haven't they?"

Conall's mouth opened to answer her, but he found no words beyond a bit of stuttering. Last they'd seen each other, she was on her way with Marared to a convent on Anglesey as punishment for misdeeds she did not commit.

It was kind of her, really, to have raised Marared as her own, since the girl was Madog's daughter by another relationship. Still, the two seemed to understand each other more than many mothers and daughters who shared blood. Conall could understand. He was far closer to his friends—Gareth and Godfrid in particular—than he had ever been to any of his brothers. Of course, the Irish had taken rivalry among brothers to absurd heights, to the point that the High King of Ireland routinely fostered brutal competitiveness in his sons. Some had died because of it. No wonder Conall hadn't ever wanted any part of that.

In reply to her own comment, Susanna laughed, a lovely bell-like sound. "I'm teasing you. Even so, we would be delighted to welcome you to Dinas Bran if your duties in Gwynedd end or if they become too onerous."

If Conall hadn't been holding the cloak above their heads, he would have bowed. "And I would be delighted to come. Thank you for the invitation."

Susanna went on. "I suppose our issues are quaint compared to what you experienced in Dublin, what with the fight for the throne and murder."

"You heard about that?"

"We do pay attention to the world beyond Powys." She smiled, and he didn't think he was mistaken to see it as coquettish.

The thought brought him up short and made him suddenly wonder who was pumping whom for information.

And he was sure it was she when she added, "Leinster has settled its disputes not only with Dublin but with Connaught. Is that why you came to Wales … to see if Leinster can take advantage of our disputes?"

"My lady, my king wishes only the best for Wales." He gathered his thoughts and redirected them on the course he'd set out along. As she'd given him an opening, he would be a fool not to take it. "Things have been going well, though less so today, of course."

Instantly her expression closed. "So you didn't seek me out to catch up on old times. Gwen sent you. I saw you talking to her a moment ago. This is about her father and brother being shut out of the singing."

"Not at all, my lady!" Conall gaped at the queen. That his approach could be misconstrued in such a way genuinely hadn't occurred to him. He had no choice now but to lay out his request boldly, so he hastened to explain: "Please forgive me if I gave you that impression or you believe me to be speaking to you under false pretenses. If I am here on Gwen's behalf, it is to ask you what you know about the attempted murder today. I have been assisting Lord Gareth in the investigation."

Susanna stopped so abruptly that his elbow almost banged into the back of her head. Fortunately, he was watching her closely and stopped in time. "Wait ... you are talking about Nest's dead dog?"

"Yes."

She frowned, apparently genuinely befuddled. "Why would that be something you would seek to ask me about?"

"The dog was murdered through poisoned food intended for Deri and Nest. Queen Cristina is particularly concerned that the wedding not be marred by such unpleasantness. Despite everything, we are continuing to search for answers."

Susanna looked at him wryly. "*Everything* being, *my brother's arrival.*"

"Yes, madam."

"Ah, I see. He does enjoy calling attention to himself."

"It is not my place to say, madam."

She looked up at him. "He is the youngest of the brothers. Growing up, I was a second mother to him. Maybe I mothered him too much. He was and is, perhaps, spoiled."

There was no *perhaps* about it, and the look on her face was less condemnatory than indulgent. Certainly Cadwaladr and Madog had been allies and co-conspirators on more than one occasion. That Susanna had brought the two men together—and genuinely encouraged their relationship—now had to be taken into account.

Conall had feared her love for Cadwaladr had blinded her to his faults, but now he saw that it was worse than that. She had the same love for Cadwaladr as Owain, despite the loss of Rhun. Even if Owain was also furious with Cadwaladr, he kept forgiving him because he loved him. And in both cases, they forgave him even though they could openly admit his faults, as Susanna had just done.

Her admission forced Conall to reassess his admiration for her—and perhaps none too soon. She was beautiful and still drew him without conscious thought, but Cadwaladr was not someone to be indulged. Doing so to the extent she'd always done—and it appeared always would do—was *dangerous*.

Their blindness gave Conall a sudden fear for Hywel, whom he also considered a friend.

He could understand loving someone even though they did bad things. Love didn't have to be—and maybe never should be—conditional. But that didn't mean she had to trust the person she loved or expose her neck to him like a defeated animal. What's more, while Owain and Susanna loved Cadwaladr, that didn't mean Cadwaladr loved *them*.

"Did you know he was coming here?"

Susanna's eyes widened. "Me? Of course not. I am glad Owain has forgiven him though. And what a miracle that Hywel led him to it." She glanced back at her nephew, just visible at the table within the tent. "I am very proud of the man he has become."

Then her attention returned to Conall. "Excuse me, Conall dear, I have guests to attend to, and, with the rain …" She canted her head. "Perhaps we will find opportunity to speak more later."

Conall could do nothing but bow and watch the queen disappear through the gatehouse, realizing as he did so that she had never responded to his query about the dog. Such was Susanna's grace and courtesy that Conall genuinely didn't know if it was merely an oversight … or intentional.

24

Hywel

"Well?" King Owain waved a hand to Hywel, indicating he should shut the door behind him.

Hywel didn't want to pretend to misunderstand, but he genuinely wasn't sure which of the possible fraught situations his father's query was referring to. Yesterday had produced so many. So he opted for straight out evasion. "How are you this morning?"

His father threw both hands out to his sides. "I have no idea what to think." He'd been sitting behind a table, upon which Taran had spread papers for his approval, but now he rose and began to pace before the fire. With the weather so warm, it was banked low, though still providing some heat. "I believed he would never return."

Hywel didn't have to ask who *he* was. *Cadwaladr.* It was what he had thought they were talking about, but it was nice to be sure.

Before Hywel could come up with a way to reply, the king flicked out a hand. "No that isn't it: I *told* myself he would never return." He fixed Hywel with a beady eye. "You knew he would."

"Yes, I knew, if it was possible to know anything at all."

"How?"

Hywel was unsure in that moment how honest he should allow himself to be. But then he decided that the two of them had come too far in the last two years to descend into lies, even of omission. "I knew Cadwaladr would eventually convince himself it was safe to come back and that he could convince you of the truth of what happened from his perspective. He would tell himself that—in his absence—you had grown to understand he never intended to murder Rhun. In his mind, it was an honest mistake anyone could have made, provided anyone else would have been intent on murdering one of my companions."

"Gareth." Owain sighed heavily.

"Yes."

"How's he taking Cadwaladr's presence and apparent reinstatement?"

Hywel raised his eyebrows. "What do you mean by *apparent*?"

Owain snorted. "Don't pretend with me, son. We both know it is only a matter of time before Cadwaladr does something heinous again. He is probably already working on a scheme to replace me, if not with himself, since it really could be that Prince Henry has taken the measure of him, but with someone more amenable to his influence."

"I was thinking along the lines of King Madog."

"Wouldn't he love to rule Gwynedd!" Owain returned to his seat, seemingly amused by the thought. "He could claim the throne through Susanna and disinherit all of you."

"Honestly, Father, if the porridge that killed Nest's dog hadn't been meant for Deri or Nest, I would have thought it was meant for *you*. I don't have any notion how to link Cadwaladr's arrival and the poisoning, but the fact they occurred on the same day gives me an itching sensation between my shoulder blades."

"While intrigue is in my brother's nature, I'm finding it difficult to see what he might have had to do with the poisoning." Owain said.

"Nor I, but I hate coincidences. Given Cadwaladr's tendencies, it would be a mistake to assume this is one." Hywel had never felt more strongly that the less his father trusted, the more likely he was to survive the coming years.

Owain's attention had been drawn to a paper before him on the table, and he spoke almost absently as he read it, "I suppose you ought to know that I do eat porridge every morning too."

Hywel took a step closer to the table. "I thought you despised porridge."

"I do, but Cristina insists, when made of oats, that it is good for my bowels. I have to admit, now I'm older, that she isn't wrong."

"How long has this been going on?"

"Some months. I tolerate her meddling because, after I eat it, I get as much bacon as I desire."

Hywel studied the top of his father's downturned head, thinking about the implications of what he'd just said. Owain genuinely appeared unconcerned by it, but Hywel found his own heart beating a little faster.

In hopes of drawing Owain's attention from his papers, Hywel said, "Father," in a heavy tone, "who knows of this?"

Owain didn't seem to be listening anymore, and Hywel was loath to repeat the question, despite his urgency. The silence lengthened until the king held out the document he'd been studying, at which point Hywel understood the reason for his preoccupation. "This is the treaty Cadwaladr brought me. I'm amazed Prince Henry was willing to put any of what he promises in writing."

Hywel took the parchment. It was all in Latin, naturally, which he'd learned as a child alongside Gwen. Even twenty years later, he could hear her youthful lisp in the words before him. The document not only appeared to be genuine, but was a justifiably momentous agreement. It was not yet signed, as it wouldn't be, but there were spaces for four signatures: Prince Henry, King David of Scotland, Earl Ranulf of Chester, and King Owain Gwynedd.

"Likely Prince Henry knew it would take a real gesture on his part to make you accept Cadwaladr back."

"To make *you* accept him back, you mean."

Hywel looked up, having finished reading, as struck by his father's words as the document before him. "I know Gareth spoke to Prince Henry about Cadwaladr, but he said nothing about my relationship with you. Cadwaladr wouldn't have told him. To admit it would be to diminish his own greatness."

"Ah, but our young prince idolizes Gareth, who serves *you*."

Hywel huffed. "I'm still at a loss."

"You aren't the only one with spies everywhere."

Hywel almost laughed out loud. "Meilyr has been talking."

"I can't fool you at all, can I?" Owain looked disgruntled. "Which makes me wonder even more why you accepted this deal before you saw the agreement. Even after all these years, I can still misjudge you."

Hywel set the parchment in front of his father with a gentle hand. "I'm not sure what you're asking."

Owain scoffed. "Let's not pretend I am anything other than I am. With Susanna here, Cadwaladr would know my acceptance of his return was all but guaranteed. He is well aware I can never say no to my sister. Truly, as Taran has said to me more than once, I say no only when I'm angry or when pressed to the wall. Cadwaladr knows me as well as anyone. Undoubtedly, this is the reason he chose this moment to return." He looked carefully up at Hywel. "I don't like being manipulated."

"I'm not saying Cadwaladr isn't manipulating you, because of course he is, but I think you're giving him too much credit in this instance. He isn't that thoughtful, even when his interests are on the line. He asked initially for Gwen because he believed her to be an ally of a sort. And as far as Prince Henry goes, even if you're right that he thinks highly of me, you can be sure he didn't share those thoughts with Cadwaladr."

"Why do you say that?"

"When we went to the church, Cadwaladr looked only at you, dismissing me, as he has always done, as an afterthought. Don't tell me he wasn't genuinely surprised to see you listening to me as you might have once done to Rhun."

"Son—"

Hywel made a gesture to cut short whatever his father was going to say. "I did not always understand fully the role I played. Since Rhun's death, I like to think I have grown into it."

"You were getting there before he died," Owain spoke without emphasis, stating a fact. "That's why I gave you Ceredigion."

"We both know you gave me Ceredigion to *make* me grow into it—and maybe to deflect Cadwaladr's ire from you to me." Again Hywel put up a hand, brushing off the fact that his father had manipulated *him* as the irrelevancy it was. "It was a clever move and not one to be regretted. Regardless, Cadwaladr is here now and returned to the fold. What comes next is up to him."

Hywel turned to look out the window, and he could feel his father's eyes on him, but he didn't turn back. They had been able to speak to each other honestly for some time now, but these events were taking that trust further than ever before.

Owain's chair creaked as he leaned back in it. "You haven't responded to my query."

"Haven't I?" He half-turned so he could glance into his father's face. "I'd say you still haven't noticed mine."

They gazed at each other for a moment, and then with a bellow of sound that split the room like a thunderclap, they both burst into laughter. Feet pounded on the other side of the door, but then stopped as their laughter continued. Hywel guessed that Taran had his ear to it, thinking first that one of them was in a rage, and was now relieved to discover Owain's famous temper remained at bay. The thought made him laugh all the harder.

In the end, Hywel gave way first, gesturing to his father with something of a courtly flourish, "Please remind me, Father. What was your question?"

"I asked how Gareth was taking your acceptance of Cadwaladr. And I also asked *why* you accepted his return to Gwynedd in a way that appears, to me at least, to be without resentment or rancor."

"Forgive me if I answer the last question first: I accepted Cadwaladr's presence in your court because his return was inevitable, and I wanted it to happen on our terms not his. Though, he will obviously think it's on his." Hywel pressed his lips together for a moment before finishing the thought. "I too think you have a soft heart—and I say that without criticism. I know you fight against it, and the last two years have been hard for you. You love your brother. You can no more stop loving him than you can stop breathing. Thus, I would rather he returned to us now, when I was here to look him in the eye, than when you were alone."

Owain grunted. "The way you speak makes me sound like I'm in my dotage, or worse, do not have the strength to make decisions that must be made, no matter how difficult."

"That isn't what I meant at all, Father! Though you've mentioned your age twice today, it isn't that you're old. It's just that you've reached an age when men start to think about their legacy. Cadwaladr's arrival has brought to the forefront what your goals and intentions for Gwynedd really are. Just as you put distrust and animosity towards Madog aside to marry Iorwerth to Marared, you put similar feelings toward Cadwaladr aside for the survival of our people. As I said yesterday, that always has to take precedence over our personal feelings."

It was a long speech for Hywel. Even then he wasn't done. "Besides which, the carrot Cadwaladr brought us is worth its weight in silver. We would not want Prince Henry as an enemy. With the treaty rejected and Cadwaladr at his side, he could truly learn to be one."

"You state things very clearly, son." Owain let out a breath. "Perhaps you could explain all that to Taran later."

"I don't think I will have to." In a few quick strides, he was at the door and pulled it open with a jerk. Sure enough, Taran was just stepping back, having overheard these last words. Fighting back a smile, Hywel gestured the steward inside.

Taran coughed a laugh. "As you wish, my lord."

Before closing the door, Hywel poked his head into the corridor, noting that Dai and Steffan remained on guard.

Steffan twirled a finger in the air. "Iago is patrolling the perimeter. Nobody else will be eavesdropping."

"Thank you."

Once back in the room, Taran was still looking embarrassed. "My lord—"

Hywel cut Taran off with another gesture and continued as if he hadn't interrupted himself. "Before Cadwaladr returned and brought you this treaty, Father, I would have said the war in England was winding down. Stephen and Maud haven't come to terms, but there's been little active fighting since Robert of Gloucester died and Henry returned to France."

"It seems that is about to change," Taran said.

"And we are about to become a part of it." Owain motioned to Taran that he should come closer and read the treaty. "And Gareth, son?"

Hywel gave his father a wry smile. "He understands why I did what I did because he is smart enough to know when peace must be made. He hates it, however. It strikes him as unjust."

"That would be because it *is* unjust. But we have long known that justice is not for princes." He drew in a long breath through his nose. "We did follow the law. Alice paid *galanas* to me for Rhun's death on Cadwaladr's behalf."

"It wasn't enough," Hywel said softly.

"No amount of cattle could make up for the loss of Rhun," Owain said simply. "I took enough for it to hurt, and I will keep a close watch on his stewardship of Merionnydd and Aberffraw forthwith, to ensure he does not pauperize his people for his own benefit. Though I'm sure Alice has been funneling him coin from his estates, he has otherwise been living off the charity of others for some time now. He will be inclined to squeeze his people while he can."

"While he can." Hywel pressed his lips together, hopeful that his father really was thinking ahead to the next time he had to eject Cadwaladr from his lands. He chose not to say anything in this moment, though he was sure his father could feel his doubts, given the wry look he and Taran exchanged immediately after.

Rather than tax his father with it now, he finished answering his father's question. "Gruffydd, on the other hand, is blindly furious with me, but I will deal with him as I need to."

Owain nodded. Such was the duty of an overlord, and it wasn't to be questioned. "What was it you asked me that I didn't answer?"

Hywel eyed his father. It was something of a relief to get off the topic of Cadwaladr. "Who knows you've started eating porridge every morning? And could the dish the dog ate have been meant for you?"

25

Conall

The weather was continuing warm for a second day, which was nice for the residents of the castle, though the downpour overnight had caused a further rise in the rivers and streams throughout the Clwyd region. Yesterday, Hywel and his men had ranged throughout the valley which the palace overlooked, in an attempt to discern the most likely areas to be flooded and warn the inhabitants to seek higher ground. Today, nobody in the palace and village on the slopes of the crag was crossing any stream, for fear of not being able to get back.

Though his conversation with Susanna had not been a success, a fact which he'd admitted to Gwen last night after returning to the pavilion, she'd told him not to worry and to persevere, effectively giving Conall his marching orders. But what he was supposed to do today he wasn't entirely sure. After the drama of the previous afternoon, the subsequent evening had turned out to be remarkably unexciting. Deri and Nest had ended up singing for over an hour in the pavilion, pleasing all the wedding guests except for Meilyr, who glowered for one song before leaving to check on Gwalchmai's health. He never returned.

Back in the great hall, Iago, who'd parked himself near the main doorway, reported that Cadwaladr had been on his best behavior throughout: at the same time jovial and expansive, on the one hand, and appropriately contrite and self-deprecating on the other.

Conall reminded himself that a murder was like an open wound. While it wasn't his purpose to be intentionally cruel, probing would make that wound bleed. And it was everyone's job today to probe. Thus, after breakfast, when he saw Nest crossing the courtyard, skirts raised against the puddles that had pooled even on the flagstones, he didn't hesitate to approach.

"Madam." Conall approached and bowed over her hand. "I am so sorry for your loss."

Nest instantly burst into tears, dropped his hand, and threw her arms around his neck.

It was one of two reactions he'd expected, the other being superior disdain and an accompanying disbelief that he could be sincere. He wasn't altogether sure the latter wouldn't have been preferable. Certainly it would have meant his neck stayed dry.

As it was, he coaxed her to accept a slightly less close embrace, so they could actually converse.

"Thank you, ambassador, for speaking so kindly to me." Nest dabbed at the corners of her eyes. As she looked up at him, they were liquid blue, just short of overflowing. "With the arrival of Prince Cadwaladr, everyone else seems to have forgotten the rest of what happened yesterday."

Conall had been counting on that. Her grief seemed real, but she had been exploiting it for attention in the hours leading up to Cadwaladr's arrival, accepting the condolences of many—in exchange for a first-hand account of the details of Annwyn's death.

"May I arrange a restoring drink for you?"

"Thank you. I have something in my wagon."

That wasn't quite what he'd had in mind, but she hooked her arm in his, leaning on him heavily such that he ended up half-walking, half-carrying her to her wagon, which had been parked at a slight angle compared to the others, of which there were six.

Conall had been inside Meilyr's wagon and was genuinely envious of his ability to lie down in familiar surroundings every night, regardless of where he traveled. He gestured to the lot of them, recognizing Meilyr's at the opposite end, but none of the others. "Whose are these?"

"Servants sleep in them and under them. Nobody important. With so many nobles here, the kings had to bring wagons full of supplies. Others are outside the walls."

"I hadn't realized so many people within the court would sleep in them. Honestly, I find it ingenious. We need to import this idea to Leinster."

"You can't expect each of the king's palaces to have room for all of us. And tents are so cold and uncomfortable. Not to mention requiring packing and unpacking." Nest smiled genuinely. "I have Manon to thank for ours. She is so clever in the way she arranges things. It's quite remarkable how much she can get inside and still leave space for us to sleep comfortably. You should see her wagon."

"I'd like that."

"It's beyond the postern gate. I'll mention it the next time I see her."

"Thank you." Conall smiled too. If he was going to use his charms, as Gwen had suggested, he couldn't have asked for a better opening.

"Of course. Come inside mine now. You may pour the mead."

It was an invitation he couldn't refuse, and he wouldn't have done so even if he hadn't intended to question her.

Conall assisted Nest up the steps that had been placed at the rear of the wagon, and was in the process of mounting them himself, when Nest, who'd made it all the way inside, screamed.

He bounded up the last steps and ducked under the overhanging tarp, squeezing past her to get into the wagon proper, since she had stopped in the opening. Then he pulled up short. Past history had prepared him for seeing a dead body, but he almost laughed instead at what he did find: Manon's careful packing had been undone, in that every one of Nest's and Deri's possessions had been thrown into the air and allowed to fall where it might.

"My beautiful dresses!" Nest tried to move past him, but he stuck out his arm to stop her.

"Don't."

"But my dresses!"

"They won't be hurt more by us looking at them for another moment." And though he could woderstand her fear, he thought she might be worrying needlessly. While many boxes had been upended and clothes were draped all over the wagon, in general the items appeared to be merely scattered about, rather than stomped on or torn. "When were you last here?"

"I woke late this morning, washed, and returned. I stayed for some time tidying up, and then went into the hall for breakfast. I was just coming back when you intercepted me."

"How long were you gone?"

"An hour, no more."

An hour was plenty of time for someone to do this much damage. The wagons themselves were set off to one side, tucked between the stables and the craft halls. And even if someone was spotted in or around them, there were so many people moving about, especially at that hour, that he had little hope they would discover the culprit.

But at this point, they had to try. "We will question everyone again. Someone has to have seen something."

"Do they? If so, wouldn't they have come to me already?"

Conall sighed, wishing he could like Nest. "Yesterday someone tried to murder you, and today your wagon has been gone through. It can't be a coincidence. You or Deri have something someone wants. Do you know what that might be?"

Nest shook her head with what appeared to be genuine confusion. "I-I have no idea."

26

Gwen

Gwen had spent the morning in the guesthouse common room, to which they'd moved Gwalchmai's pallet for the day, since he was still finding it difficult to rise. Saran and Meilyr had relieved her a moment ago—Saran to change his bandage and Meilyr to take charge of Tangwen. Taran was in the midst of one of his several daily naps, under the watchful eye of Marged. Gareth, meanwhile, had gone to the hall, and likely was glowering at Cadwaladr, who remained irrepressible, holding court at the high table as he'd done the night before.

Thus, left to her own devices, Gwen found Deri sitting on a bench with a large flagon of mead at his side and a cup cradled in his hands. It wasn't actively raining at the moment, and the sun was shining weakly through the cloud cover. It was still early in the day, not yet noon, but even so, she was surprised to see him without an instrument in his hands.

"May I ask what you're doing out here?"

Deri held up the cup. "What does it look like I'm doing?"

She wrinkled her nose as the air around her became saturated with alcohol. Really, it was her fault he'd spoken mockingly back at her because her first question had been accusing. So was her second.

"Perhaps I should have asked, *why are you not rehearsing?* The wedding is tomorrow, and you have a grand performance tonight in the hall."

"Didn't you hear? Someone went through our wagon. Nest is distraught again and refuses to practice. She refuses to *sing.*" He narrowed his eyes at her. "Don't think I don't know what you did yesterday. Your husband told *me* that she was ready to perform alone if I didn't sing, and you told *her* the same thing about me."

Gwen didn't bother to look sheepish. "You do realize what is at stake here, don't you? If you don't sing, the wedding is off."

"*I* know that. Nest simply puts her nose in the air and prances away from me when I mention it. *How can you think about singing at a time like this?* she says."

"Would quitting also mean you didn't get paid?" Gwen held her breath as she looked into Deri's face.

"Of-of course."

But as he spoke, he didn't meet her eyes and took a long swig of his mead.

A chill went through Gwen at the way she didn't believe him, and that likely they were right to think Madog wanted the wedding called off. He didn't want to prevent the marriage so badly that he was willing to be open about it, however, and risk renewed hostilities with Gwynedd.

Deri shot Gwen a beady look under his bushy brows. "And you can march right back to your father and tell him it changes nothing. *He* doesn't get to sing no matter what."

That Deri would be so overt in his comments was both a reflection of his hostility to her family and the amount he'd drunk. She wished again that music hadn't been the linchpin in the leverage King Madog was using against Owain. It would have been perfectly reasonable for Meilyr to share the load with Deri, with or without Nest. But the terms of the contract, absurd as they were, loomed large over the proceedings.

And since Gwen knew about them, she didn't rise to the bait and instead took the opportunity to return to the subject of the death of Nest's dog: "Have you had any further thoughts about who might have tried to kill you yesterday?"

"Your father," Deri said instantly.

Gwen pulled in a long breath through her nose, striving for patience. "According to the contract my king signed, if you die, your king has the right to cancel the wedding. My father would gain nothing from your death."

Deri's expression turned mutinous. "Then I don't know."

"How about Nest?"

"What about Nest?"

His attitude was worse than what Gareth had described. She was asking essentially the same questions too, and getting fewer answers. "Did you see anyone suspicious in or around the wagon this morning?"

"No."

It was too bad Gareth's talk with Deri yesterday had had so little effect. Deri had not softened towards Meilyr at all and, by the looks, was drinking more than ever.

To that end, he took a long swig from his cup and drained it, after which he tried to pour more from the flagon, but it was empty too. He peered forlornly into the interior as if it would miraculously fill up with mead if he looked long enough.

Then, in an apparent decision, he set the cup and flagon on the bench beside him, clapped both hands on his thighs, and stood up. "Let's take a walk."

Gwen was startled by his sudden change of attitude, though at least this one was slightly more accommodating. He could hardly be less so. But if he was willing to talk to her some more, she was certainly willing to talk to him.

"You are very lovely." Taking her hand, Deri tucked it into the crook of his elbow.

Thank you was the appropriate response to any compliment, but Deri was keeping his hand on top of hers, and his thigh was brushing her leg as they walked. While Gwen was perfectly capable of extricating herself, she was also puzzled by the sudden interest.

"Just how drunk are you?"

He scoffed. "No more than usual."

But Gwen wondered. Gareth had been more drunk than he'd expected from his drinking two nights ago. While Deri was perfectly capable of drinking to excess between breakfast and the noon meal, he would have had to have drunk gallons to have reached this point already today.

Still, her abrupt query served the purpose she'd initially intended, which was for him to stop behaving so solicitously, drop the hand that had held hers, and move slightly away. Then she took advantage of an upcoming puddle in the courtyard to loosen her hold on his elbow in order to skirt it. She didn't walk away from him entirely, however. She wanted information from him and was willing to put up with his foul breath and even fouler attention a while longer in order to learn something more if she could.

Grimacing slightly to herself, she softened her tone. "Things aren't quite what they ought to be with you, are they?"

"My dog died."

Last Gwen had heard it was Nest's dog, and Deri didn't like it anyway, but she didn't contradict him. "I meant earlier. Something is wrong with you. Are you … unwell?" An illness he was trying to cover up would explain a great deal.

"I'm perfectly fine." He put his nose into the air.

"I'm sorry," she said. "I didn't mean to intrude."

"Yes, you did."

He was right, of course. And also right that his health wasn't any of her business. She had no right to pry into his personal affairs if what was going on with him had nothing to do with the poisoning of the dog or the attack on Gwalchmai.

But she'd always been of the mind that if you didn't ask, you didn't learn anything—and being lied to was informative in and of itself.

Rather than lie anymore, Deri didn't talk to her at all, instead escorting her all the way across the courtyard and through the gatehouse. Initially, it appeared to Gwen that he was heading for the church, but then he took the path past it, down the hill towards the river that ran at the base of the escarpment upon which the palace was built.

Gwen could hear the water rushing before they saw it, and she said as much to Deri.

"Can you? I don't hear anything."

They had entered the town by now, and came around a cluster of houses, only to stop dead in surprise at the raging torrent before them. While a river had always meandered past Denbigh to the west, all of a sudden it had been joined by one from the east, arising out of nothing overnight and doubling the size of the first. The road that came from the north had disappeared beneath the flow. The western stream had entirely burst its banks and taken out the little wooden bridge that crossed it. The combined force of the two rivers was threatening homes that yesterday had seemed well out of danger.

Most of the village lay on the eastern bank on slightly higher ground, while their pastures resided on the other side of the river, which the bridge had accessed. While Gwen watched, a man urged his herd of sheep onto a rise farther west.

Quite a crowd had gathered too, not only villagers but residents of the palace, who had nothing better to do between now and Iorwerth's wedding than gape at the flood.

A woman nudged Gwen. "You should see the fields to the east. The River Clwyd has overflowed as well. I've never seen so much water."

His hand at the small of her back, Deri urged Gwen along the bank to a better vantage point.

Gwen didn't share his enthusiasm. "I don't need to get any closer."

He didn't respond, and such was the crush of the crowd that she had no choice but to be dragged along, with him elbowing several villagers out of the way in his haste to see what he could. Ultimately, he stopped in the first row of onlookers, many yards east of the road, and pointed almost giddily at the high flow and the debris within it.

From behind them, a woman shouted, "Watch out!"

The crowd convulsed as an almost intact thatched roof of a house came roaring down the river. It was the largest of the detritus, which included whole trees, overturned boats, and even a sheep, struggling to keep its head above the rushing waters.

But Deri, of all the people in the crowd, hadn't startled at the woman's shout.

Gwen glanced at him and said, "We should take a step back."

His eyes were on the flood, and he didn't reply. Like when the woman shouted her warning, he didn't seem to hear her.

Deri was going deaf.

And maybe blind.

The conclusion was an obvious one, now that she thought about it. The latter could be encompassed, but for a musician, the possibility of losing one's hearing was tantamount to losing one's life.

Then he smiled at her and used one hand to pull her closer, while resting the other at the small of her back. The people around them were jostling one another in their excitement, pressing close and then retreating as they shouted to their friends, some of whom were running along the opposite bank.

After the roof passed, a young man some yards to the west tossed a rope to an older man on Gwen's side of the river near the road down from the castle. The pair shouted back and forth, words Gwen couldn't hear, but she could guess that it was about the possibility of using the rope to cross.

"Don't! You can't!" Gwen put her hands around her mouth, trying to shout above the rushing river, though of course there was no way they could hear her.

Then Gwen felt a hard shove at her back. Between one heartbeat and the next, she lost her balance and fell towards the water, her arms flailing. Deri shouted and reached for her, but he was too late. She hit the water and went under.

27

Gareth

Gareth stopped brushing his horse's coat and leaned into his forearm, watching Hywel, who was holding the horse's head. "Why on earth is your father eating porridge for breakfast, and when did this begin?"

"It's been a few months," Hywel said, "and he started forcing it down only at Cristina's insistence that it was good for his innards."

Gareth had already heard from Conall about the sacking of Nest and Deri's wagon, inspected it with Nest, and could make nothing of it. Until she repacked everything, which she was currently doing, she couldn't tell him what, if anything, had been stolen. Earlier, he had also shared a moment with Gwen before she set out to corner Deri once again. They had the mutual feeling that they needed to approach their suspects/victims, few as they were, in succession, in hopes that one of them might shake loose a bit of truth that would move the investigation forward.

Gareth had otherwise spent the morning keeping a beady eye on Cadwaladr, who'd done nothing of note beyond talking to everyone he encountered, a smile on his face and an easy laugh on his lips.

When Gareth could stand sitting in the hall no longer, he'd retreated to the stables. It wasn't quiet, not with so many men and horses to see to, but it gave him space to think. And, until Hywel arrived, nobody had approached him.

"I have given no thought ever in my life to the king's innards, and wish I hadn't now." Gareth patted the horse's neck. "So is it attempted regicide? That would certainly explain the escalation of events, with the attack on Gwalchmai, the theft of the dog, and now the situation with Nest's wagon."

"Though the latter makes no sense in the context of an attack on my father," Hywel said. "Have you talked to the kitchen staff since yesterday?"

"They were more than cooperative the first time when Llelo questioned them, and I gave him the same task today, to see if any of them remembered anything new, now that they've had a day to consider. Your stepmother told me yesterday that her porridge had come from the common pot, and thus, if it was poisoned, not only would your father and stepmother be dead, but so would half the people in the hall. Still, if your father was the intended target, it would bring to the fore some attributes of our would-be killer."

"As in, he knew enough to know my father ate porridge, but not enough to know that Deri and Nest did too."

"Exactly," Gareth said. "Again, if your father was the intended target, the would-be killer put poison in a bowl that was set aside, thinking it was intended for the king's breakfast."

Hywel drew in a breath. "My father wasn't in the hall when the dog died. Why would the killer believe the bowl was intended for him?"

"Because Cristina had already spoken to the kitchen about his breakfast, as she does every morning."

"He really does hate porridge. If she didn't force it on him, he wouldn't eat it ever." Hywel managed a laugh. "That the first victim was a dog blinded me to the danger this person represents. We must be very careful now."

"Blinded all of us," Gareth said, "though I was trying not to let it. We have discussed the poisoning all along as attempted murder—just of Deri or Nest. And once Cadwaladr arrived, I really did lose my mind for a bit."

"You aren't the only one." Hywel paused. "I don't want to call off the wedding, but how else to keep my father safe?"

"I'm not sure what difference leaving Denbigh would make. He has his men around him here as much as anywhere. I assume one of them is tasting his food before he eats it."

"Yes, though I know he is often a bit lax on the matter. I impressed upon him this morning the importance of not letting down his guard."

"Good." Gareth gave a sharp nod. "The kitchen is now off-limits to anyone but the two queens and the servants who work in it. I have posted men at both entrances."

"One of the servants could be the culprit," Hywel said.

"True, but all of them are long-time residents of Denbigh or known to us. If they poisoned the porridge, it's because they were paid to do so. The tightness of the circle should be enough to expose him if he acts again. Honestly, I don't think he will. Unless the dog was the intended target, which at this point I find highly unlikely, the poisoner knows he failed. He might try again, but it will be by a different means."

"And who will he try for?" Hywel looked away, out the door of the stables. Children were playing tag in the courtyard, bare armed and bareheaded, spurning any of the warm gear their mothers might normally force upon them at this time of year. The clouds on the horizon were heavy with rain, but it wasn't raining yet. "Was the target Deri or Nest? Or my father?"

"I can't make sense of a motive for the bards, other than if they were trying to murder each other." Gareth rubbed his forehead. "Most murders arise from anger, passion, or greed. I haven't been able to dig deeply enough into either bard's life to know what might cause one to murder the other."

"Neither attacked Gwalchmai."

"True."

"So we're back to my father."

"Except for the ransacking of Nest and Deri's wagon."

Hywel snorted. "Except for that."

More movement beyond where Hywel stood in the doorway caught Gareth's eye, and he stepped beside his prince in time to see Gwen walking with Deri towards the gatehouse.

Hywel saw them too and frowned. "He's holding your wife too close."

Gareth trusted Gwen absolutely, so his frown wasn't due to concern that she was somehow attracted to Deri and thinking unfaithful thoughts. If Deri was holding onto Gwen, it was because she had let him and was hoping to lull him into giving her good answers because of it.

Still ...

Gareth growled low in his chest, feeling protective, which was normal, and uncertain as to what he should do about it, which wasn't. He allowed himself to waver a moment between his desire to interfere and the surety that his wife was a capable investigator and knew what she was about. Then he set the brush on a nearby shelf and started after them.

Up ahead, Gwen skirted a puddle and put some space between herself and Deri, though she didn't drop his arm. Gareth's mouth twitched at how well he knew his wife. She didn't like Deri. He reminded her too much of her own father as he'd been years ago, before Gareth's marriage to Gwen and Meilyr's to Saran. Gareth didn't like Deri either, of course, though recently he'd been leaning towards feeling sorry for him.

Hywel fell in beside Gareth, his expression amused. He was perceptive enough to be thinking similar thoughts. Having grown up with Gwen, Hywel was like a brother to her and was as protective as Gareth.

"About this contract my father signed with Madog. I haven't had a chance yet to tell Gwen how sorry I am that my father signed it and also sorry that I wasn't able to tell her about it sooner. He swore both Meilyr and me to secrecy." Hywel raised one shoulder in a half-shrug. "Obviously, Meilyr saw fit to break that vow, as he needed to and I should have done sooner. My father knows that you know, by the way. Have no fear of him."

King Owain had imprisoned Gareth once, but, since then, Gareth had rarely feared him. Now, he said, "I can't speak for her, and while I know she would appreciate you mentioning it, she doesn't need you to. If anything, she is resentful of King Madog, not King Owain. And Meilyr, more than anyone, seems to be taking his usurpation in stride."

"Slighting Meilyr at this wedding is a far worse offense for my father to have perpetrated than what drove him and Meilyr apart after my grandfather died. I'm glad to see they have come out of it friends. It speaks to how they have changed." Hywel shot Gareth a grin. "Your father-in-law has been telling tales about you, by the way."

"I fear what he has said!" Gareth laughed.

"Nothing but good, I assure you."

Gareth was feeling much more content than a few moments ago. "If, for some reason, Madog decides he'd rather have music instead of dealing with his own feuding bards, Meilyr and Gwalchmai would be happy to step in."

"*I'd* be happy to step in."

They'd followed Gwen and Deri down the slope towards the village, and for a moment Gareth lost sight of his wife amidst the crowd that had gathered, since it was stretched three or four deep for fifty yards along the bank. Deri had pulled her all the way to the right, near an old tree. Then Gareth's view was blocked by people filling in the gaps and crowding closer together.

As he gazed at the number of people clustered on the bank, his concern deepened. "Should we be doing something about this?" he asked Hywel.

"Do you mean the flood or the crowd?" Hywel barked a laugh. "Yesterday, the Dragons and I spent half the day urging people to move themselves and their herds to higher ground. Nobody would believe these creeks and streams would flood to this extent. Floods happen less often here than in Gwynedd. And now all they want to do is stand around and watch."

"They don't have our mountains, and people rarely believe what's possible until they see it with their own eyes." Gareth finally spotted Gwen again, Deri still beside her, the water practically lapping at their feet. He wanted to tell her to step back, but the noise from the river was too loud to be heard over such a great distance. He moved downriver to somewhat higher ground so he could see her better, even if it meant he was farther away. The last thing he wanted was to interfere if Gwen was getting somewhere questioning Deri.

As to the flood, Gareth could understand people's desire to gawk. Looking at the river now, it was difficult to believe that a few days ago it had been hardly more than a creek, and the flow coming from the east had been little more than a trickle. Gareth skirted a few more onlookers on the western side of the crowd, trying himself to get a better view.

"Watch out!" Someone off to Gareth's right shouted, and he took a step back, startled by the sight of half a house coming towards them down the river.

"This flood would be momentous even in Gwynedd." Hywel coughed as he took an elbow in the stomach, followed by a very contrite, "Pardon me, my lord, I didn't see you," from the offender, who'd just finished tying one end of a rope to a hitching post attached to a tavern, which two days ago had been safely out of the flood zone but in another hour might be under water.

On the opposite bank, another man was tying the other end of the rope at head height around an oak tree, the roots of which would be severely undermined if the flood kept up its current pace and if the heavy black clouds on the horizon were as complete as they presently appeared. It was only a matter of time.

As it was, the river had risen another foot since Gareth and Hywel had arrived and was starting to lap even at Gareth's feet.

"Where's Gwen?" Hywel wasn't quite as tall as Gareth, and he was on his toes, trying to see over the heads of the onlookers between them and her.

"She was on the bank with Deri—" Gareth spied her at the exact instant she fell into the rushing water, and he was moving before his mind had time to process what he'd seen.

One moment he was standing on the bank, and the next he'd thrown himself forward, both hands catching the rope that had just been tied across the water. His weight stretched it down so it was barely above the rushing river, but both ends held. For now.

"Christ, Gareth!"

Hywel held onto the near end of the rope with both hands, trying to steady it. Gareth had gone under in the first instant, but he bobbed back up, still holding the rope, now essentially at the level of the water. At first he couldn't see Gwen, and he didn't know if it was because she'd gone under too or if the curve of the river was obscuring his vision.

Then, just ahead, her head bobbed up, and she was a good enough swimmer to right herself and point her feet downstream.

He fought the current himself, trying to become as large a target as possible for his wife, who was barreling towards him at a terrific pace. He could find no purchase with his feet, so pushed down on the rope with both hands, attempting to get more of his upper body out of the water.

If Gwen had fallen into the center of the river, with the current moving as fast as a horse could gallop, Gareth wouldn't have been able to help her, but they'd each been standing at two ends of an inside curve of the river, meaning the river was slower here than along the outer bank.

Ten frantic heartbeats and a lifetime later, Gwen hit Gareth full on, and he managed to take most of her weight on his torso. Because he was on the downstream side of the rope and she was on the upstream, the rope caught her around the waist as well. The water buffeted them with force, like standing underneath a waterfall.

"I'm so cold, Gareth." Gwen spoke through chattering teeth.

Gareth himself was already so cold that he couldn't feel his fingers, and he was afraid he would lose his grip on the rope.

"Hang on!" Hywel's voice rang above them. "You'd better hang on!"

"We're trying!" Gareth was shouting, but Hywel didn't reply, and Gareth wasn't sure his words could be heard over the rushing of the river.

Far too long later, though it might have been only a hundred heartbeats, the men on the bank dropped a log the width of Gareth's upper arm in front of him. Four men held it steady, two to a side, with Iago taking the anchor point at the back end. Steffan and Gruffydd were on their knees on the muddy bank, each with a ready hand if either Gareth or Gwen got that far.

"Grab on!" Hywel was still holding the end of the rope to keep it steady, by now joined by more helpers.

Gareth was both afraid to unstick his hand from the rope and afraid not to. But he managed to wrap it around his left arm, and that allowed him to grasp Gwen's right wrist. He wasn't going to let go no matter what. "Left hand first, *cariad.*"

"I don't know if I can. I can't feel my fingers."

Gareth moved his right hand to cover hers and then helped her work her fingers free. With a gasp, she threw out one arm and then the other to the log and hung on for dear life as the men pulled her towards the bank and up it. Steffan and Gruffydd grabbed her by her upper arms and carried her to safety.

Hywel took their place, looking as if he was going to get into the water himself to help. Gareth waved him off. He had little strength left, but the last thing they wanted was to lose their prince in an attempt to save his steward.

The sight of Gwen sitting on the bank, wrapped in a blanket and surrounded by caring hands, each desperate to help, had Gareth marshaling every last ounce of strength. Cadoc had come down to the water's edge to join Prince Hywel, bow in hand, and he held it out to Gareth as far as he could reach.

Laboriously, hand over hand, Gareth moved down the rope towards the bank, finally grasping the end of the bow for the last few feet. He had never been so cold in his life, and it was only when Hywel bent to him and said, "You're safe," that he realized he was out of the water.

Then Cadoc and Hywel dragged him up the bank to Gwen.

28

Hywel

Hywel thought he'd been angry yesterday. He'd certainly been angry for the whole of the last two years since Rhun had died. But all that felt like nothing compared to what he was feeling right now. It was one thing for someone to try to murder his father, or Gareth, or him. It was quite another for Gwen to almost die, and he didn't for one instant believe what Deri was telling him.

"It was an accident, my lord! I couldn't do anything to stop it! One moment she was beside me, and the next she was in the water. I almost fell in myself." The bard stood before him by the door to the guesthouse common room, wringing his hands, his eyes on Saran, who was tending to Gwen and Gareth by the fire. "It wasn't my fault!"

Hywel wasn't having it. He was just managing to speak without shouting because he didn't want to disturb his friends. "You were the one who took her down there and chose to stand on the bank. I saw you with your hand on her."

"If she was nervous, she should have said something."

It was a cowardly thing to blame Gwen, and Deri knew it, because he ducked his head. He did not, however, take it back.

"You were taking advantage of her desire to ask you questions about the dog's death to stay close to her." For the life of him, Hywel couldn't remember the name of the dog, if he'd ever known it. "She is a beautiful woman, and you wanted to touch her."

"I know. I know." Deri wrung his hands some more.

Hywel made a sound of disgust and dismissed him. It hadn't escaped his notice that Deri had been drinking—possibly quite a lot, given the fumes that wafted over Hywel. He was also disgusted that he couldn't tell if Deri's current contrition was due to horror at what he'd done or genuine concern for Gwen. Deri had long experience with drinking and performing, and both activities, by definition, made good liars.

As the bard departed, undoubtedly to drink some more in the hall, Conall stepped nearer and looked intently into Hywel's face. "She's alive, my prince. They both are."

"I know. By luck."

"By training. The rope across the river was luck. Gareth would have jumped in anyway, and I have no doubt found a way to save them both, even if they'd had to float two miles downstream to do it."

"He would have tried." Hywel turned his head to look at Gareth, who was practically sitting in the fire, wrapped in Hywel's own goose-down blanket. "If they weren't crushed by the debris first."

It had been a real fear. The river was full of branches and rocks—and whole houses it seemed. Hywel himself hadn't seen a flood like it in his lifetime. Nor had anyone younger than fifty. They had to go all the way back to his grandfather's time for anyone to remember anything like it. A thaw in December wasn't unusual in Wales, but it was Aron, who knew most about the weather, because he knew the most about most things, who'd guessed it had been a perfect storm, quite literally, of snow, rain, thaw, and more rain.

First thing, Gareth and Gwen had been taken back to the guesthouse. Helpers had then stripped them of their wet garments, dried them off, and dressed them again in layers of clothing and warm blankets. Gwen was currently rocking in a chair by the hearth, nursing Taran, who was (unbeknownst to him) warming his mother with his own body heat. These days, he was nursing less often than he'd been a few months ago, but he would be sensing his mother's distress, and would want to nurse as comfort for them both.

Mari, Hywel's wife, sat next to Gwen, a protective hand on her knee, and Saran was bustling about, checking heads and backs and legs, waiting for a sign that they were warming. Gwalchmai was sitting up on his pallet, watching everyone with concerned eyes, though he still wasn't feeling at all well either.

Llelo remained on guard at the door, as if someone might make another attempt to murder Gwen from within the palace. Dai had run back and forth to the kitchen six times, keeping everyone in the room, not just his parents, supplied with soup and warm bread. All of the Dragons, in fact, had been close by since they'd brought Gareth and Gwen up from the river. They were family. It warmed Hywel's heart to know it. But all of them were angry. And all of them were feeling ineffective and impotent.

Meanwhile, likely knowing it, Meilyr had found a spot in one corner, at first tuning his harp, and then playing a soothing melody. Hywel could see the way the music lessened the anxiety of everyone in the room. Their actions slowed and became less jerky and manic. Catching his eye, Gareth rose and came closer, though still hugging the blanket around himself, though the room was quite warm now, with the fire blazing.

Hywel made to protest, but Gareth waved him off, in much the same gesture he'd used when he was in the river. Hywel had a thought to watch for it from now on. When the time was right, he would tease him about how predictable he was.

But not yet.

"If I sit any longer, I'll be too stiff to move for the rest of the day." At least Gareth's color was better, pink instead of white.

The two of them moved towards the stairs, and Conall came over too and sat on the fourth stair up.

"Do you believe Deri?" Hywel said.

Even if Hywel hadn't been shouting, Deri's protests had rung around the room, so Gareth had to have heard at least some of his interrogation.

"I genuinely don't know." Gareth shook his head, not so much to say *no* as because he didn't know. "Gwen says she felt pressure between her shoulder blades and then a shove that forced her into the river. Deri's hand had been on her back, as we ourselves saw, but the crowd was large and jostling. She doesn't know who pushed her. It could have been an accident."

Hywel blew out a puff of air. "Accidents do happen, as do coincidences, but I don't like to see them around Gwen, especially not in the middle of an investigation."

"A *murder* investigation, my lord," Conall said, reverting to a moment of formality. He occasionally called Hywel by his given name and much of the time called him nothing at all. Hywel was the son of a king and heir to the throne of Gwynedd. Conall was the nephew of the King of Leinster. In this moment, Conall was conceding Hywel's higher rank, but usually there was no rank between them.

Now that he thought about it, since Cadwaladr's arrival, everyone had been treating Hywel like he was going to break apart at any moment. He could have been annoyed, but instead felt a rush of love for them, combatting some of his anger.

And really, that anger more rightfully belonged to Gareth, as Gwen's husband. Oddly, Gareth had been far more overtly angry yesterday; today, he was almost disturbingly calm. It occurred to Hywel that the two of them had become such close companions that Gareth's anger was more for *him*, and Hywel's might be more for *Gareth*. If true, it said something immense about both of them and their relationship.

Then Gwen called from across the room. "Come over here and talk to me. I'm fine. You don't need to protect me, and I want to hear what you're saying. We all do."

Gareth's face showed a reluctance that matched Hywel's own, but they did as she bid. Gwen had long experience with murder, and this wasn't the first time her life had been in jeopardy. It hadn't happened for several years, and every time it did happen, Hywel swore he wouldn't ask for her help again. Always, he failed to keep that promise. Again and again. That made Hywel angry too, though this time at himself for being such a hypocrite.

Of course, though he was her lord, as well as her friend, Gwen herself had told him many times that she was a grown woman who knew the risks. Like a soldier, sometimes a capable person had to take on risk to save others.

Mari smiled as Hywel approached; he put a hand on her shoulder and squeezed. Although they'd been in danger together once too, since their marriage, Mari had mostly stayed out of these investigations. She would bend an ear to Gwen or Hywel when they needed someone to listen, but her first priority was—and had to be—their boys.

Gareth propped himself up against the wall near the fire, still wrapped in his blanket, though he appeared warmer now because he wasn't hugging it so closely around his body.

Gwen rocked gently in her chair. "I know you boys like being secretive over there in your corner, but figuring out what is going on here takes priority over misguided notions of protecting me, and you know we do better when we put everybody's mind to a problem. Let's start at the beginning with what we know."

This was familiar territory—so familiar, in fact, that Llelo and Dai drifted closer too. All families—the ones that loved each other and enjoyed each other's company anyway—had little traditions and rituals. Music played a large role in both Hywel's family and Gwen's and, for better or for worse, so did murder.

"The first thing we know is that Nest's dog died from eating poisoned porridge," Hywel said.

Gwen frowned. "Do we know that, in fact? We have no body and no porridge, so even that can't be ascertained."

"I stand corrected." Hywel cleared his throat. "Nest's dog died after eating porridge."

"That's better." Gwen nodded. "And that's where we came in, but is it really the beginning?"

They all thought about that for a moment. "We can't know right now. We might not be able to determine when this all started until the end," Llelo finally said.

Gwen nodded. "For us, that's a more common situation than not. So then what happened?"

"Gareth sent the porridge away with Gwalchmai, so Saran could check it, and he was attacked and left unconscious," Llelo continued, as his mother had meant him to. "The porridge was stolen by a person or persons unknown."

"After which the corpse was stolen, also by someone as yet unidentified," Gareth said, "and then Cadwaladr arrived and threw us all into turmoil. If nothing else, he provided our killer with an excellent distraction."

"Which may or may not be part of the story," Hywel said. "As yet, we don't know that either."

"Then, this morning, someone went through Nest and Deri's wagon," Conall said, "but who is responsible remains a mystery."

Gwen huffed. "We have far too many unknowns."

"We have *only* unknowns," Llelo said.

"What we have," Gareth said, with a gentle look at his son, implying he wasn't correcting his statement so much as augmenting it, "is events but no culprits. Do we have *any* suspects?"

"Who do we include? Who do we *not* include." Hywel laughed and answered his own question. "Nobody knows anything about anything—or at least not enough."

"Someone has to know something." Mari had so far been keeping silent, though she'd been observing the rest of them talk. "Nobody saw anything unusual in the kitchen? Nobody was around when someone took the dog's corpse? Nobody went near the wagon?"

There were headshakes all around.

Mari pursed her lips. "I don't believe it."

Dai had been chewing on his lower lip while his elders conferred and now said, "How about instead of thinking about who did any of these things, we look at who *couldn't* have done them—in other words, the people who were somewhere else or otherwise occupied when these events were taking place."

"That's a good idea." Gareth nodded. "We did a little of this before, early on, but not with everyone participating, and we have more events now to work with."

"I'll go first." Llelo straightened in his seat, having shot his younger brother an approving look, unoffended that Dai had thought of something he hadn't. "Deri couldn't have wrecked the wagon because he was in the hall before Nest arrived to eat breakfast and stayed long after she left. I sat watching the whole time too, so it wasn't me." He grinned somewhat mischievously.

Dai shoved his shoulder. "Why would he have wrecked his own wagon?"

Llelo shrugged, still not offended. "I'm just saying. If we are worried Deri pushed Mam into the river, and our goal is to eliminate suspects, he couldn't have wrecked the wagon too. That's all I'm saying."

Hywel cleared his throat. "Leave off, you two. Dai's idea is a good one and so is Llelo's. While I am not convinced the porridge that killed the dog was meant for Deri or Nest, since it turns out my father is also eating porridge in the morning, the fact that someone went through their wagon indicates they are involved."

"Nest accused Deri of trying to murder her and vice versa," Gareth said.

"But Nest never went into the kitchen yesterday morning," Gwen said.

"As the kitchen workers confirm." Llelo nodded at his mother.

"And according even to Deri, she didn't touch the porridge before Annwyn did." Gareth looked at Hywel and said, having read his mind, as usual, "That's the name of the dog."

"If King Owain was the intended victim, things look a little different, as do the list of suspects," Gwen said.

"Cadwaladr being the most obvious," Gareth put in.

"Yes, but he wasn't here," Gwen looked lovingly at her husband, "as you well know."

"That doesn't mean someone couldn't have meant to poison the king for him."

"I know, my love, so let's talk about who might have had a motive to do that, beginning with Susanna, Cristina, and Alice, all of whom had access to the kitchen in a way other guests do not—and all of whom have a relationship with the king."

Conall's expression turned thoughtful. "Susanna didn't seem to want to answer my questions last night."

Hywel had decided he wasn't going to touch this topic and to keep his mouth firmly shut, if only because he was interested in what his friends and co-conspirators had to say, but right away, he had to intervene. "I object to the idea that my aunt would attempt to kill my father at the behest of my uncle. If anything, you need to replace Cadwaladr with Madog."

"If Madog is behind this, he definitely would have to be working through someone else so as not to get his hands dirty," Mari said flatly. "As with Cadwaladr, I say we have to consider him separately."

Hywel subsided at his wife's forceful tone.

Gareth glanced at Hywel, perhaps a little nervously, before continuing. "Cristina was present at the initial poisoning and took charge of it. She certainly had access to the kitchen, but I would have said she has a vested interest in keeping King Owain alive, at least until her sons are grown enough to make a bid for the throne."

All around, heads nodded in agreement.

"Does she have a motive for getting rid of Nest and Deri?" Llelo asked.

"Only to disrupt the wedding, which she appears, otherwise, to be in favor of," Gwen said.

"And then we have Alice, who never entered the kitchen," Gareth said. "I have a hard time picturing her sacking Nest's wagon, but she *is* Cadwaladr's wife, and he is here."

"As much as I would like to blame any of this on him," Gwen said, "I can't see a way to do so, but I did learn that Alice is acquainted with Manon, the wife of Nest and Deri's steward, Andreas."

"And those are two more people close to Deri and Nest who have been in and around all these events, though neither could have committed all of them," Gareth said. "They also have no clear motive, since Andreas would surely lose his position if anything happened to Deri."

"And Manon is married to Andreas, who would lose his position if anything happened to Deri," Gwen said. "I can see her being jealous of Nest, but she is newly pregnant. Why murder Nest now—and so publicly?"

"And again, we can pinpoint where they were at the time of the dog's death," Conall said. "They were in the hall."

Gareth tipped his head. "Manon was in the hall. Andreas arrived later, having been in consultation with the priest."

"Do we believe him?" Dai asked.

"We do." Gwen sighed. "I spoke with the priest yesterday evening. He concurs."

"And Andreas never went into the kitchen to assure the creation of the porridge," Llelo said.

Gwen made a dismissive motion with her hand. "It's remotely possible he could have seen Gwalchmai leaving the hall with the porridge, attacked him, hidden the bowl, and then gone into the hall. But unless he has the *sight*, he couldn't have known what had happened in the hall before entering it, after which he stayed within sight of Nest and Deri." She looked at Gareth. "When was the corpse stolen?"

"That has a longer time frame," Gareth said.

"Provided we believe the servant delivered the corpse in the first place," Conall said.

"And if he's the murderer, we have an even larger problem on our hands," Gareth said, "because he's a boy of nineteen."

"I met him in the kitchen," Llelo said. "He seemed as bewildered as the rest. He wasn't there to witness what happened in the hall either."

"Maybe it's a mistake to think these events are all related," Conall said, though even as he spoke he sounded dubious. "If the poison was meant for King Owain, then the attack on Gwalchmai and the theft of the dog's corpse are, of course, connected. But what if the ransacking of Nest's wagon has nothing to do with any of this and was just a thief using the upheaval as cover?"

"What does that make of Gwen's trip into the river?" Meilyr asked, speaking for the first time.

Hywel had a moment's pause to realize that, while Hywel himself had almost lost one of his closest friends in life, and Gareth had almost lost his wife, Meilyr would have lost his daughter. As a parent himself, Hywel had no trouble imagining the enormity of that grief.

Thus, he said, "If Deri pushed her, then he is, indeed, a villain and a would-be murderer, making him the likeliest culprit for the poisoning of the porridge and the theft of the corpse. He certainly had opportunity for the latter since he spends much of his time in the chapel, which is adjacent to the laying out room."

"But he didn't attack Gwalchmai," Gwen said. "And he was in the hall all morning, so he isn't responsible for the state of his own wagon."

"He also had a spoonful of porridge ready for his mouth as the dog died," Gareth said. "I don't see him trying to kill himself."

"At least not by poison," Gwen said. "I find it much more likely he's going to drink himself to death instead."

"Which brings us all the way back around," Hywel said. "With no one person among those closest to these incidents responsible for all of them, we have to consider now how many ways we are looking at this all wrong."

29

Gareth

Gareth woke early the next morning, determined to do *something* before the wedding that would propel the investigation forward. By his reckoning, he had about six hours. It was so early in the day, in fact, that it was still dark, and the courtyard was deserted. It had also stopped raining, however briefly, but it had rained long and hard in the night. The flood below the castle was so large he could hear it from where he stood.

He didn't care to venture down the hill, however. Even with the lantern he carried, it was too dark to see well, and he had no interest in a repeat of the adventure of yesterday. Whether or not he had openly admitted it to Gwen, that had been as close a call as they had ever experienced. He still didn't know whether to blame Deri, to search for another culprit, or to accept that it was an accident. If they didn't discover who was responsible soon, he might never know. The wedding was today. Flood permitting, tomorrow the people would disperse.

Rather than dwelling further on the progress of the investigation, or lack thereof, he turned slowly on one heel in order to take in all the permanent buildings within the palace walls: the guesthouse, the barracks, the great hall, the king's quarters, the blacksmith's works, the kitchen, a series of craft halls, the public latrine (the king's own latrine was located behind his quarters so Gareth couldn't see it), the laundry, the stables, the granary, and the chapel. All in all, the walls encompassed ground about eighty yards by sixty. Denbigh was actually one of the smaller of King Owain's palaces, since it was circumscribed by the size of the plateau upon which it had been built. Both Llys Rhosyr and Llanfaes on Anglesey were built in the lowlands, and were a third again as large.

The laying out room sat beside the chapel, and he made his way towards it—not because he expected to find the dog miraculously reappeared, but because it was the only place he knew to start. He stepped inside the room, still with no dog in evidence or anything else of note. Even the sacking that had been bundled into the shape of the dog under the sheet told him nothing, as it came from the storage room at the back of the stables. By the lingering smell, it had once held oats for the horses, to supplement their hay.

The thought pricked at him, reminding him of the porridge that had started this investigation. While oats made Gareth's usual kind of porridge, and apparently King Owain's too, Deri and Nest had been very particular about not eating Welsh grain for theirs, heaven knew why.

Gareth spread out the sacking and studied the lettering on the side, consisting of a sheaf crossed with a sickle. Gareth had a fine hand with a brush himself, and this was well done. He bent closer, noting the use of a tar-based paint. Some farmers weaved a colored band into their sacks to identify their farm for the mill where their grain was processed and at the market where it was sold, so payment could go to the right place. This farmer had woven a black double stripe around the top.

Rather than leave the sack behind this time, Gareth folded it and tucked it into his belt at his waist to keep it with him in order to show Gwen later. Then he went back outside and stood in the shadow of the eaves.

It took a few moments for his eyes to adjust to the darkness. In that time, a slender figure came through the postern gate to his right, holding a laundry basket on her hip. From a distance and in the dark, he couldn't have said for certain who it was, but her shape and stride were such that he could make a good guess. Quickly dousing the lantern, he became one with the wall at his back, unmoving and barely breathing, as she walked past within twenty feet of him.

As soon as she had gone by, he moved from his hiding place, keeping to the shadows and following her progress across the courtyard. She didn't go to the laundry room, which was on the other side of the laying out room from the church, but by-passed it in favor of the back door of the stables. A moment later, she disappeared inside.

He gave her a count of ten before he followed. Inside the stables, it was warmer and much darker than out. Dawn was still an hour off, but the sky had begun leaning to gray rather than black, and anyway torches burned all night at the gatehouse and the front of the hall.

At first, Gareth could hear or see nothing, and he feared the woman had realized he was following her and had given him the slip, entering by one door and leaving by another.

But then he noticed a flickering light at the far end of the stables, past the last horse box. He followed it and the rustling sounds that emanated from the back corner storage area, from whence he'd guessed the wadded up sacking that had doubled for the dog's corpse had come. He hadn't had any cause to come back here in all the times he'd been to Denbigh—though years ago he'd been locked in a similar room at Aber when King Owain had accused him of a crime he hadn't committed.

As he came through the doorway, Manon was on her knees within the circle of the lantern light and was in the process of dumping her linens back into the basket she'd brought.

She didn't hear him, and since her back was to him, didn't see him either. Gareth watched her hurried movements for a few heartbeats before deciding it was time to make himself known.

"Hello, Manon." To his own ears, his voice sounded unnaturally loud and echoey.

Manon visibly startled and was on her feet a moment later, backing away from the basket and from Gareth. "I-I-I—" That was as far as she got, either unable or unwilling to complete the thought.

Gareth simply lounged in the doorway, effecting a casual attitude, his arms folded across his chest and his shoulder braced against the frame. "What do you have there?"

"N-n-nothing!"

He made a gesture towards the basket. "Really?"

She stared at him, wide-eyed.

"If I were to empty it, what would I find?"

She shook her head, still not speaking.

He would much prefer she tell him, rather than staying mute while he went through her things. It would establish a bad precedent, though since she'd already been spoken to several times, her ability to lie was well-established. He could guess what was in the basket, but it would be far better if she told him herself.

So he waited, his eyes on her face.

She stared back for a full count of ten, and then she capitulated, her shoulders shaking and tears coming to her eyes and voice. "It's the dog. Nest's dead dog."

He canted his head, silently telling her to continue.

"I was passing by the stables, and I smelled something terrible."

He was disappointed that she had already progressed to the next stage after being caught: lying. Again.

She waved a hand in front of her face. "Can't you smell it too?"

He could. The dog was, fortunately, very small, but it had been dead for two days, which meant rigor would have passed and the decay of the body would be well under way. Likely, if Manon hadn't decided to move the dog this morning, someone would have found it anyway.

But he didn't tell her that, instead musing, "Interesting that you were able to smell it all the way across the courtyard. Perhaps even more interesting, instead of informing someone—say *me*—you chose to bury it within your laundry basket."

"I—I—" She tried again to deny or to lie, but then began to sob.

Gareth felt a bit of an ogre for calling to account a pregnant lady. In the early stages of her pregnancies, Gwen had cried at the slightest change in his tone, and he'd been his most censorious with Manon. He couldn't believe she was a natural villain. He'd found her with the dog, it was true, and he was all but certain she was the one who'd stolen it in the first place, but he was looking at tears of desperation.

So he softened his tone slightly, in hopes of getting some actual truth out of her. "Was it Deri you wanted to murder, or Nest?"

"I didn't! I didn't want to murder anyone!"

Gareth noted the use of the word *want*, implying, again, desperation. He gestured to the laundry basket. "That isn't what it looks like from where I'm standing."

Manon shook her head vigorously.

"Does that mean you didn't do it or you didn't *want* to do it?"

Still no answer. She was proving to be more stubborn than he'd hoped, which also made him more suspicious. Her protests seemed genuine, but he had been lied to so often and so well by so many people, that he didn't trust anymore that he could tell the difference between tears at being wrongly accused and those at being caught.

"The longer you refuse to talk, the more suspicious I become of you. You do realize that?"

She shook her head mutely.

He really didn't want to lock her up, but he would if he had to. In his head, he was already lining up participants. Conall was very good at playing off Gareth. Iago made an excellent and menacing bar for the door.

He swept aside the image. "Why did you steal the dog's body, Manon?"

"I—I—" He'd asked a question she couldn't deny outright. But instead of answering, she bent her head and sobbed some more.

Most people were bad liars, but many improved once caught and once they warmed to their subject—and if their survival was at stake. While he couldn't tell where Manon fell on the spectrum, something had driven her to steal the corpse, and that same something was keeping her quiet. It might be purely self-preservation, but he thought there was more to it than that.

It was a truism that women were different from men, but it was worth reiterating. They didn't think the same way, and they didn't care about the same things. According to Gwen, Manon was pregnant—finally—and overjoyed at the fact. A woman in that state would do anything to protect her child.

The question before Gareth now was *how was this protecting her child?*

While he wanted an outright confession to put the case to bed, it wasn't forthcoming, so he picked up the basket, peeked under the linens to confirm the dog was, in fact, there, and jerked his head at Manon. "Come with me."

At first she didn't move, and he feared she wasn't going to comply, which would mean he had a whole new problem. But as he left the stables, he glanced back to see her trailing dejectedly after him.

The sky was beginning to turn gray, which meant he could see perfectly well without a lantern, and he led Manon to the laying out room. She balked at entering, prompting him to snap impatiently, "You entered before. You weren't so squeamish that you couldn't put a dead animal in your laundry basket."

When she hovered in the doorway, he set the basket on the table and walked back to her. She shrank away, but all he did was reach past her and shut the door behind her. "I'm not going to hurt you."

She was paler even than Gwen had been when she'd come out of the water yesterday.

"I didn't mean to hurt anyone."

That was a slightly different way to phrase her denial, and he eyed her before saying softly. "You could have killed Gwalchmai, you know."

The tears that had been in abeyance during the walk from the stables flowed again with real force as she sobbed, bent over at the waist. He was glad he'd closed the door, since it blocked some of the sound. Hopefully, most people outside would confuse her weeping with the rush of wind and water. And then, to nobody's surprise, the rain began to fall again, rat-a-tat-tatting on the roof. Its arrival bought him time, which he was going to use.

"Why don't I tell you what I'm thinking, and you can tell me if I'm right: you poisoned the porridge and then, when I sent Gwalchmai off with the bowl, you followed, struck him on the head, and took the bowl."

"Yes! Yes, I did that!" The words burst out of her, accompanied by more sobs. "I took the honey too and threw it in the river. That's why you couldn't find it."

That was something he could actually believe. "And then you stole the dog's corpse."

She wasn't looking at him, but she nodded.

He tapped a finger to his lips, considering the best way to ask his many questions.

"Are you saying you wrecked Nest's wagon too?"

"I wanted to frighten Nest." Suddenly she looked up, the tears abating and her face screwed up. "I hate her!"

It was a bold statement, one she hadn't needed to think about, and Gareth thought she was again telling him a portion of the truth. But only a portion.

"Why would that be?"

"I am jealous of her." Then Manon swallowed hard. It was a moment of delay, when earlier the words had come easily. He couldn't help thinking she was about to lie to him again—or at the very least tell him partial truths. It was as if she was searching for an answer that would satisfy him.

"Before my marriage, my voice was as lovely as hers, but she is the one on the dais, not me."

"You thought if she was dead, you could replace her?"

"I didn't want her dead! I wanted to make her ill or frighten her enough that it would keep her from singing. It would have worked too if your wife hadn't convinced her that Deri would go on without her." Her lower lip stuck out like she was a child caught stealing a sweet. "She deserved to have her pretty things ruined."

Truthfully, Manon had done a poor job in that regard, since none of Nest's dresses had actually been despoiled or even damaged.

"Poison seems a little extreme. You could have killed her, and then this would be a very different conversation. You were lucky the dog got to the porridge first."

"I know." Manon hung her head.

"What poison did you use?"

Manon kept her eyes downcast, reverting to silence.

The answer was important enough, however, that he asked his question again.

Finally, she whispered, "Badger's bane." She said the words in English, as if she didn't know the Welsh word for the poison and was parroting what someone else had told her.

Then she wiped a last tear from her cheek. "What are you going to do with me?"

"I will think on it." Gareth sighed as he studied her down-turned head. "The death of the dog is one issue that needs to be addressed. You will have to atone to Nest for that. Your attack on Gwalchmai is another matter, one our family will have to consider together."

He paused. "What did you hit him with?"

Her head jerked up so she met his eyes for one brief moment before she looked away again. "A piece of wood."

"Square or round?"

"I don't remember." She swallowed hard. "What are you going to do about the dog?"

He rested a hand on the top of the pile of laundry. "Leave this with me. You might as well go back to bed. I'm sure you're exhausted."

She drew in a breath. "Aren't you going to put me in a cell?"

"I could, but what difference would it make?"

"I-I might try to run away."

"Where? We are on a plateau surrounded by water."

That flummoxed her for a moment. Some villains were relieved once they'd confessed and *wanted* to be punished. It was looking as if Manon fell into that category, but he thought there was still something strange about her entire confession.

"I expect you to confine yourself to the palace until I confer with King Madog."

After another pained stare, Manon gave him a quick curtsey, turned on her heel, and fled.

Part of him was sorry the river was in flood, because it would be far easier on everyone if she did run away. A dog was dead, yes, and attempted murder was not something to be disregarded, but he had no interest in bringing judgment on a pregnant woman, no matter how misguided. The dog was dead, but Gwalchmai would live, as would he and Gwen, though since Manon had not been at the river when Gwen had gone in, he could hardly blame her for that.

Gareth watched her go, hoping he wouldn't regret his decision later. Then he decided he could do only so many things at once, and the dog took precedence now. With a sigh, he began removing the bundle of linens from the basket.

30

Llelo

As Llelo arrived in the laying out room, Gareth had just set a basket aside on a nearby table next to his leather tool roll, which lay flat, revealing tweezers, a narrow knife, a metal pick, and a needle. Then he turned back to the body of the dead dog. Though it was still wrapped in a last layer of sacking, Llelo knew it was Annwyn because one paw stuck out. He had seen Manon leave moments before as if being chased by hounds.

He stared at the paw and then looked at his father, who made a rueful face. "At long last."

He glanced out the door and then back to the table, putting two and two together and wondering if he'd just reached four. "Did *Manon* take it?"

"So she says. And so I found her."

Having woken to find his father gone again, Llelo had been determined to track him down so he didn't work alone today. None of them should be working alone, not with two attacks on members of their family within as many days. He had neglected to suggest it the previous night, and he was honestly surprised nobody else had thought to say something.

Now, even while shaking his head over the re-emergence of the dog, he said as much to his father.

"Then it's just as well you're here."

Gareth tossed Llelo an herb sachet from a basket on a side table, kept at the ready in case of need, and Llelo hung it around his neck.

"In the past, you always made sure I was with Mam."

"Who's with her now?"

"Dai said he would stick to her like tree sap."

Gareth laughed. "Good."

"It's Cadwaladr, really, isn't it? He has everyone wound up tight like harp string. It's as if all the time you have half your mind on him and half on the investigation."

"Earlier, I'd soaked my brain with too much mead. Sadly, sobering up hasn't helped." Then, in a few sentences, Gareth explained what he'd learned from Manon.

"So that's it? It's over? She confessed to everything?" To Llelo, it was a mundane and unsatisfying ending to the mystery.

"It seems so, if we discount the attack on your mother—if it even was an attack."

"You're saying I don't need to be here to protect you?"

"Unless we have it wrong again."

"Do you not believe Manon?"

Gareth made a noncommittal noise. "There are bits of her story we'll have to confirm. When your grandmother wakes up, she can look at the dog and see if she concurs Annwyn was poisoned with Badger's bane—that's Monkshood to you and Aconite to *Mamgu*. When I questioned Manon, I had a strong feeling she was mixing lies with occasional truths, and I don't know which bits go where."

"She really hit Gwalchmai on the head?"

"So she claims. At this point, that crime is the most serious of all of them. When your mother told Manon and Andreas what had happened to Gwalchmai, Manon paled and swayed. At the time, Gwen assumed it was shock at the ferocity of the attack."

"Manon *is* pregnant." Llelo frowned. "She must have been truly desperate to do all this."

"Such was my exact thought." Gareth took in a last deep breath and then, rather than pulling the dog out of the hemp sacking, began to cut through it with his belt knife, which Llelo himself had sharpened for him the day before. "That's why I am withholding judgment until we have more information. Desperation and jealousy are not the same motive. She claims she is jealous, but her acts are desperate."

Thankfully, the dog proved to be less bloated than Llelo had feared. Maybe that was still coming. As with a human, a dead animal went through stages of rigor, and the dog's corpse had reached the point of being cold and soft—and smelly.

Llelo tried to ignore his nose, and he was glad he'd left the door to the laying out room open. "All except messing up Nest's wagon."

"Except for that, yes. That looks like jealousy. So while Manon might have meant to poison Nest instead of her dog, I don't believe she did it because she wanted to replace her on the dais. Poison takes a level of forethought and malice that's different from petty vandalism."

Llelo stood with his arms folded across his chest, not feeling particularly forgiving towards Manon at the moment, pregnant or not. It was hard to feel anything but anger towards her with the sad little corpse in front of him. "Monkshood is a powerful poison."

"It is, and not something to be trifled with. You can't really poison someone with it just a little bit. Not everyone will die, but many will, and Manon would have had no way of knowing how much or how little of the porridge Nest would eat."

"Unless she knew in advance that Nest wasn't planning to eat that day so she could fit into the dress."

"Then she would have most certainly murdered Deri instead, since he had no such restrictions. If that was the plan, it was an insane one."

"Pregnant women can sometimes not think clearly," Llelo tried, more than a little tentatively.

Gareth let out a laugh. "Don't let your mother hear you say that." Then he sobered. "What's bothering me the most about Manon's confession is that it took a bit for her to admit to it. It was almost as if her initial denials were closer to the truth, and she just needed time to think. I have found, with liars, that they don't usually succumb that quickly. The pressure has to build, at least for a few hours, until their consciences can't stand the guilt. By the next morning, either they have embraced the lie or given it up."

"I stutter when I lie."

"Yes, you do." His father shot him a grin. "It is something to be proud of. Manon stuttered a great deal too, at least at first."

"And then what did she do?"

"Cried. And that's a difficult response to navigate as well. She's pregnant, which means she cries easily anyway." He rubbed his chin with the back of his hand. "I am dismayed at how little convinced I am."

"She confessed." Llelo said flatly.

"True." Gareth stepped back from the dog. "Come here, son, and take my place. I had set you to do this job, and you still should."

Llelo hesitated. "Tell me this isn't because of the offensive smell, which is far worse than it would have been two days ago."

Gareth grinned. "Think what you like. It still has to be done."

"Ha!" Llelo laughed, but still took his father's place. It was a trust, and he was comforted by the knowledge that Gareth *had* given him the task initially.

"What do we do first?" Gareth said softly.

"The same as with people, though with a little more leeway. We should cut her open if we have to. The smell of decay is overwhelming everything else right now, but it would be good to confirm that the cause of death was poison."

Llelo bent closer, his fingers opening one closed eye and then the other. His frown returned as he noted the way they were bloodshot.

"Will you look with me, Father? This doesn't look like death from Badger's bane to me."

"Why do you say that?" Gareth walked around to the other side of the table so he could see better.

"An infusion of Aconite results in trembling limbs, sweating, nausea, vomiting, diarrhea, intense pain, paralysis, and ultimately death. At first the pupils of the eye will alternately contract and dilate. Towards death, they remain dilated. Symptoms appear a quarter of an hour to two hours after ingestion."

Gareth eyed his son. "You've been spending time with your grandmother."

Llelo couldn't help looking pleased with himself. He had recited from memory a passage from his grandmother's herb book. "She knows things."

"And because she does, you do too." Gareth gestured that Llelo should continue. "If you don't see that, what do you see?"

Llelo ran his hands along the dog's fur. "I see no sign of vomiting or diarrhea, not even a froth in the mouth, which Deri said he saw." He glanced at his father, a questioning expression on his face.

Gareth nodded. "I concur."

Llelo was going to have to touch the dog more. Steeling himself, he pried open the dog's mouth and immediately saw what looked like a bone obstructing its throat. "Can you lift the lantern for me?"

Gareth did as Llelo asked, shining the light as directly as possible into the dog's mouth.

Sure now, Llelo turned to the side table and rummaged through his father's tools, looking for tweezers, because he didn't want to stick his hand in the dog's mouth if he could help it. Another thing his grandmother had warned him was that many poisons could be absorbed through the skin.

Tweezers in hand, he turned back to the dog. Really, they needed a third person: one to hold the lantern, one to hold the dog's mouth open, and one to work the tweezers. In the end, Gareth hung the lantern on a hook above the table and tilted the dog's head until the light illuminated the interior of the dog's mouth. Then Llelo reached inside with the tweezers. After some effort, he pulled out a shard of chicken bone that had been lodged in the dog's throat, blocking his windpipe. He thought it was part of a leg bone. Regardless it was splintered and bloody on one end.

Father and son stared at the bone held at the end of the tweezers.

"What does this mean?" Llelo said. "The dog didn't die from poison after all?"

"I've been a fool." Gareth appeared equally surprised. "We took the witnesses at their word—including Queen Cristina—that the dog could have died so suddenly only from poison. Otherwise we would have looked for other causes right away."

Llelo met his father's eyes. "What then, has Manon actually confessed to?"

31

Gwen

"Wait a moment. You went into the examination of the dog's body thinking we were done with the investigation because Manon had confessed to all of it, and now we might be done because no murder was ever attempted?"

A good night's sleep had done wonders for Gwen's state of mind, and she was able to laugh out loud as Gareth related how the dog had died. They were sitting again at the table in the guesthouse common room, and she was glad she hadn't taken the children to eat in the great hall, avoiding it not because she had a premonition of the news Gareth would bring, but because people would be discussing her near-death experience yesterday, and she didn't want to be the object of their stares. They would have to put the investigation aside soon, to prepare themselves for the wedding, but Gwen was enjoying the company of her family, even with the topic at hand.

Saran had already examined the body too and come to the same conclusion as Gareth and Llelo: the dog did not die of poisoning and, more bluntly, had never been poisoned at all.

"Well, murder was done only if Manon gave the dog the chicken bone," Dai said dryly, apparently trying for levity. It hadn't escaped Gwen's notice that he hadn't left her side this morning, even following her to the latrine and back. If the protectiveness kept up for too long, it would become annoying, but for now, it warmed her heart.

"I wouldn't have thought a dog choking on a bone would try to eat something else," Gwen said.

"In point of fact, it would," Gareth said. "I conferred with King Owain's dogsman, and he said a dog in distress knows something is wrong but not what, and might try to eat, which can explain why Annwyn took a bite or two and then gave up and retreated under the table."

"Where did Annwyn get the chicken bone?" Dai asked.

Llelo lifted a hand to indicate he would answer. "I asked in the kitchen while Father was talking to the dogsman. The bones were boiled for stock and to loosen the remainder of the meat, and then thrown in the waste pile. One of the kitchen staff remembers chasing Annwyn away from it that morning. Nobody would murder a dog with a chicken bone anyway."

"Cristina would," Meilyr said. "And the dog *did* defecate under the high table."

Gwen coughed and laughed at the same time. "You're not wrong, but Queen Cristina was the one who set this investigation in motion, and she wouldn't have had us looking into a poisoning if she already knew the dog had died from eating a chicken bone. Nobody would have known she gave it to Annwyn. Cristina could merely have pointed it out—and that would have been the end of it."

"As far as our investigation goes, this would have been the end of it if not for the attack on Gwalchmai," Gareth said. "Legally, Manon owes him payment for the crime."

Gwen sighed. "She owes Nest too, for the destruction of her things."

"Except she couldn't have done it," Dai sat a little straighter on his bench. "Manon was in the hall all morning yesterday. I saw her. She arrived before Nest and left after."

Gareth ran a hand through his hair. "Then I don't know what's going on."

Gwen began ticking items off her fingers. "One, Manon confessed to putting poison in the porridge in an attempt to do away with Nest. Two, the dog died, but not from poison, so these two things are not related. How is that possible?"

Llelo's expression cleared. "Because the dog died, neither Nest nor Deri ate of the porridge, so Manon's attempt to harm Nest was foiled. Manon simply *assumed* the dog had died of the poison she'd put into the porridge."

"That's possible, Llelo," Gwen said, "but given the questionable nature of aspects of Manon's confession, I think we have to wonder if the porridge was ever poisoned at all. People have been known to confess to crimes they didn't commit."

"They have?"

Gareth smiled ruefully. "We have neglected your education, son. Yes, they sometimes do."

"Why would they do that?"

"It can be out of a strange desire to get attention, even if it's bad attention," Gwen said. "Sometimes it's because they are miserable and exhausted and feel guilty about something else they've done, so feel they should be punished. And sometimes it's because they are trying to protect someone else."

"She said she poisoned the dog with Badger's bane," Llelo said. "That's very specific."

"It's always the specificity that trips liars up. If they were better at it, they'd know to keep things as vague as possible." Gwen looked at her stepmother. "Anything I should know about Badger's bane that I don't?"

"I don't know what you know," Saran said, "but even if the dog had been poisoned, Badger's bane would have been an unlikely candidate—"

"—because even if the initial signs are immediate, it takes time to kill!" Llelo spoke triumphantly. "I thought that from the start, especially since it didn't seem the dog had eaten more than a bite or two of the porridge."

"I see someone has been paying attention when I speak." Saran smiled.

"What poison could have killed more quickly?" Gareth asked.

"Badger's bane, which we call Monkshood, and Hemlock are the most deadly plants I know of. Neither kills instantly. You need a sword for that."

"Poison is often viewed as a woman's weapon because it works more slowly and from a distance, so it gives the murderer time to get away." Gwen put down the bread she'd been eating, no longer hungry, and moved to the chair by the fire. Taran climbed into her lap. "Often it's difficult to discover the source of the poison and the identity of the poisoner, because too much time has elapsed between the poisoning and the death."

"I knew I married into this family for a reason. It wasn't just your father's music." Saran shot a loving glance in Meilyr's direction.

As usual, he'd been working away silently on his food, but now he looked up. "I know a person or two I'd like to poison if I thought I could get away with it."

Gwen wasn't sure if he was referring to Cadwaladr, her first choice, or Deri—or even King Madog, who'd forced this hiatus on the bards of Gwynedd.

"If we don't figure out more about what happened in the next few hours," Llelo said, "by tomorrow everyone could be gone. Unless the flood stops them, of course."

"Even then we'd have another day, two at most," Meilyr said. "According to the villager I spoke with last night, by now, all the snow in the mountains has melted. Even if the rains continue, the flow will be well down by tomorrow. People *will* start leaving."

"If one of those people is Cadwaladr, it can't come too soon." But then Gareth gestured with one hand. "Don't mind me. I'll get over this."

"He tried to kill you," Meilyr said simply. "You've earned the right to never want to see him again." Then he looked around at the rest of them gathered about the table. "Will you let me take a crack at Manon? I knew her father well."

"I'll take Deri again," Gwen said, rocking Taran gently. "If he feels bad enough about my swim in the river, he might talk to me."

Meilyr nodded. "Even more, he'll be preoccupied getting ready to perform. It will make his temper short but make it difficult for him to lie."

"I think I know what's going on with him anyway," Gwen said, realizing with the events of yesterday she hadn't mentioned it yet. "He's losing his hearing."

"Oh no." Meilyr sat back in his chair, shocked and genuinely sympathetic. "No wonder he's short-tempered and drinking too much. To lose one's hearing is disastrous for a bard."

"It also makes him more dependent on Nest, rather than less, which makes him even less likely to want to see her dead." Gareth pursed his lips. "I'll talk to her."

Gwen gave a low laugh. "You do realize she likes you."

"She doesn't. I've done nothing but hound her for the last three days."

All Gwen did was raise her eyebrows, laughter still on her lips.

Gareth eyed her back. "And Deri doesn't like you?"

"I would say not, since he may have tried to drown me yesterday." Gwen meant to speak lightly, but her words came out with an edge she hadn't intended.

Instantly Gareth was on his feet. "I know, *cariad*." He crouched in front of her and kissed the back of her hand. "You won't be seeing him alone."

"I wasn't alone yesterday!" But then her tone gentled. "I will be careful."

"I'll stay with her, Father," Dai said.

The sound of heavy boots on the flagstones in the courtyard came to them through the open window. Hearing the urgency in the footfalls, all but Gwen and Taran were on their feet before Conall appeared in the doorway. "Manon tried to cross the river. She's alive, but I think you need to come."

32

Gareth

Gareth could feel the anxiety all around him. The wedding was two hours away, but the news of Manon's near drowning, hard on the heels of Gwen's, had the entire community in an uproar.

He also knew this was partially his fault. He had pushed Manon to the edge, and so she had tried to run. That was, of course, if she hadn't meant to kill herself as a way to escape her troubles. Regardless, now that he knew the dog hadn't been poisoned, it was long past time he got truthful answers to his questions.

Conall led them to the headman's house, which was located higher up the bank and thus safe from the floods. The house was also substantial, built in wood, with two rooms and a wooden floor instead of dirt.

By the time they arrived, Manon had been stripped of her clothing and dressed again. She was wrapped in blankets and sat on a stool before the hearth. Half a dozen people hovered around her, including Andreas, Deri, and Nest. Even Queen Cristina had come down. This close to the start of the wedding, none of them had time to be here, and none of them looked like they were being particularly helpful either.

For his part, Gareth saw the opportunity in front of him.

"My queen, all of you, please take seats on that bench against the wall." The house was square, and the bench was behind where Manon was currently sitting. He didn't want her looking at her companions while he talked, and he didn't want them seeing her face either, if she ever raised it to look at him. "While Saran tends to Manon, I'd like to discuss what has happened."

Andreas was the first to protest. "I don't know what you're about, Gareth, but this isn't the time or the place."

"Yes, it really is. Please."

"Do as he says." Cristina strolled to the bench and sat, apparently resigned, but also looking amused. "He won't let this go until you do."

The rest obeyed, because she was a queen rather than because they wanted anything to do with talking to Gareth, and all with evident reluctance.

He positioned himself so he faced both them and Manon.

"I will start at the beginning as I understand it: I was woken by my brother-in-law, Gwalchmai, two mornings ago with a request from Queen Cristina to come to the hall. He informed me that Nest's dog, Annwyn, was dead. I arrived to find Nest and Deri accusing each other of murder—of the dog, certainly, but also of each other— through poison in the porridge. I was told the dog had eaten a few bites and died."

"She had!" Nest made a move to rise to her feet, but Deri grabbed her arm and pulled her down.

"Let the man talk. The sooner we listen, the sooner we can be done with all this."

Gareth gave him a nod in thanks. "My first act was to secure the bowl of porridge. I gave it to Gwalchmai to take to Saran, to determine what poison had been used and to prevent anyone else from eating it. I sent my son Llelo to the kitchen to requisition any leftovers and speak to the staff there, and then I myself questioned Deri and Nest. In all of this, the assumption remained that the porridge had been poisoned and was the cause of the dog's death."

"It was!" Again, it was Nest who interrupted.

This time it was Cristina who told her to keep quiet.

Gareth coughed into his fist, returning the attention to himself. "This assumption was further supported when we discovered Gwalchmai had never reached Saran but had been bashed over the head with a piece of wood and the porridge stolen, and again when the dog's corpse was stolen from the laying out room."

Manon gave an audible sob and put her face into her hands.

Gareth wasn't ready to speak to her and carried on as if he hadn't noticed. "The next day brought the sacking of Nest's wagon—" here Nest preened a bit, though nobody was looking at her, "—and the near-drowning of my wife in the river."

At this point, Gareth paused, looking from one person to another, trying to read what was in their faces. He settled on Manon's.

"Will you tell them, please, what happened this morning, Manon?"

Manon looked as if she'd been struck in the face. "What-what-what do you mean?"

"You stutter when you lie, Manon," Gareth said. "And you know very well what I'm asking."

Cristina tsked. "Just tell him, Manon, before we ourselves expire."

But Manon merely looked down at her feet. Her refusal, more than anything else she could have done, told him that he was finally on the right track in doubting her story.

Gareth sighed. "This morning, I encountered Manon trying to sneak the dog's corpse out of the palace in her laundry basket. She confessed to poisoning the dog, attacking Gwalchmai and stealing the porridge, stealing the dog's corpse, and ransacking Nest's wagon."

Nest, Deri, and Andreas were on their feet in the same instant, each protesting in their own way.

"Don't be a fool!" Deri looked as if he might launch himself at Gareth.

Andreas was equally outraged. "That's a lie! My wife would never hurt anyone!" His words were for Gareth, but his face had drained of color and his eyes had gone to his wife. For a moment, Gareth saw doubt there.

Nest too was looking at Manon, but her expression was extraordinarily odd—a mixture of surprise and amusement. She opened her mouth to speak, but then closed it and sat back down on the bench. For Nest, a woman who desired always to be the center of attention, it was very strange behavior indeed.

Then Gareth cut through the hubbub of conversation that had ensued. "Do you stand by your confession, Manon?"

Andreas had stepped to Manon's side and put an arm around her shoulders, pulling her to him. "Don't be absurd, she doesn't know what she's saying."

"Manon?" Gareth raised his eyebrows.

Manon had turned her face into Andreas's chest. Though she again didn't speak, she did nod emphatically.

Gareth looked at the others. "Our problem now is that very little of what Manon has confessed to makes sense. For example, she was in the hall when Nest and Deri's wagon was ransacked, as well as when Gwen went into the river, so she could not be responsible for either. She was unable to give specifics about the attack on Gwalchmai, and, most importantly, the dog didn't die from poison."

"What?" Every one of the people in front of him gasped in unison at this news.

Gareth couldn't help but relish their full attention at long last. "Annwyn died from a chicken bone stuck in her throat."

33

Gwen

"You can't mean that." Manon finally turned from Andreas to face Gareth and spoke actual words. "She was poisoned. Of course she was."

"She was not," Gareth said.

Manon continued to look blankly at him. "She has to have been."

"No."

"But—" she looked up at Andreas, "but you—" and then she broke off to look at Nest. "You said she was!"

Nest was having none of it. "Of course she was poisoned. You have no idea what you're talking about."

Saran took exception to her disbelief. "I myself examined the dog's body. She died of a chicken bone in her throat. There can be no doubt."

Gwen had been watching everyone's expressions and she thought she was beginning to understand a few things. She began by stepping into Andreas's line of sight. "Do you have something to tell us, Andreas?"

He swallowed. "Me?" His recovery was quick. "Why would I have something to tell you?"

Manon's emotions were still running very high, and Gwen saw her lips form the shape of *but you* before she caught herself again.

Everyone else was looking at Andreas, so Gwen motioned broadly to draw their attention back to her. "Let me tell you what I think happened, and you can tell me if I'm right."

All but Cristina had risen to their feet at the mention of the chicken bone and hadn't subsided. Now the queen spoke serenely. "Go on, Gwen. Tell us what you're thinking. I, for one, would very much like to know the truth."

Her words could have been sarcastic, but Cristina was sitting with her hands folded in her lap, watching the proceedings with an apparent detachment.

Gwen couldn't refuse her and didn't want to anyway. "We have facts that are indisputable: the dog died from choking on a chicken bone; Gwalchmai was attacked; the dog's corpse was stolen and Manon caught with it; Nest's wagon was sacked. We can agree those things *happened*. But let's suppose the inciting incident, the poisoning of the porridge, did not happen, and Manon confessed to something she didn't do."

"Why would she confess to something she didn't do!" Nest wasn't ready to stop shouting.

"Because she wanted to protect the person she assumed *had* poisoned the porridge." Gwen looked at Andreas. "She was lying to protect you."

"I didn't poison the porridge." Andreas blinked twice very fast. "Why on earth would *anyone* think I wanted Nest or Deri dead? They are my livelihood."

"It only matters that Manon thought you had done it," Gwen said. "One of the many things that has been different about this investigation is that much of what has happened was done out of love, not hate."

She paused to take a breath and gather her thoughts, at which point Gareth leaned down to her and whispered in her ear. "You'll have to elaborate, my love, because I'm not seeing it yet."

Gwen was just opening her mouth to continue when Cristina jumped in. "Oh, I see." She pointed at Manon. "You attacked Gwalchmai and stole the dog's corpse to protect Andreas, whom you thought had poisoned the porridge and whom you love."

Cristina had never been involved more than peripherally in any investigation, but she was proving herself observant, clever, and well versed in intrigue, which wasn't in any way comforting. The queen then moved her pointing finger to Deri. "You spend your time in the chapel, which is next to the laying out room. *You* saw Manon steal the dog's corpse. You didn't know why she would do such a thing, but you wanted to protect her from the repercussions of her actions because *you* are in love with Manon. That is why you shoved Gwen into the river: you thought she was getting close to the truth and you wanted to deter her from asking any more questions."

Deri's mouth fell open, and he was making sounds of denial, but they were belied by the flushing of his face. Gwen moved to within his line of sight, and, as he saw her, his face crumpled. Then he bent forward, his shoulders shaking, and Gwen realized he was weeping.

Gwen stood looking at him a moment longer and then took a few steps closer in order to put a hand on his shoulder. "I could have died."

"I know!" Deri's voice came out a wail, and he wrapped his arms around Gwen's waist and hung on, truly sobbing now. "I'm sorry. I'm so sorry. I'm a foolish, pathetic drunk, who should be put down like an old dog."

At that point, Meilyr, who'd been leaning against one wall, pushed off and came closer. After separating Deri from Gwen with gentle but forceful movements, he got Deri to his feet and walked him back to his corner. Once there, Meilyr urged a long drink from Deri's own flask on the dejected bard, which finally got him to stop weeping. It would definitely be a moment of irony if, after all this, the wedding couldn't take place because *Deri* was too dejected to sing.

Because her father could be trusted to do what needed to be done, Gwen turned back to the room. "And last of all, love explains why Nest ransacked her own wagon."

"What!" Nest was all outrage, but Gwen had the measure of her now and pinned her with her gaze.

"You love yourself more than anyone, except perhaps Annwyn. You had been reveling in the attention paid to you up until the arrival of Prince Cadwaladr—and you wanted it back." She looked around at the others. "While every box and carton was upended, not a single item was in any way damaged, including all her lovely dresses."

"Manon sacked my wagon. She confessed to it!"

"As Gareth pointed out earlier, Manon was in the hall all morning, as witnesses will testify."

"Then why did she say she did it?"

Gwen turned slowly on her heel to look at Manon. "That is a very good question, and worth reiterating. Why, Manon? And why did you think Andreas had poisoned the porridge in the first place?"

As usual, Manon remained mute.

Then Llelo's voice came from the doorway to the house. "Cian and I may be able to answer that."

34

Llelo

"I found a vial in their wagon, one I would not want to drink of myself." Llelo stepped forward, the small vial clutched in his hand. The letters *BB* were written on a paper stuck to its side.

From the looks, they'd timed things nicely. Llelo would have liked to claim he'd planned to appear at just the right moment, but it had been Cian's idea to search through Manon's and Andreas's belongings at a time they knew the owners would be otherwise occupied. When Cian had dragged him out the postern gate and over to the wagon, Llelo hadn't even gone inside at first because he was so anxious about violating their privacy and, truth be told, breaking the law.

That the wagon was so neatly organized had been helpful. They had gone through everything as carefully and quickly as possible, and it had been Llelo, once he'd worked up the nerve to enter, who'd found the vial in a small wooden box underneath one of the beds.

Llelo had known for a while that Cian had a bit of a wild streak. Llelo's lack of one might have been the reason they were such good friends, since Llelo's caution prevented Cian from leaping before he looked, and Cian's daring pushed Llelo to risk more than he otherwise would.

"*Mamgu,* can you say what this is?" He handed the vial to his grandmother.

She took it and held it up to the light. It was a brownish liquid in a glass container. "Not without opening it, and if it really is Badger's bane, I would rather not." She looked directly at Manon. "It is the most deadly poison known to man."

Manon immediately dropped her eyes to the floor. Andreas opted for outrage. "How dare your son search my wagon! I will speak to my king about it!"

To Llelo's complete shock and surprise, his father not only defended him, but lied outright: "Llelo did so on my orders, and I will be happy to discuss the events of the last few days with your king. For now, this vial was found in your wagon. Thus, you should know what's in it. What does BB stand for?"

As if they all didn't know.

"I've never seen it before in my life! I say it's yours, and your son pretended to find it in my wagon."

It was such an obvious lie, that more than one person in the room guffawed.

"That isn't true!" Cian stepped to the fore and spoke with utter and transparent sincerity. "I was there, and he found it under one of your beds!"

Cristina was never one to suffer fools and had been among those who'd mocked Andreas's initial denial. "Of course it's yours, Andreas. Llelo is the most honest man one could ever meet, and that's even knowing his father. The vial is yours. What is in it?"

Andreas was still looking mutinous, but Cristina was not to be put off. "What if we asked for a cup of mead from the headman and poured the contents of the vial into it. I would expect you to drink it."

"This is absurd," Andreas said.

In the distance, a bell tolled, calling the people to ready themselves because the wedding would begin within the hour.

Cristina studied the arrayed suspects. "You two," she pointed to Nest and Deri, who had stopped sobbing and was standing with his head resting against the wall and his eyes closed, "will come with me. You have a wedding to attend, as do I. Manon and Andreas, you are not needed and will stay with Gareth and Gwen." She made a motion in Gareth's direction. "Get to the bottom of this, will you?"

Then she stood and swept from the room. She was followed by all the others she'd indicated. As usual, nobody defied the Queen of Gwynedd.

Once they were gone, Gareth blew out a breath. "Time to stop your fruitless denials, Andreas. The vial contains Badger's bane. Who were you meant to poison with it and for whom are you working?"

35

Gareth

E ven as Gareth asked the final question, he was answering it internally: *Cadwaladr.*

And then he brought himself up short. Even though he wanted to and it was always his first instinct, he couldn't blame everything on the treacherous prince. The obvious answer should really be *King Madog*, since, of course, he was openly Andreas's employer. Its very obviousness, however, argued against it. King Madog would know that if Andreas was found to have poisoned someone, everyone would immediately look to Madog himself as the real culprit.

While Gwen and Queen Cristina had been talking, bits and pieces of the investigation had begun rising to the surface of Gareth's mind, like oil separating from water. *Badger's bane,* as a term for aconite, was not common in Wales, but instead was a name someone who had spent time in England would know. That person wasn't Manon, who hadn't known the poison for what it was, and had pronounced the term in fractured English. Then there were Gareth's conversations with Andreas and Cadwaladr. The two men had separately used the exact same turn of phrase in the exact same way, though Andreas had been talking about the death of the dog and Cadwaladr had been talking about the death of Rhun.

Gareth had no doubt anymore that Manon had been trying to protect Andreas because she thought he was the poisoner. What remained unclear was why it made sense to her that he would poison Deri and Nest. And if she thought he'd made a mistake in poisoning their porridge when his real target was someone else, King Owain for example, how she thought that her husband, of all people, could have made that mistake.

Thus, the logic of this chain of events still eluded him. Past experience told him pressing Manon might yield him little, so he said to Gwen, "Could you take Manon away? You too, Saran, Meilyr, Cian." He looked at each one in turn. "Thank you for your help."

The expression on Cian's face said he didn't want to leave, and he exchanged something of a pleading look with Llelo, who simply nodded, prompting Cian to wrinkle his nose in protest.

Meilyr put an arm around his shoulders and walked with him to the door. "You did good work, but this isn't our job anymore, son."

Gwen, meanwhile, went to Manon and took her arm, ignoring her protesting "Andreas!" as she did so.

Moving to her other side, Saran spoke soothingly to her, and the three of them left as well.

Andreas took a step to follow, but Gareth said in a harsh voice, "Do you really want her to hear what you are about to tell me?"

"I don't know what you mean." Andreas stopped moving. He hardly seemed to be breathing.

Gareth laid bare his thoughts: "Manon knew you had the aconite in your possession and feared you had poisoned the porridge, which was why she tried to protect you from discovery. We of Gwynedd think now that your real target was King Owain, who also eats porridge in the morning."

Andreas coughed, which was the last thing he should have done. It was a stalling tactic, so when the outright denial came a few heartbeats later, Gareth didn't believe him.

"That's absurd."

Gareth held up the vial, which Saran had passed to him on her way by. He was almost afraid to hold it, but since Llelo and Saran were still alive, he supposed he would stay that way too, and the poison couldn't reach him through the glass.

"This is Badger's bane. You can't deny it. I could have Manon arrested for the attack on Gwalchmai. He is bard to King Owain. If proved, and her own confession would be enough to ensure it, the required payment to Gwalchmai would be considerable. I don't want to put a pregnant woman in a cell while she awaits her trial, but I will if you don't tell me what this is about."

Andreas's lips pressed together. He looked at Gareth and then at the floor. Gareth took a moment to glance behind him. Llelo and Dai were standing on either side of the door, guarding it. Conall was leaned against a pillar supporting the roof, in his classic stance—arms folded across his chest and feet crossed at the ankles, looking for all the world as if he'd be perfectly happy to stay that way for the rest of the day.

"Manon knows the truth." Gareth turned back to Andreas, who was working very hard to keep his expression neutral. "You might as well tell me. Gwen will get it out of her eventually. Your wife is strong enough to lie for you, but she won't be able to lie forever."

In point of fact, Gareth knew no such thing. Manon had managed to keep quiet about a great many things up until now, far past the point he thought a basically honest person should have been able to do so. She must really love Andreas—and fear for the future of her child—to have gone so far to protect him. Her love gave her power.

For his part, Andreas still didn't speak.

"You're a spy. Tell me who for." Though Gareth needed to hear Cadwaladr's name, this was a delicate moment, and he didn't want to lead Andreas by putting the name in his mouth. "You might as well get this over with. I don't see why you care so much about your employer that you would go to such lengths to protect him!"

Andreas blinked, surprise evident on his face, akin to his look when it was revealed that Manon had thought he'd poisoned the porridge.

"Think of Manon," Gareth urged.

"My God." Conall spoke from behind Gareth, and his voice was full of awe. "It isn't Cadwaladr!"

Andreas wet his lip as Conall said the prince's name. Then his expression turned quickly to horror and then to utterly nothing as Conall finished his sentence.

"Nor is he doing King Madog's bidding. We've been looking at this all wrong. It isn't a *him* he's protecting. Andreas works for Susanna."

36

Gwen

With the wedding underway, Gwen, Saran, and Manon passed the church just as Nest's soprano soared into the air. It was a spectacular sound, though one they didn't stop to listen to as they hurried past, hoping nobody in the churchyard would notice them. The singing continued, audible even from a distance, as they passed through the palace gate, heading for the chapel, which Gwen thought would afford them a quiet place to talk.

Manon kept her head down and slightly turned away from Gwen. She wasn't crying anymore, but neither was she talking. She had lied repeatedly to Gareth, and now Gwen needed her to tell the truth, but she didn't know how to make her.

Once inside the chapel, Manon stopped and at last her shoulders sagged. "I don't understand how it has come to this."

"Sit down, Manon." Gwen pointed to Deri's bench, and Manon obeyed, plopping down as if all fight had left her.

Gwen noted, however, that she still wasn't talking.

Outside, singing birds replaced Nest's voice, indicating the marriage vows were being said at the church door. In another moment, the wedding party would enter the church for mass.

Saran, who'd come with Gwen from the headman's hut, settled herself on the bench beside Manon and took her hand. "It's all right, my dear. Whatever you did, nobody has died."

Manon hung her head. "Gwalchmai could have."

"But he did not. You must have been truly desperate to have picked up that piece of wood and bashed him on the head with it."

Internally, Gwen applauded Saran's bold statement. The more she and Saran talked openly about what Manon had done, the more Gwen hoped Manon would follow their example.

Instead, she seemed to shrink further into herself. "I-I-I was. Desperate, that is." Manon was stuttering again, and she shook off Saran's comforting hand. "You should lock me up. I am a danger to myself and others."

Gwen and Saran exchanged a look, and Gwen started to feel a little desperate herself. The longer the lies went on, and the more obvious it was that Manon was lying, the more sure in them she became.

"Leave the poor child alone. The person you want to talk to is me."

Gwen spun around. She had thought she'd recognized the voice, but she was still stunned to find Queen Susanna standing in the doorway of the chapel.

"My queen—" Manon started to speak, but Susanna made a slicing motion with her hand.

"By all that is holy, child, go find yourself something to eat in the kitchen. You're as pale as my nightdress." Then Susanna's eyes met Gwen's. "Enough is enough."

Manon scurried away, passing Susanna in the doorway, and then, after another motion of the queen's hand, Saran went with her. What Susanna had to say was for Gwen's ears alone. That the queen was here at all indicated the wedding mass had started, since she wouldn't have been able to leave sooner without her departure being painfully obvious.

Susanna began walking towards Gwen. "Marared is safely married to a man who loves her with his whole heart. Nothing can stop that now, not even my death."

Gwen didn't reply. She didn't even move, so afraid to say anything—think anything—that would deter Susanna from speaking.

And then Gwen noticed the tears streaming down the queen's cheeks. She put a hand to her heart to see the other woman's grief.

"As I'm sure you realize by now, Manon is lying about virtually everything. This morning, after Gareth let her go, she came to me and told me what she'd said to him. I assured her all would be well and that I would deal with it after the wedding, but I should have known such a gentle soul could not live with such deception."

Susanna paced up the nave to the altar and stared at the cross upon it. "I have prayed for deliverance so many times. When it did not come, I decided to take matters into my own hands. The poison is mine, and it was intended for my husband, were he to refuse to go through with the wedding." She gave a little laugh. "There, I said it. Do with me as you will."

The queen was still looking at the cross, and since Gwen found her knees trembling, she backed into the bench on which Manon had been sitting and sat herself. "Why would you want to kill your husband? What has he done?"

"What has he *not* done?" This time Susanna's laugh was mocking. "Don't answer that. I know what you mean. If his attempt to murder Hywel in our own castle wasn't enough to push me over the edge, what did?" She took in a breath. "When Marared was thirteen, I caught him in her bed with his arms around her."

At Gwen's protesting cry, Susanna gave her a quelling look. "My husband said he heard her weeping in the night, beset by a bad dream, and went to comfort her. Marared confirmed his story, and I wanted to believe him—and her. But then I decided I could not look the other way even if he spoke the truth about *that* night. She had to be protected, and I have done so to the best of my ability ever since. It was the reason she came with me to Llanfaes. I would not leave her alone with him ever again."

Their investigation into the death of Annwyn had taken a very dark turn. Gwen was shocked by what Susanna was accusing her husband of, so she had to ask, "Do you have further—" She was unsure how to finish the question.

Susanna did it for her. "Proof? I would not have trod this path if I didn't. I don't *think* my husband is evil. I don't *suspect*. I *know*. I have learned a great deal since then, because I have watched him and followed him and asked questions of the right people. I had never been ignorant of how little he came to my bed, but I allowed myself to ignore the women who shared his instead. And then I wrenched the truth of who he really is from two of his other daughters, both grown with families of their own, but upon whom he forced himself during their early womanhood. This is the reason Madog wrote the marriage contract as he did, in a last attempt to stop Marared's marriage to Iorwerth."

Gwen's hand was to her mouth, struggling for something to say, some condolence, but nothing else came to her beyond a plea to the Virgin Mary.

Susanna let out a huff of air. "You might call upon her. She has given me strength all these years to do what must be done. At first, I railed against God for not delivering Marared from danger—until I realized that He had delivered her by waking me that night and sending me to her room. Normally I never wake at that hour, and I hadn't checked on her in the night in years."

"Why did you that time?"

"I don't know. I was on the way back from the latrine, passed her door, and stopped, thinking of a conversation we'd had earlier that day. Thirteen is such a fragile age for a girl. I needed to look upon her sweet face." Susanna's expression turned grim. "Instead, I found my husband *comforting* her. I believe with all my heart it wouldn't have taken him long to do far more than that."

"I assume, then, that Manon knows what you asked Andreas to do, and that's why she suspected him of poisoning the porridge?"

"What did Manon tell you?"

"Little of use, and nothing true, except for the part about stealing the dog's corpse. Early on, we wondered if King Madog wanted to stop the wedding and was using poison to do it by murdering his own bards."

Susanna gave a surprised grunt. "In the end, you may have arrived at the right answer without me."

"I guarantee you we would not have. We discarded that theory, deciding instead that the porridge had been poisoned by mistake, and the real target was King Owain, not Nest or Deri."

Susanna frowned. "Why on earth would you think—" She stopped and then, after a pause, laughed. "You thought Andreas was working for … Cadwaladr?" She laughed again. "Of course you did. And why wouldn't you? But no. Manon is such a sweet thing, so innocent until recently. She came to the same conclusion I did, and for much the same reason: we believed Andreas had betrayed me to Madog, who had ordered him to use the poison on Deri and Nest to stop the wedding."

Gwen felt the revelation like a physical blow. "That's why neither of you talked to Andreas!"

"It seems now, that if we had, it would have cleared up a great many things, and much pain could have been avoided."

Gwen felt as if she was being buffeted by increasingly stronger waves. "Manon wanted to protect Andreas and her life with him, but even more, she was trying to protect *you*!"

"Ah. I knew you were clever. You guessed the rest already? Yes, you are right: after the dog died, Manon followed Gwalchmai from the hall and encountered me just entering it. It is I who bashed him on the back of the head and stole the porridge. It is I, not Manon, who owes your brother *galanas*."

* * * * *

"It is all very well and good that Susanna has confessed, my love, but we have some loose ends to tie up."

Gareth lay flat on his back with one hand across his eyes. They were alone in their bed chamber, except for their two children, who'd fallen asleep at the wedding feast, despite their best efforts to remain awake. Below them in the guesthouse common room, a raucous party was continuing.

Gwen was quite sure she wasn't going to be able to sleep with it going on, so she rolled onto her side and studied her husband's profile. "Such as?"

"How could Susanna hurt Gwalchmai? And once she did, how could she leave him lying alone by the herb hut?"

"She was desperate and hit him far harder than she intended. She meant simply to surprise him from behind, to drop him to his knees so she could take the porridge and run. And she did check on him every hour to make sure he was breathing. She's the reason he stayed warm in his cloak."

"I suppose I can see that. Men in battle have been known to find strength far beyond the usual." Gareth rolled onto his side too.

"That doesn't excuse her," Gwen said, "but I'm finding it hard to see her as the villain of this piece."

"You like her." Gareth studied Gwen's face.

"It's hard not to admire her courage, even with what she did to Gwalchmai."

Gareth reached out a hand and curled a strand of Gwen's hair behind her ear. "I'm sorry for my part in this."

Gwen's brow furrowed. "Which part is that?"

"I was befuddled by drink from the start. I never should have drunk so much that night."

"You did drink more than normal, I'm quite sure, but perhaps not quite as much as you think."

Gareth's lip curled in his skepticism. "How so?"

"With all that has happened, I forgot to tell you that I had a chat with the cellarer after the wedding. A mistake was made with the mead that was served that night. I remember you saying it was excellent?"

"Yes, it was. That was the problem."

"It was only a problem because you didn't realize it was different from what has been served in the past. Our drink is always watered down, which you well know. However, that night, by mistake several tables were served the fully potent mead. Yours was not the only head suffering unduly the next morning. As it turned out, one of the servants was taking carafes from the wrong area of the cellar—and continued to do so up until this afternoon when his mistake was discovered." She patted her husband's arm. "All week, Deri has been going to that servant, whether by mistake or design, for refills for his flask."

37

Gareth

They were sitting within the large pavilion, which in another hour would be taken down, since it was no longer needed. Most of the revelers were on their way home, including the contingent from Powys.

Hywel had chosen this spot to confer so there would be no chance they could be overheard. This was made doubly sure by the ring of Dragons who patrolled the exterior of the pavilion. King Owain trusted the captain of his own personal guard, just as Hywel trusted his, but these secrets could not be spread beyond those who were already involved.

"I am going to *kill* him." Typically, King Owain was raging about, unable to sit still at the summary Gareth had given him of the conclusion of the investigation. "Marared is my daughter now. If Madog were to lay a single finger on her—"

Also typically, Taran was able to be a little more circumspect. "You can't kill him. Not yet. He's the King of Powys. There will come a time, however, when it can be done *without* suspicion falling on you."

It was a little daunting to realize this was almost the same conclusion the Dragons and Gareth had come to about murdering Cadwaladr.

"Poor Susanna." Hywel had heard the whole story earlier, so he'd had time to feel something besides anger.

"Poor *Susanna!*" King Owain turned on his son. "Don't pity her. She is as strong a woman as God ever created. She's right to believe she is where she is because no other woman could be as brave as she and the Lord works through her." Then his chin wrinkled. "That said, Cristina would have murdered me outright." He sounded proud, as honestly he should be.

Gareth thought it was safe to agree with that assessment out loud. "It is because of Cristina's quick action that I became involved in the first place. Without her, Nest and Deri might not have sung at all, the wedding would have been called off, and none of this would have come to light."

"You forget that Susanna would have murdered Madog!" King Owain stopped his pacing and flopped onto a chair. "Are we sure my sister isn't again taking the blame for something she didn't do?"

Gwen shook her head. "The accusations Susanna laid at Madog's feet are far worse than a mere attempt at murder, even of you, my lord. This time, she is not protecting her husband."

Nodding, King Owain looked around the pavilion thoughtfully, and when he spoke next, his words were softer. "We sat very similarly in Aberystwyth two years ago before we rode north to counter Ranulf and take Mold."

That had been in the halcyon days before Rhun's death. Here at Denbigh, they all gave the memory of Rhun the moment of respect it deserved before Hywel said, in one of the most cheerful voices Gareth had heard him use since then, "Today, we are all alive and well, Father." The prince leaned forward. "We are *here*. Now. Truly, how wonderful is that! Rhun would be so happy to know it."

The love in Owain's face as he looked at his heir soothed Gareth's own heart. "By all that is holy, son, you are right." For a moment, the king might have been blinking back tears, but he quickly swallowed them down, and his voice strengthened. "We survived another wedding."

"Meanwhile," Taran said, "Madog has gone back to Dinas Bran to sulk, and Cadwaladr is off to Anglesey to wreak God-knows-what-havoc in Gwynedd."

Owain refused to deflate, and he clapped Taran on the shoulder. "I know you've missed him."

Taran's expression turned sour indeed.

Owain laughed to see it, and he then turned back to his son. "No need to ask if you'll be keeping an eye on your uncle?"

Hywel laughed too, a big, round sound that could have been cynical but instead was full of joy.

Gareth knew the reason why because all of a sudden he felt the same: They *were* alive. Hywel was the *edling* of Gwynedd. And Cadwaladr was right where they wanted him.

"Yes, Father," Hywel said. "Have no fears on that score."

Historical Note

Medieval pets were not something I spent a great deal of time researching before I began writing this book. I knew cats and dogs were kept for their utility: cats in order to suppress the mouse and rat population and dogs for hunting and herding, especially in Wales with the prevalence of sheep and cattle. I was not entirely aware, however, of the extent to which dogs permeated medieval society.

As Gareth observes in *The Prince's Man*, dogs came in all colors, shapes, and sizes, including spaniels, terriers, and a wide variety of hounds. Not all dogs were kept purely for work either, and ladies' dogs like Annwyn were not rare, to the point that one medieval thirteenth century writer lamented that many such dogs died from an overly rich diet. Dogs were so common, in fact, that William Greenfield, the Archbishop of York, complained in the early fourteenth century that bringing little dogs into the choir during divine services would "impede the service and hinder the devotion of the nuns." link

Cats too, while mousers, were also appreciated as pets and companions. A ninth century poet wrote about his cat:

I and Pangur Bán my cat,
'Tis a like task we are at:

Hunting mice is his delight,
Hunting words I sit all night.

Less appreciatively, a scribe, writing around 1420, found his manuscript ruined by a urine stain left by a cat in the night. He was forced to leave the rest of the page empty, drew a picture of a cat, and cursed the creature with the following words:

"Hic non defectus est, sed cattus minxit desuper nocte quadam. Confundatur pessimus cattus qui minxit super librum istum in nocte Daventrie, et consimiliter omnes alii propter illum. Et cavendum valde ne permittantur libri aperti per noctem ubi cattie venire possunt."

[Here is nothing missing, but a cat urinated on this during a certain night. Cursed be the pesty cat that urinated over this book during the night in Deventer and because of it many others [other cats] too. And beware well not to leave open books at night where cats can come.] link

On a further historical note, the circumstances surrounding this book are also rooted in history: Prince Cadwaladr was returned to favor in Gwynedd around this time; Prince Henry plotted to over-throw King Stephen with the help of his uncle King David of Scotland

and Ranulf of Chester, with whom he planned to split the rule of England; Iorwerth married Marared, the daughter of Madog of Powys; and Welsh bards did hold such a high station in Welsh society that they had their own order, policies, and laws associated with them. As one author writes:

The poet always held an exalted position among the Welsh and his highest achievement was to become the chief poet at the court of a wealthy prince or king. The symbol of the Bardic Chair probably came from the fact that the *pencerdd* sat next to the king. This exalted position resulted in considerable rivalry, and many poets attempted to obtain this exalted position. Many studied under older and superior poets in order to learn the complicated rules, *cynghanedd*, or the system of alliteration in Welsh poetry.

Eventually, since this was similar to a craft in that it was the poet's livelihood, it was inevitable that a type of guild was formed. This led to the formation of three orders of bards: *pencerdd*, the chief poet; *bardd tellu*, or family poet; and, lastly, *cerddor* or minstrel. By law the *pencerdd* was described as "a bard who has won the chair." He exercised authority over the lesser bards. When Wales lost its independence in 1282, these legal rights disappeared. link

About the Author

With two historian parents, Sarah couldn't help but develop an interest in the past. She went on to get more than enough education herself (in anthropology) and began writing fiction when the stories in her head overflowed and demanded she let them out. While her ancestry is Welsh, she only visited Wales for the first time while in college. She has been in love with the country, language, and people ever since. She even convinced her husband to give all four of their children Welsh names.

She makes her home in Oregon.

www.sarahwoodbury.com